Kelly Creighton facilitates community groups and sch include: *The Sleeping Season* Bones of It, Bank Holiday Hu*rricane* and *Three Primes*. Her work is widely anthologised and has been noted in many poetry and short fiction prizes. She co-edited *Underneath the Tree*: an anthology of Twelve Christmas Stories from writers in Northern Ireland. In 2014, she founded The Incubator literary journal, showcasing the contemporary Irish short story. Kelly was the recipient of a 2017/18 ACES Award from the Arts Council of Northern Ireland. She lives with her family in Newtownards, County Down.

kellycreighton.com

@KellyCreighto16

'Creighton has a poet's eye for imagery and a novelist's understanding of the value of a good plot.'
The Irish Times

'Creighton a writer to reckon with.'
The Irish Examiner

Praise for *The Sleeping Season*

'The people, their places and everything they say is totally credible. Highly recommended.'
Books Ireland

'This is a novel of style and verve, that explores the darkness within relationships and the choices we make to protect those we love.'
Sharon Dempsey

'A breath of fresh air for the genre. The novel holds a spotlight to difficult societal issues. I'm already a fan of the series.'
James Murphy

'There is heart along the mystery and it is wrapped in a narrative that is both tight and lyrical.'
Simon Maltman

'What I loved most about The Sleeping Season is how much of a feminist anthem it is. I'll definitely be anxiously waiting as each book releases.'
Geek Herring

Praise for *Bank Holiday Hurricane*

'The 16 stories are by turns gritty and moving.'
The Irish Times

'Distinctive, powerful and filled, at times, with an electric high-wire tension, they contain a lyricism that comes at you sideways and will knock the wind right out of you.'
Bernie McGill

'sophisticatedly nervy, bruised, moving, memorable short stories.'
Damian Smyth

'Dark, witty and cleverly observed.'
Jane Talbot

'It's a compelling collection that you will read quickly – and then want to immediately read again.'
Claire Savage

'Kelly Creighton is a fearless writer with an impressive range. Sharp on impact these stories give voice to characters other writers shy away from.'

Paul McVeigh

Praise for *The Bones of It*

'A brilliant crime debut, chilling, compulsive and beautifully written. A hugely impressive addition to the growing body of Irish crime fiction.'
Brian McGilloway

'Blackly comic in tone. A Bildungsroman that evolves into a slow-burning psychological exploration of the mind.'
The Irish Times

'… true discovered masterpiece of fiction. *The Bones of It* is not just a novel to read, it is a novel to experience.'
San Diego Book Review

'Scott's is an authentic voice, and Creighton a writer to reckon with.'
The Irish Examiner

'This finely written thriller keeps the reader gripped and intrigued … a meaty, fascinating work of fiction.'
CultureHub Magazine

'Incredibly well written.'
Sinead Crowley

ALSO BY KELLY CREIGHTON

POETRY
Three Primes

FICTION
The Bones of It
Bank Holiday Hurricane: short stories
(co-editor) Underneath the Tree

DI SLOANE BOOKS
The Sleeping Season

PROBLEMS WITH GIRLS

DI Harriet Sloane Book 2

Kelly Creighton

FRIDAY
PRESS

First published in 2020
by Friday Press
Belfast

Copyright © 2020 Kelly Creighton

The moral right of the author has been asserted.

All characters and events in this publication, other than those clearly in the public domain, are fictitious and any resemblance to real persons, living or dead, is purely coincidental.

All rights reserved.

No part of this publication may be reproduced, stored in a retrieval system, or transmitted in any form or by any means, without the prior permission in writing of the publisher, nor be otherwise circulated in any form of binding or cover other than that in which it is published and without a similar condition including this condition being imposed on the subsequent purchaser.

ISBN: 9798605106081

www.fridaypressbooks.com
@friday_press

For Maddie and Martha

Prologue

It is early evening. We are coming home.

Flying over the lights of London, past the horizon of clouds that looks like a mouth, lips parted. Flying away from the glowing teeth of an orange sun. I am the only one awake for the turbulence warning. I grip my armrest and wish I'd ordered that glass of Merlot. I don't know when I became so afraid of flying.

The young boy in front, whose unselfconscious burps have been the elevator music of this flight, is my distraction. He reaches his hand back and pulls the shutter down on my window. The snap awakens Rowan. The plane dips then straightens, less obviously this time. I breathe my relief into Rowan's dry fragrant head. He doesn't know we are not on the ground anymore, that we are no longer in America, no longer in England.

'We're almost home,' I tell him, although he is not listening but is looking at the iPad while we fumble in the sky again. I open my shutter to look out at the clouds. Jared is asleep on Paul's knee. Paul is sleeping too. He hasn't even felt that turbulence.

Rowan reaches for his twin, paws at his hand. I encourage him to sit back. He is strapped to my lap by the loop around my seatbelt. Who are they kidding that this will save anyone, if it needs to?

The woman who has dozed beside me cuts across to look out at the clouds. 'That was hairy,' she says in a soft Northern Irish accent.

'I hate flying,' I say.

'I can tell. Did the babies like the big smoke?'

'We were in Florida,' I say. 'My partner suggested we do this for their first birthday. One last hurrah before I go back to work after maternity leave.'

'That's nice,' she says and smiles at Rowan, who lifts his head from my chest to look at her. He smiles coyly, both hands coming up to hide his face.

'Sweet boy,' she says.

The plane plummets, this time waking Paul. 'What's happening?' he says.

'Turbulence,' the woman says.

Paul rearranges himself, holds onto Jared as he fixes his shirt. 'At least this flight is short,' he says.

Most of the people around us are without children. They are in business suits and reading papers, tapping on laptops or sleeping, and gradually waking. The woman beside me wants to talk, trying to distract me. 'I haven't been home in years,' she says.

'Where are you from, originally?' I ask her. Anxiety creeps up on me.

'Belfast. Have lived in London for thirty-odd years,' she says.

Jared wakes. He cries, was already asleep when we boarded and now he doesn't know where we are. I keep looking at Paul for reassurance, but he is dealing with the baby. The woman beside me takes my hand in hers. 'It will be over soon,' she says.

'I know,' I say. But I let our hands stay like that.

Soon I see the festive lights of the runway, then we are on home ground, then collecting baggage at the carousel. I get the boys into the double buggy and leave Paul to wait for our cases when I see the woman struggling with a suitcase. No one else seems to want to help her.

It is heavier than I would have thought. It takes both of us.

'Oh, thanks for that,' she says.

I realise I haven't asked her a thing about herself. 'Are you back for business or pleasure?' I ask, much calmer now.

'Neither,' she says.

'Well, good luck.'

'Good luck to you, too.' She nods at the babies who are fussing, pulling hats off one another. She laughs mildly and walks off.

Paul joins me and we carry on through the airport, to the car park, to our car.

Outside it is close and warm, cloudy with a chance of rain. Our people carrier looks like a stone at this time of day. How different things will be now, I think, setting Rowan into the car seat, and Paul, putting Jared into his. We start for home.

I pull down my visor, look in the mirror to make sure everything is as it should be. But I hardly recognise any of this. Least of all, myself.

Chapter 1

It was a beautiful Wednesday morning in May when I went back to the job. We had brought the Florida weather home to Belfast with us. My babysitter and sister-in-law, Sylvia, stood in her hallway with her arms out for my boys like she was being handed a gift. She and my brother Addam, the minister, were done asking God for a child of their own and were planning to adopt. In the meantime, she was borrowing my two.

Which is not to say that I didn't see fear in Sylvia's eyes the day I left Rowan and Jared with her for the duration of my shift and drove away, heading back to the day job at Strandtown PSNI station.

When I entered the office Chief Dunne did not flinch.

'You're back already,' said Carl Higgins, fixing his flicked-out Oasis-style hair and looking every bit as trendy as I remembered. 'I thought you were avoiding us.'

'I couldn't stay away,' I said.

There was a woman standing in the corner looking at the message board, her chin in her hand. She glanced at me, carried on with what she was doing, then she called over to the chief.

'Harriet, how are you?' Fergus Simon greeted me, wrapping his arms around me for a second or three.

'Great! Where's Diane?' I asked after my old partner; her car was missing from the parking area.

'Diane requested a transfer, didn't the chief tell you? Secret service. All very hush-hush,' said Fergus tapping the side of his nose.

'Was it something I said?'

I was watching the chief in conversation with the new woman when he caught my eye and finally came over. 'DI Sloane, welcome.' Then he called over to her: she still had her eyes glued to the board. 'Hewitt, come here and introduce yourself to Sloane.'

Hewitt approached us. She was a bit younger than me, mid-thirties I'd have thought, and serious as hell looking. She had a long face, thin lips and eyes that you do not want on you if you are in a phase of self-doubt, which I was.

'Sloane; Hewitt. Hewitt; Sloane,' Chief Dunne said. 'I'll leave you to do the formalities yourselves.'

Hewitt shook my hand. 'Fleur,' she said in a thick Scottish accent, 'and you're Harriet. Heard a lot about you.'

'You're looking at the new Superintendent,' said Higgins, unpeeling a satsuma. I looked sharply at him. 'Not me,' he said. 'Fleur.' He popped a segment in his mouth.

'Congratulations,' I said to Hewitt, could barely get the word out.

'Cheers,' said Hewitt. 'We're having a meeting soon, I expect it'll get you up to date. Welcome back, I suppose.'

I gave her an insincere smile, waited until she was away before I said, 'Welcome back, *I suppose*?'

'She's a toughie,' Higgins said out of the side of his mouth.

'I'll be back in a minute,' I said. I stood in the toilets, looked at myself in the mirror and wondered if I looked as stupid as I felt. How did I think I could leave for a year on maternity leave and they wouldn't have given the job to someone else?

Dunne and Hewitt were across the room talking about an initiative only they were privy to that would be filtered down to the team in the coming weeks. I felt like a gooseberry.

I skim-read all the recent caseloads for our district pretending I wasn't listening to the two of them. Diane's words came back to me from when we'd been working on the case of River Reede, the four-year-old who had gone missing from his home in Witham Street.

Diane said Chief Dunne was infamous for bedding younger women, despite having been married for decades. When I thought about it I couldn't help but see a fresher version of his wife Jocelyn in Superintendent Fleur Hewitt; they both had fine features and unruly brown hair. Both had this earthy superior thing going on. Plus, not once did he clear his throat impatiently with Fleur.

They were fucking. That was as clear as day. But what did anyone care? Greg Dunne was old by now and wasn't I living with a beautiful man who was not only an anaesthetist but a good and dependable person. Didn't Paul dote on the boys and even put a wrapped present in my bag when I wasn't looking?

I'd heard enough about Dunne and Hewitt's cosy little number and decided to tear open the present: a framed photo of the babies. I set it on my desk and ran my finger along the attached card, which read:

It's your turn now, Harry/Mummy, knock 'em dead!
Love you, Paul, Jared and Rowan xx

Chapter 2

Reading local case files was making me edgy. I felt this void inside that I could not place, it felt new. I much preferred to look forward those days than back. But I was reading up nevertheless: drugs, robberies and assaults, protests and arrogant rugby players. Superintendent Hewitt appeared by my side and abruptly proceeded to tell me that she hadn't had the time before to say but Sarge Higgins and I would be working together. I called bullshit. Hadn't made the time, more like.

Sergeant Higgins? I almost said, but I didn't want to look surprised when this was my patch, this office was as mundanely familiar as my own living room – more familiar, actually. Yes, I'd been away but I was back. This team was mine, even Higgins, pain in the ass or not. I'd take him as a partner. So be it.

'Great,' I said. Hewitt walked off and it was just Simon and I. 'Carl passed his sergeant exams then?' I asked him. 'Any more surprises? What are you, the new Chief Constable?'

'I'm happy where I am, ta muchly,' said Simon. I was convinced he meant that.

'What's she like?' I nodded at the door Fleur Hewitt had just left through. 'Aren't Scottish procedures different from ours?'

'She's alright. Dead clued up. Anyway, she's lived here for years.'

'I've never seen her before.'

'You should have applied, Harry.'

'I did apply, but don't tell anyone.'

'I thought you were a shoo-in.'

'I think someone is trying to force me out.'

'You're kidding! Who?' he asked.

'Yeah, I'm kidding,' I said. I was not.

*

It was gone noon when a woman walked into the station. She stood by the window waiting for a desk sarge to take her query. I saw her through the glass and knew I knew her.

'I'm here to speak to Superintendent Hewitt,' she said.

'I think you're for me,' Hewitt said, swanning past. She went out into the hall and opened the side door into an interview room.

'Oh hello,' the woman called out to me. 'Where could I possibly know your face from?'

'The flight, last night,' I said, remembering. Sixteen hours before, my hand had been in hers.

'Wow, how do you like that!' she said.

Hewitt looked at her watch, catching the woman's eye. 'Ready?' she asked.

'As I'll ever be,' the woman said, looking back at me. A smile of relief swept across her face, and I couldn't tell why I felt relieved too. There was something comfortable about her.

That pleasant thought was all too short-lived when a call came through from dispatch:

A dead body had been found in the PACT office on the Upper Newtownards Road.

Higgins was already at the service car when I got outside. It was sunny and breezy, but despite that, there was no mistaking I was back in Belfast and back to work as I jumped into the marked Skoda beside him and we set down the Holywood Road.

Siren on, turning left onto the ankle of the Upper Newtownards Road, near *Fat Factory*: a shop of sorts that hired out their toning beds, which supposedly 'sculpted' the body through vibrations alone.

Beside that was Wee Buns, a bakery. And beside that, was the PACT office. The acronym stood for Progressive Active Community Together; a party not popular on a road where most folk still voted for their choice of the *big two*. And usually the orange option.

Outside the office stood Mike Birch, a local MP, he was in a grey suit. He held his glasses in his hand. Two red marks tracked the bridge of his nose. Higgins let the siren die and we got out of the car.

'I can't believe she is in there like that,' said Mike.

'When did you arrive?' I asked him.

'Ten minutes ago. I can't believe it.'

The office was small with only a desk and a filing cabinet, behind the desk was a flurry of sheets strewn over the floor. Staplers, paper clips and pens that had been scattered everywhere. Despite the disruption to all the paperwork, it was clear the deceased had not fallen on top of it. I stepped over the pages to better see the soles of two lime green Converse trainers that were prodding out from the desk.

On the floor was the body of a woman. She was lying face down with three oozing stab wounds to her back. She was wearing a sleeveless blood-dyed T-shirt. On her lower half were three-quarter length jeans. She had her hair cut in a bob and coloured rose petal pink. Her young face was turned slightly sideways so I could see her cloudy green eyes that were fixed and staring blindly. She looked like a teenager.

Chloe Taylor.

'Chloe Taylor is her name, twenty-one years old,' Mike Birch said, he reeked of booze and aftershave. 'She was a volunteer here with PACT.'

On the desk were two cups of coffee that had not been touched, they had square brown logos on the front. I held my hand above the cups. They were a little over room temperature.

'Are these yours?' I asked Mike.

'Nope. There has been a lot of political unrest here ... Not that I'm telling you how to do your job.'

I'd seen the demonstrations on the telly. I had no need to be in the area since I wasn't working and had moved into my twin sister Charly's old house at Mount Eden Road off Malone, while she and her family moved only around the corner into my parents' old house, and my father out of there and into an apartment at New Forge, just five minutes from Bethany Nursing Home where my mother had already languished for years due to Huntington's.

But I knew the protests were outside PACT for months and had only ceased one week before Chloe Taylor's body was found there.

I got Mike to show me where I would find the surveillance tapes. He walked past Chloe, trying not to look at her, located the tape deck which was open and empty. 'No, this isn't right,' Mike said, perturbed. 'Someone has opened this and taken the tape. We tape everything. Bit old-fashioned but we don't waste taxpayers' money on high-tech gadgetry. We've been more vigilant since there've been threats to the office. Most protests are peaceful, people wanting the union upheld and we want to move beyond that, be progressive. Some people want to go backward, so there have been threats, mostly online.'

'Did you report them?' asked Higgins.

'Oh, yeah. I have a reference number.' Mike looked at the papers on the floor hopelessly, then at the empty tape deck.

Outside grew a crush of nosey sods who were asked to move along while the road was closed off and cordoned by tape that shook behind a curtain of air.

In that crush was a man who wore an apron that had the same name and logo as the coffee cup, the same brown square and swirling font. I slipped under the cordon and went to have a word with him.

His name was Boyd Matchett, nickname Bap, he was a man in his thirties and owner of the bakery/coffee shop next door. Boyd told me he ran the place with his wife, Lyndsey, co-owner of Wee Buns and sole proprietor of thickly drawn on eyebrows.

She also was outside, rubbernecking with the rest of the crowd.

Lyndsey followed me into the bakery again. 'Can I get you something to eat or drink, love?' she said in that endearing yet condescending manner I sometimes like, but because she was younger than me, and I was jetlagged, I found it irritating.

'Just a few minutes of your time,' I said.

'Is someone dead in there? That's the impression I get with the police tape and everything.'

'Yes.'

'When did it happen?'

'We don't have answers for any questions people may have at the moment.'

'No, of course not,' said Boyd. He sat down.

'Did you notice anything suspicious this morning?' I asked him.

'No.'

'Did you see the young woman enter the office?'

'No.'

'I could hear someone in there when I was in our storeroom,' said Lyndsey. 'I could hear life in PACT.'

'What did you hear?'

'Like a chair scraping on the floor and footsteps, no voices or anything. And no music; usually Birchy likes to get the radio on first thing. It's not loud, but when we're getting set up, before we put our own radio on, you can generally hear the humming noise of the radio next door. Sure you don't want something, love? A wee cappuccino?'

'No thanks,' I said. 'The office was opened by a volunteer this morning.'

'The young girl?'

'A young woman.'

'Oh, God, it's not her, is it? I've seen her there loads of times. I didn't see her today.'

'I'm afraid a young woman has been killed next door.'

Lyndsey covered her open mouth with her hand. Boyd's pale eyes grew wide in shock.

'So, she didn't come in here and get two coffees?' I asked.

'I don't think I'd know her to see,' said Boyd.

'Ah, you would,' said Lyndsey, 'wee young girl, she's only about nineteen or twenty, dyes her hair different colours. Sometimes it's pink, sometimes it's that washed out grey.'

'I know who you mean. She wasn't in the bakery today.'

'Someone was,' I said. 'There are two cups of your coffee in there and they are still warm.'

'You're joking!' said Lyndsey.

'Well, they're not cold. They aren't yesterday's.'

'Who have we had in here?' Lyndsey flicked her hand at her husband.

'Some school kids buying sausage rolls for their lunch,' he said. 'Not many people, those protests have lost us a lot of business. The usual trade, workers in the area are keeping away.'

'Has business picked up in the last week, since the last protest?' asked Higgins.

'Not really,' said Lyndsey.

'But you said you were busy,' I reminded Boyd. 'Busy doing what?'

'Making phone calls. Making orders. And we did have some customers.'

'Can you give me a list of all the people who have been here in the last couple of hours?'

'Yes,' he said, sighing. 'But, can I tell ya, this isn't our coffee. We don't sell that coffee since we were messed about by the supplier, we use something else but we just have all those cups and aren't wasting old ones when they're perfectly fine.'

'And we're not the only coffee shop that does this type of coffee, you know,' said Lyndsey. 'There's probably ... how many, Boyd?'

'You're looking at fifty, sixty, easy in Belfast alone.'

I reiterated my request for a list. Boyd held a pen then set it down. 'There were a few mums in, groups of couples, these ones who leave the kids to school and do some messages, pop in and grab a coffee on the way back for pick up. Mostly women and kids. Women who come out of the Fat Factory and pop straight in here for a fresh cream bun after.'

Lyndsey shook her head at his poor timing for a joke. 'No one who'd go in and ... kill someone, put it that way,' she said. 'If I think of anything, can I let you know, love?'

'Please do, even if you don't think it's important.'

'Every little helps, doesn't it?'

'Is that Tesco or Asda?' Boyd said.

'Tesco,' she said.

I gave Lyndsey Matchett my card and walked back towards the scene. Mike was standing in the office, still speaking with Higgins. 'A really good, decent person,' said Mike. 'She doesn't deserve to be lying there like that.'

'Let's get you out of here,' I said.

We brought him to the station to give us a statement. There he wouldn't be able to look at the body anymore. Mike Birch told us the same details in the interview room, repeatedly, and with the same steady disbelief at the remarkable and remarkably sad day he had found himself living. We soon sent Birch home.

*

'She's been dead a while,' said Brian Quinn when we met him back at PACT's East Belfast office. 'Look at her arms, they're blotchy. Lividity has set in.'

'When do you think she was killed?' asked Higgins.

'Going on for an hour and a half ago.' Quinn bent down and looked at her hands and arms. 'No defensive wounds, she hasn't seen this coming at all.'

'What else can you tell?' I asked.

'Straight off the bat? The perp is above average height, which you can tell because of the direction of the blood spatter.' Quinn pointed at the wall and floor. 'And when we look closer at her stab wounds I bet that will verify it; the angle the knife entered the victim's body.'

'There was a knifepoint robbery at Mayhew's pharmacy up the road yesterday,' said Higgins.

'Do they hold money here, though?' I said, thinking the pharmacy sounded like a robbery. What was there to steal in a political office?

'They were looking for pills up there, or money,' said Higgins.

On the short drive back to the station again he was still talking about the robbery but I doubted the person who robbed Mayhew's was thinking so clearly. Whereas PACT looked like someone had put thought into it. The disruption of the office looked staged to me.

'Don't know if you heard,' said Higgins, 'but that particular individual from the pharmacy didn't leave with anything, he was scared off by this little, ballsy, middle-aged pharmacist who told him where to sling his hook.'

'Can't be the same perp, can it?'

I watched the woman, my aeroplane neighbour, walk down the Holywood Road dabbing her eyes with a tissue. Hay fever was my first instinct, then I saw her face clearly and saw that she was in floods of tears.

'A dead woman?' asked Superintendent Hewitt inside the station.

'Yes,' I said. 'A stabbing. Young woman called Chloe Taylor. What happened with your visitor?'

'That was Janet Ward,' said Hewitt, 'her sister Karen was strangled almost forty years ago. Janet wanted to talk to us about the possibility of reopening the case.'

'Christ, what a burden,' I said. 'Must still be so upsetting.'

'I'm sure it is, but I think she was more upset I said no.'

'You said no?'

'We can't just reopen it now.'

'But she flew all the way from London.'

Hewitt frowned. 'She could have phoned and saved herself the hassle.'

I went to my desk and watched Hewitt, trying to get the measure of the woman.

Chapter 3

Some places you'd rather not be. I'd rather be doing the Orlando flight with two babies five times over than standing in the hospital mortuary next to Jackie Taylor. Jackie stared at the girl on the cold silver table, his face simmering like water. He opened his mouth and a noise came out that made me look away from him and at the girl again.

'Is this your daughter?' the medic asked him. 'Can you confirm that you are looking at Chloe Taylor?'

'I can confirm it,' said Jackie, a squarely built grim-faced man. He was wearing a pale silver-grey shirt with the sleeves rolled up and sweat patches under his arms, he had a swallow tattooed on his forearm.

His face did not register anything. We left the room and I thanked him, and before we were about to bring him back home he said he needed to use the toilet. When he came out and re-joined Higgins and I, his face was reddest around the eyes. I don't know how he held it together.

'What about Chloe's mother?' I asked him in the car. 'Is she still living?'

Jackie glanced out of the window, he flinched a bit then composed himself. 'She wouldn't be interested. She hasn't seen Chloe in years.'

'So, she doesn't know that Chloe has been killed?' He looked at me in shock, and I tried to pedal backwards, '…attacked.'

The word *killed* seemed too harsh, even though he had seen the outcome with his own two.

Jackie said nothing.

He was shivering as we passed Stormont Hotel and the parliament building that late afternoon after four P.M. when the place was leafy, lush and peaceful.

We took a right, just facing the civil service grounds, and drove until we reached the Taylors' home: a lovely detached house with the long sweeping pavior driveway full of cars. An Audi, a Fiesta, the arse of a silver BMW was hanging out into the street, blocking the footpath. There were magnolias in bloom in the well-kept garden, and a bike leaning against the wall.

I opened the back door of the service car to let Jackie out. Once inside the house, he went upstairs and left Higgins and me to fend for ourselves.

There were four people in the house. Drew Taylor, for one. He was standing with his fingers tucked in his armpits looking out of the conservatory and at the tree in the back garden that gently swayed in the breeze, there was a flour sift of light coming in through the leaves. Drew turned and looked at us and stared. There was another man, younger than Drew; he was lifting huge boards and carrying them out of the room and upstairs. And two women: the dark-haired one was standing looking at her phone in the kitchen and the other one, with the streaming long blond hair approached me, a forlorn look shaping her face.

'I'm Lizzie,' she said in a husky voice. 'Chloe's best friend.' She put her hand out to shake mine, then Higgins'.

'DI Sloane,' I said. 'This is Consta … *Sergeant* Higgins.'

'Pleased to meet you both,' she said. 'Pity about the circumstances.' Lizzie glanced at Drew and was silent.

Seeing him there the usual assumptions came to me; he was a prominent loyalist. Where trouble was, Drew Taylor was never far away.

Diane Linskey and I had once interviewed him over the possibility that he'd thrown – or knew who had thrown – a pipe bomb into the service car of one of our colleagues.

Fortunately it didn't detonate.

Didn't harm Detective Amy Campbell, who was sitting guard outside the PACT offices around the time of the flag debacle in 2013.

We never got a conviction, as is infuriatingly often the case with this kind of crime. No one wants to talk and sometimes you understand. I remembered him, and Drew sure as hell remembered me, he exhaled noisily and looked back at the tree.

'We want to get a better knowledge of Chloe,' Higgins said to Lizzie, 'what she did on a daily basis … who she was in contact with. Can we have a chat with you, with you being her best friend?' He smiled then, laying the charm on thick.

'Oh, sure,' said Lizzie, unable to resist. He was pretty for a copper, even I had to admit that.

'Her father told us Chloe was studying at Queens,' said Higgins.

'Yes, first year Social Anthropology.'

The young man with the boards came back and lingered near us.

'Are you Chloe's brother?' I asked him.

'Yes,' he said.

'This is Thomas,' said Lizzie.

'Thomas!' Drew gestured him over. Thomas hesitated then he chose us, he paused in front of me. He was rangy with curly brown hair and a cute but pimple-stippled face. He looked at me open-mouthed.

'I'm very sorry for your loss,' I said and he mumbled something, looking unsure whether to walk off or not. Drew joined us instead. He wanted to hear everything. 'Hello again, Mr. Taylor. What is your connection?'

'We're cousins,' he said full of his usual bad attitude.

'Thomas, I've given the kitchen a clean,' said Lizzie with her hand on his back. 'You'll have callers. I thought your dad wouldn't want the place messy.'

'Yeah,' said Thomas rubbing the back of his head, uncomfortable with being touched, I understood it; when you are having a baby, or two, or when you are grieving, people think they can touch you, friends, strangers, enemies.

'We were all working this morning, it was a mess,' Thomas said to me apologetically, then he thanked Lizzie.

'You weren't planning on this,' said Drew, throwing a dirty look Lizzie's way.

'You want to see my own house at the moment, Thomas. Complete bombsite.' Lizzie gave a helpless little laugh and Drew gave her another dirty look.

Out of the kitchen came the other woman, the one with the long dark brown hair, she was far smaller than the blonde, she stood by Drew to let everyone know who she belonged to and rocked on the spot as if she were holding a tired baby. 'I put the soup in the fridge,' she said, fake-yawning.

'When did you last see Chloe?' I asked Thomas.

'This morning,' he said without meeting my eye, 'she was getting ready to leave.'

'How was she feeling?'

He stared blankly at me.

'Anxious, happy?'

He looked at Drew for an answer; Drew looked back at him.

'Just her normal self,' Thomas decided on. After a pause he added, 'She was going to the office to volunteer. She has no class on a Wednesday till late afternoon.'

'Did Chloe drive to the PACT office?'

'Yes.'

'And whose cars are those outside?'

'The Audi is Dad's. The Fiesta is mine.'

'The BMW?'

The brunette nodded at Drew. 'Ours.'

'Oh, and you are?' asked Higgins. 'We haven't been introduced.' Smooth bastard!

'Roxanne. I'm married to Drew; Drew is cousins with Chloe.'

'I last saw Chloe last night,' said Lizzie. 'She had a drink at mine. What about you, Drew?'

'Huh?'

'When did you last see your cousin?'

'Chloe?'

'Yes.' Lizzie gave him a benevolent smile.

'Must have been months ago now. Christmas.' He thumbed the corner of his mouth.

Lizzie sat on the brown leather sofa in the light blue living room, she squirmed then put her hand down beside her. 'Is this your bag?' she asked me.

'It's mine,' said Roxanne.

Lizzie stood and handed Roxanne the handbag before she sat down again. Roxanne pinched it like a sample of piss. Drew nodded to the kitchen where they all went, except for Lizzie who stayed with Higgins and me.

'I keep asking myself if this is real,' she said. 'Chloe was so humble, such a sweetheart.'

'Did everyone think so?' I asked her.

'No one gets a clean sweep, do they? Have you talked to Lewis?'

'Who is Lewis?' asked Higgins.

'I thought he might have shown up here, and since he hasn't, looks like a red flag to me.'

'Who is he?' I said.

'Lewis… Chloe's on-again, off-again.'

'And they were…'

'Off at the moment, but they've been together for years. I thought he would have called. I asked Thomas, but he hasn't heard from him.'

'He sounds like a person we need to speak to,' said Higgins. 'Do you have a surname for Lewis?'

'Skelly. He studies at the Belfast Met; so does Thomas, actually.'

'Thank you, Lizzie,' I said and went over to Thomas. 'Could you tell your dad that we'll get in touch tomorrow? He has my number.'

'Are you leaving now, Inspector?' Drew asked me.

'Detective Inspector; yes. For now.'

'Great, take her with you. She's doing my head in.' He meant Lizzie, who was standing at the front window looking out.

'Here's my babe now,' she said. I was unsure if she'd heard Drew, if she was ignoring him. 'We'd already planned to go out for a bite to eat, and I should try to keep to a routine, shouldn't I? Even though it's the last thing I want to do. Look, anything I can do…'

We followed her outside. Out of an old silver Mercedes that was bumped up ahead of our service car came a man, early thirties, maybe older, he was in a white shirt and black trousers, a broad white smile on his chops, tanned skin and black hair. He smiled at us as she lifted her bike from against the house and strapped it to the back of his car rack.

Drew came out now too and lit up a cigarette. He stared at Lizzie and the man whose car she was getting into, her *babe*. Drew's eyes followed them out of the street. Then he put the cigarette out on the wall. And stared at me as he did it.

*

Higgins drove, cut out onto Stormont Road back toward the station. 'When are we going to acknowledge what happened at the Christmas party?' he asked me.

'What are you on about?' I muttered.

He made a kissing sound.

'It won't be repeated,' I said.

'No, I know that. It just came out of nowhere. Like a bat out of hell.'

'Let's stick a pin in it.'

'What, no post-mortems?'

'None,' I said and Higgins laughed.

Fuck, so it did happen. I'd hit the Merlot hard that night and told myself I'd imagined it.

Chapter 4

My shift was done by six. I travelled along the Outer Ring to Forestside. Sylvia greeted me at the door. She had the boys' bags ready to go, their coats on. 'Let's take those off you two,' I said. 'It's even warmer in the car.'

'I couldn't get dinner made, Harriet,' she said. 'Now Addam will come home wondering where his dinner is and he shouldn't have to.'

'Can't he bring something in?' I asked her.

'That's not how we do things in this house, Harriet,' she said, which felt like a verbal spanking.

'My brother's a big boy,' I said. 'Can't he make something?'

'No, he can't. He's not been feeling the best lately, maybe you haven't noticed. And he's had a busy day, too.'

'Yeah, busy day drinking tea with pensioners.'

Sylvia seemed nervous, like always. Perhaps that's just around me. She always liked my brothers, obviously, being married to one. But there was Brooks, the eldest, whom Sylvia liked especially. Addam never approved, Brooks being a drug addict, though impossibly sweet with it. Neither of them had to worry about seeing him, anyway, not since Brooks had taken up with some old pal of his again and disappeared out of our lives again. He had been staying with me in my old apartment in St George's Harbour overlooking the Lagan when one day he went out to meet a friend, for coffee, he said, and never came back. Must have been some coffee!

I was six months pregnant with the boys at the time. It was shortly after that I caved to Paul's invites of a date. Which was weird, getting to know someone else when I was already pregnant.

But not strange to Paul, who always wanted kids and couldn't have them since he'd had treatment for a childhood cancer that had made him infertile. I wasn't so keen on him to begin with but I was lucky to have Paul and I now knew it, especially when my sisters, Coral and Charlotte, had gone missing out of my life because, after the initial attraction of newborns, babies – as I was learning – made everyone (but Paul) retreat.

'Twins,' they both said. 'I'm going to be the best aunt. I love them already.'

And then, screw all! And after all I did for their kids over the years! They were both over it, and now if I hadn't have had Paul, I would have no one. Except the twins. I don't know that one-year-olds are much company, or a support system of any sort. They were the reason I needed support, and I always hated to need help.

But Sylvia was as intimidated by my sisters as she was by me, which made it too easy to tell her what I wanted her to do with the boys. It made accepting her help easier. We had a conversation about what she'd feed the boys, after which I discovered she had done her own thing and ignored my rules. Sylvia had some idea that when they were with her for those few hours, the boys were hers and she would feed them whatever she wanted to; she didn't take any notice of how I'd been doing it over the past year.

I must say though, she looked wrecked. Felt wrecked enough to be ratty with me; which was really saying something.

'Try to be on time tomorrow when you collect them,' she said as she held the bags out. I lifted Jared and put him in the car and then Rowan. Sylvia stretched back and gripped her side. I had two fat and active little guys and they'd given her a battering. She did not even wave at us as we drove away. That was just day one.

The boys fell asleep, dewy and briny with sweat, bubbles of it on their noses, their lashes webby and wet as I drove in the sour heat along the Outer Ring toward home. They were hard work but thank goodness they were cute. They really were the most beautiful things I'd ever seen and I'm not being biased.

At home, Paul and I gave them a bottle each and put them to bed. Thinking about Jackie looking at Chloe, his once-baby, on the table that day, I felt the blowback of his pain rip through me. I usually try to be present in body and spirit myself out of the hospital emotionally.

'How did the boys get on?' Paul asked.

'Sylvia had coats on them in that heat!'

'Typical exam weather, remember studying for exams in the garden?'

'Yes, I know. If someone else says, "I suppose this is our summer" again, I'll crack.'

'But it is … always nicer in May than July and August.'

'I know.'

'Come here.' He kissed me on the lips. 'Want a salad?'

'Yes.'

We sat at the table as we ate.

'Maybe I'll ask Sylvia to let the boys sleep longer during the day so I'll see more of them in the evening,' I said.

'You can't make them sleep, you know that.'

'Yes, but I can tell her to try.'

'How did she get on?' Paul asked, wanting more detail.

'She looked massively stressed. Especially about dinner. She'll just have to prepare better, like we did when we knew I was going back to work.'

'But Sylvia doesn't work, she's not used to it.'

'She helps out at the church,' I said. 'Being a minister's wife is a sort of job, no?'

Paul shrugged.

'She was snappy when I questioned some of her choices.'

'Well, you need to ease up on some things when someone else is minding your kids.'

'Are you taking her side?' I asked him.

'No, never. Do you want to watch some TV?'

'No, catch up on your programmes, I want to look some things up.'

'I was hoping you'd tell me about your day.'

I had never, not in fifteen months of being with him, asked Paul about his day. I vowed to do it the next one.

I'd written *Lewis Skelly, Belfast Met* on my notebook. I was going to look him up but instead I looked up 'dead girl found' and ended up sidetracked by a new search of a different girl; her coverage far outweighed Chloe's. This victim was found in April, five days before Paul, the kids and I left for Florida.

Erica McClelland.

Erica was nineteen years old and a music fan who had been in the live music venue, *The Night Kitchen* on Ormeau Avenue, Belfast. She had been watching a band called Vacant Aluminium. She was found dead in shallow water at Ballyholme beach in Bangor, fifteen miles away, at six a.m. on the morning of Thursday 26 April. She'd been stabbed three times in the back.

I wasn't sure how similar her death was to Chloe Taylor's. Erica was from Lisburn and had no Bangor connections; Chloe was killed in her place of work, in broad daylight. They were both young women who had been stabbed three times and killed. But that was not enough to link the two.

'Okay,' I said to Paul. 'Let's see what's on Netflix.'

Chapter 5

'The victim was stabbed with a hunting knife,' Brian Quinn confirmed the next morning. 'This is a slightly taller than usual man we were looking for. The victim was injured in the heart and died a quick death, she wouldn't have known what was happening.'

'Motives,' said Chief Dunne. 'Who do we suspect and why would they want to harm Chloe Taylor?'

'There was the political angle,' Carl Higgins said.

'Now we need to investigate the personal,' said Fleur Hewitt.

'Couldn't it have been random? What kind of knife was used at the pharmacy robbery?' I asked.

'A machete,' said Sarge Simon.

'Stop it! A machete? But what about Erica McClelland?' I said. 'Wasn't she stabbed three times in the back?'

'That was a kitchen knife, this was a hunting knife,' said Higgins.

'Does that matter?' I asked. 'Maybe the different weapons are an attempt to throw us off the scent.'

'Go talk to the pharmacist again,' said Superintendent Hewitt. 'Sloane and Higgins, go this morning.'

*

'I recognise her,' Higgins said in the car.

'Who?'

'Erica McClelland.'

'Where from?'

'My gigs, and just the music scene in general.'

'She *was* at the gig at The Night Kitchen; Vacant Aluminium,' I said.

'With her friends one minute, then gone. Eleven p.m. was the last anyone saw her,' said Higgins, 'they thought she'd gone to the toilets or something, then they thought she'd gone home ... until she was found dead the next morning. In Bangor.'

'What is your gut saying?' I asked.

'I doubt highly these are linked.'

'Who is it usually, Carl? The murderer of young women?'

'Intimate partner. Or the ex ...'

'Did you ever see Erica at any gigs with a partner?'

'No. I'm not thinking about her though, she's Bangor's problem.'

'Very sweet of you!' I said. 'And there was me thinking you'd grown up a lot since we last worked together.'

'I didn't mean it to sound rude.'

'It did.'

'I'm just thinking about our case. About Chloe.'

'And I'm thinking about her ex,' I said, taking a left. 'We need to track down Lewis Skelly and see what he has to say for himself.'

'Harry, Mayhew's is back there,' said Higgins, turning to look over his shoulder.

'We'll go later.' Fleur Hewitt was not going to tell me what to do. 'We're going to see Lewis. Lizzie called the station this morning.'

'Lizzie who?'

'Chloe's best friend,' I said. 'That's how I got Lewis' address. She also wanted to know if we had found the killer yet.'

He scoffed. 'Hasn't been twenty-four hours.'

'Lizzie obviously cared for the girl. And not only that, people get mildly edgy when there's a killer on the loose.'

'I suppose they do,' he said.

A young man sat smoking in front of the Orangefield address Lizzie had given me. He had jaw-length hair and wore a Pink Floyd tee.

'Ah,' said Higgins, 'Floyd man, like him already.'

'Thought you were strictly brit pop, Carl.'

'Strictly rock and roll, Harry.'

I tried not to smirk in front of the young man. 'Lewis Skelly?' I asked him.

'That's me.' He invited us inside.

'How long did you date Chloe for?' Higgins asked him, going straight for the kill.

'Three years,' Lewis said. 'From sixteen years old to nineteen, or twenty.'

'How did you meet?'

'At a protest.'

'What were you protesting?' I asked.

'The G8 summit meetings.' He must have been uncomfortable when we stared at him, so he elaborated, 'You know, putting profit before people, before our planet. I'm not so involved now, Chloe was. First time I saw her she was holding her placard over her head in Custom House Square.'

'Unusual place to meet a potential date,' I said, adding a smile to try to put him at ease, trying to slow it down a tad.

I thought of Paul and how we first met in the kitchen that is now ours, and how random life is, how it is impossible to tell who will mean anything to you when you first meet them.

'Tell us more,' I urged Lewis; I wanted his words at his pace. He seemed calm but his hands were shaking. He needed to trust us. 'Get them to trust you, but don't let them think you're their friend,' Father used to tell me.

'She stood out,' said Lewis. 'Her hair was dyed teal. That's what she called it, I called it blue. It was raining and Chloe was worried the colour would run. That's what we were talking about.'

'What month was that?' Higgins asked.

'June, five years ago, going on,' said Lewis.

'The summit, 2013,' said Higgins. Impressive that he remembered.

'We were friends for a couple of months,' said Lewis, 'then we became something more serious.'

'When did your relationship change?' I asked.

'Yeah. Definitely that September.'

'And ultimately, you split up?'

'Uh-huh.'

'Why was that?' I asked.

'I don't know.'

'Did Chloe finish things?' asked Higgins.

'She did.'

'And you have no idea why?'

'Yes and no; lots of things happened.'

'Like what, Lewis?'

'It was never easy.'

'You were young, too,' I said.

'Yeah, I suppose. There was that …' said Lewis, stopping.

'You're twenty-one now, same as Chloe?'

'Right.'

'And what do you do with yourself, Lewis? Work? Study?'

'I am studying a foundation degree, it's at, erm, Belfast Met.'

'Which campus?' asked Higgins.

'Millfield.'

'Had you any concerns about Chloe?'

'Yeah, always. The first day I met her, for a date, proper date, that September, her mum Glynis had just been sectioned and that was difficult for Chloe.'

'How long was Mrs. Taylor in hospital?'

'A month, something like that.'

'And this affected Chloe quite a lot?'

'Yes. A few months later her mum moved out completely. She would refuse to take her medication, so it was hard for all of them.'

'Did she keep in touch?' I asked.

'They tried for a while. At least, Chloe tried. Jackie didn't want Glynis mentioned in the house. Chloe couldn't talk to him about her … or anything else.'

'And after that?'

'Two years later … Chloe started studying Law at Queens, then she was selected to be on the Young Leaders UK programme. Chloe had the chance then to question world leaders and travel a bit.'

'That sounds positive.'

'It was. At that stage.'

'What changed?'

'It probably changed when she was studying for exams and she received these Facebook messages.'

'Okay …'

'They were really nasty, and I don't know, Chloe sort of had a breakdown over it.'

'A mental breakdown?' asked Higgins.

Lewis nodded. 'She saw what happened to her mum and she got depressed, tried to sign herself into a mental ward but they wouldn't take her.'

'How did Chloe seem to you at this stage, looking back?' I asked.

'Sad. Crying all the time. Not like herself.'

'What did her family say?' asked Higgins.

'I told Jackie, he sat and listened, but he looked really angry. He always looks angry. He took her, made sure she got help, but the waiting list was crazy, so they went private. He helped Chloe, but I think he held that against me, me telling him.'

'What were the Facebook messages about?' I asked Lewis.

'Just sexist shit. Some sad keyboard warrior. No name. I had a look to see if we could work out who it was.'

'Did Chloe go to the police?' asked Higgins.

'No. She didn't think it was something you could do anything about.'

'We would have tried our best,' I said weakly.

'Cool.' Lewis raised his eyebrows with a disbelieving look.

'Have you been to the Taylors' house since?'

'Doubt I'm welcome. Jackie never acknowledged me at hospital, or anywhere else.'

'You mean the mental health hospital,' said Higgins.

'That's what I mean. Not that she was in for long, she was an outpatient, in the main.'

'Her brother? Thomas? Do you talk to him?'

'No. Thomas is painfully shy, like, and a bit of a loner.'

'How long was Chloe in hospital?' asked Higgins.

'A few days here and there … then she was an outpatient. Then she disappeared.'

'Where to?'

'Took a gap year and went travelling.'

'Nice. Where did she go?'

'Around Europe. France, Spain. I hardly heard from her then. When she came home that March she called things off, but we hadn't spoken in so long I knew it was over.'

'Who did she go away with?'

'I have no idea. She just got distant and weird.'

'You fell out?'

'No. Chloe never fell out with people. She did … she did … *love* me.' Lewis' voice cracked on the word. 'It was mutual when we ended. We decided that if it was meant to be … but that we'd focus on ourselves for a while.' We were about to leave him when he said, 'Detective, tell Thomas I'm sorry.'

'I'll pass on your condolences, Lewis.'

*

'I like him, he seems sweet,' I said as I drove away.

Higgins laughed.

'What?' I asked.

'You're a judge of his character now, are you?'

'No, obviously I get it wrong, from time to time.'

'You talking about me?'

'No, I am not talking about you. You're *obviously* an ass.'

'Thanks,' Higgins said. 'Textbook Sloane.'

'No worries,' I told him. 'And I don't want to pull rank on you, Carl, but in future ease up on the interruptions.'

'Yessir.'

'And slow it up a bit.'

But I was flattered. I knew Carl was trying to impress me.

We went to Summerhill to talk to Jackie.

'We've spoken to Lewis Skelly,' Higgins told him.

'Is he okay?' Jackie replied in a whisper. He had a delay in his movements.

'He's upset,' I said.

'Lew's a good kid,' said Jackie.

'You like him?' asked Higgins.

Jackie turned and looked at us properly, became more alert. 'Like him a lot. Why do you seem surprised?'

I changed the subject, 'Lewis mentioned that Chloe went travelling in her gap year.'

'That's right.'

'Where did she go?'

'Europe.'

'Whereabouts?'

'All over,' Jackie said before taking a deep breath. 'She asked for her bank account details, it was a trust fund for her wedding one day. Chloe said she didn't believe in marriage, and I said, "Go on then, go to Europe, if it's something you have to do".'

'And her friends went too?'

'It was organised through her university. I remember … a June, and a Beatrice … they're names that stand out, like, old-fashioned names, I thought at the time. A handful of them took a gap year and did this.'

'What about Lizzie?'

'Oh, her. No. She's a lot older and not at university.'

'Do you know Lizzie well?' I asked.

'I don't know Lizzie at all. That was the first time I met her, yesterday.'

'I heard Chloe had a spell where she was worried about her mental health.'

'Do you think she stabbed herself three times in the back?' There was a fast turn in mood and tone from Jackie. He became suddenly sharp, suddenly aware.

'Well, no, but …'

'I don't want to hear about that. It's irrelevant.'

'Can we speak to Thomas?'

'Why? He knows nothing either.'

'We need to speak to everyone who is close to Chloe,' I reminded him.

'You mean everyone who *was* close to Chloe.' He looked broken. 'Thomas is out. I'll tell him you called.'

'Just one more thing, Mr. Taylor,' I said. 'We located your daughter's car in Lena Street.'

'I don't want it back at the house.'

'What do you want us to do with it?'

'Give me the keys,' said Jackie.

'They were in Chloe's bag,' I said. 'We'll give you everything together, at the same time.'

'Drew will sell the car, he'll sort it out. Where's the clothes she was wearing?'

'We need to keep them, for now. Sorry,' I told Jackie. 'Then you can get them back.'

'Okay.'

'And you want them?'

'I don't know. I don't know what I'll do with them, or any of her ... stuff. I can't face her room.'

'We just have to make you aware that the clothes she was wearing during the attack—'

'The attack,' he said, 'the *murder.*'

I inhaled. 'They had to be cut off ... and they'll have blood on them.'

'I don't want them,' he said. 'Her coat, though, Thomas says she went out wearing it in the morning. It had a picture of a tiger on the back.'

'There was no coat at the scene,' I said.

'It wasn't in her car?' asked Higgins.

'No,' I told him.

'When you find it, Thomas wants it.'

'Can you describe it for me in more detail, please?'

'Black, but light material, it had a tiger's face on the back, red trim on the belt and the cuffs. Chloe got it on her travels. It was special to her, and he'd like it for that very reason.'

Chapter 6

By two p.m. we went to Mayhew's pharmacy located on Newtownards Road, where the pharmacist told me what I had already read: a man dressed in jeans, a black jumper and balaclava, and brandishing a machete, said, 'Give me everything, money, pills, or I'll swipe your fucken head off.'

The pharmacist showed me the whole show on their CCTV.

'It was on the news all evening,' he said, amused.

I had been travelling home and had not seen it when it happened. Even I gasped when Jennifer Crothers, the woman who worked behind the counter, grabbed the machete from the would-be thief.

Just then she came out of the ladies drying her hands on a paper towel.

'Here's the hero herself,' the pharmacist said, excusing himself to go and help a customer.

'That was very brave of you,' I told Jennifer, 'but for future reference, we don't recommend doing that.'

She scoffed. Jennifer was very slight, dainty looking with a hoarse voice and devilish laugh.

'It's done now.' Jennifer laughed. 'Too late for what-ifs. But, would I do it again? No, I probably wouldn't.'

'Congratulations, it worked,' said Higgins.

'Maybe you'll see fit to nominate me for a wee medal, son. And I was on the TV all night.' She laughed then Carl laughed.

'God, are the police getting younger or what?' she said to me, and I realised it was not me she was talking about but Carl.

'I don't think so,' I said. I looked at him again and saw how young he did look.

I'd thought I didn't look much older. Maybe I'm weathered now with raising twins. 'We're testing the machete for prints. We'll be in touch as soon as we hear anything. Likelihood is that this person is in the system.'

'Pitiful creature all the same,' Jennifer said. 'Must be hard-up. He was never going to use that thing, you know the way you can sense danger? He was no danger. Not that I wanna deal with that shite every day, a machete waved about in my face, but, let's just say, I'm not fucken stupid, detective. I'm not gonna risk my life for the sake of a few quid,' and out of the side of her mouth, 'that isn't even mine but your man's.' Jennifer rolled her eyes in the direction of the pharmacist.

Higgins laughed. 'We'll see what we can do about a medal all the same.'

'You don't think this was the same person that killed the girl up the road?' she asked. 'Now that would scare me, alright.'

'That wasn't a machete.'

'There's a glut of crime up and down this road,' she said. 'But imagine ... Hey, maybe I should have taken some time off.' Jennifer looked at me with concern.

'You've been through a traumatic experience. No one would think poorly of you if you did.' I understood, it was easy to say, but hard to do.

'I don't care what any one them thinks of me,' she said then she deliberated for a while. 'Hmm, maybe I have been through a traumatic experience. There are people who have received claims for less. But you know what I believe? If you live like that it comes back to bite you. I know people claim on their home insurance every year and then bad stuff is going on in their personal lives and I just think, there's your payout. I truly believe that.'

'It would make things much easier,' I agreed. 'Stick to the right side of the law and you'll be fine.'

'Aye, but there's those that do and have hard lives too.'

Make up your bloody mind, I thought. I thought, you're crazy, woman. Not brave but fully mad.

'Let's hope he gets his comeuppance,' said Higgins.

'Or help, Officer,' Jennifer said. 'As I say, must be desperate. It's usually depression disguised, deep down.'

What could I say to that? Wasn't she right? Maybe not so mad after all.

And I thought a lot about what she said when, shortly after, we went along Kings Road to Tullycarnet: a housing estate in Dundonald near the Ice Bowl. There we pulled up at Drew Taylor's house: a red brick end semi with an extension that filled most of their previously-sizeable garden. There was a balding hedge closing off a small grassy area. A paved area which held a selection of small tricycles. Plant pots were dotted about. And in the corner, a wooden loveseat.

Two months shy of 'silly season' a loyalist flag waved over the front door, so I suspected that was where it lived all year round, just to shout, 'Here, look at us, we support the union, proudly, every day of the year. They can take our flag down at the City Hall, but here it is. And it's never coming down.'

Roxanne opened the door to us. In the living room on a cream-coloured sofa sat Drew playing with his phone, only looking up to see us before looking back down and straightening his legs out with a restless motion that carried up to his face.

It was an interesting face. Angular, pouty, photogenic. Any time he was ever in trouble, I would look at his picture a little too long.

Drew was sandwiched between two small sleeping children.

They lay kipping among purple and black cushions that matched the paper on the feature wall, where similarly coloured horizontal lines became waves the more you looked at them. The type that would make you seasick after a few bevvies. A massive pop art canvas depicting both the kids together and awake sat on the mantel.

In real life both children's faces were crusty with red spots and pink splotches. The house smelled of calamine lotion.

'Chicken pox,' explained Roxanne.

The little girl was around three, and the little boy around the age of my twins. He had a beloved and abused teddy under his arm. It seemed the boy had a cold too, his face was also streaked with whitened snot-whiskers that Roxanne took to with a wet wipe when she noticed, careful not to wake him. She looked even more tired than Sylvia had.

'Put that phone away, Drew, it's so antisocial. I bloody hate it,' Roxanne whispered, annoyed.

Drew looked at her and slowly turned off his phone and got to his feet. 'Come in here,' he said. In the kitchen scales were sitting out.

'Doing some baking?' I asked.

'Yes,' he said, running his tongue over his teeth. 'If I'd known you were coming I'd have baked you a cake.'

I raised my eyebrows at him and he leaned against the kitchen counter and blinked with disinterest.

He was a prolific drug dealer in the area, well known to us for his dealing and paramilitary activity. His guys liked him as a heavy but from what we could glean they didn't love his dealing ways.

That was where his organisation drew the line, or some of them. The older brigade was not so keen on their officialdom being used as a vehicle to get kids hooked on narcotics.

'What can I do you for?' Drew said.

'We just want to elaborate on what we were talking about. We want to find the individual who murdered Chloe.'

'We all want that, sure.'

'Are you close?'

'I'm close to Jackie. His kids are alright, they aren't my kind of people.'

'In what way?'

'Look at where they grew up and look at me.'

Roxanne had come into the kitchen to hear what was being said. 'They're the poor cousins, Drew's side,' she said in a lyrical voice, plaiting her hair that was swept over one shoulder. Avoiding looking me in the eye.

'We need to hear from you, and you too ...' I said to the pair.

'What do you want to hear?' asked Drew jutting his chin.

'Anything you think might be useful about your cousin.'

'Surely Jackie told you all that.'

'He told us quite a bit but we need to get a more rounded picture than one person's point of view.'

'But why come here?' said Roxanne.

'Chloe's blonde mate told you everything you need to know,' said Drew.

'I don't need you to be defensive, Mr. Taylor,' I said. 'We need justice for Chloe.'

'He gets that,' said Roxanne. 'We're here to help in any way we can, but I just don't think we can ... we barely ever saw her.'

Drew grumbled.

'You last saw Chloe at Christmas?' I asked.

'I can't remember. Officer …'

'Detective Inspector,' I corrected him when I noticed him wait for me to do it. But I didn't think he was trying to wind me up, he seemed like he wanted to get it right and show us some form of respect, as people.

For the job we were trying to do.

'You can see that I'm at home with my unwell children.' Drew shrugged.

'You are off work today?' asked Higgins.

'Yeah.'

'Where do you work?'

'The bakery, sure,' he said.

'Which one?'

'Big Baps, in the village.'

Big Baps – ridiculous name – had closed down years before in Dundonald. I knew he was having a laugh, he didn't work at all, only in being a member of a different kind of force.

'I just want to leave my number with you,' I said as kindly as I could, 'so that if there's anything you remember, or that you think to tell us, no matter how small it seems, you can call us.'

'Yeah, I have your number: 999,' Drew said and refused my card, so I handed it to Roxanne who was tutting at her husband's ill manners.

'We'll get in touch if we can think of anything,' she said, throwing her undone plait over her shoulder to unravel.

'Are you friendly with Chloe?' Higgins asked her.

'Me? No,' said Roxanne.

Drew looked angry.

'Are you coping okay?' I asked him.

'Why wouldn't I be?' Drew said, looking spooked.

'You've had a loss, even if you aren't close Chloe's still family.'

'That's true,' said Roxanne, looking toward the door, to where the kids lay.

'They are zonked out,' I said.

'Itch medicine wipes them out.'

Drew's face softened a bit. 'Sorry,' he said, 'but it boils down to this: I can't even take the kids to the park, I'm being stopped by your mates.' He was staring at me. 'They want to look at my phone. Cause me hassle. I'm sick of it, hear me?' There was a slight threat in his tone and the momentary respect he'd just shown me was gone.

'Why do you think that is?' asked Higgins.

'I appreciate that, Mr. Taylor,' I interjected. 'We're all on the same side here, today.'

Drew nodded, closing his eyes slowly.

'Before we go I'd like to just ask what were you doing yesterday?'

'You saw what I was doing yesterday.'

'Early. Between ten and twelve in the morning.'

'We went to The Bell,' said Roxanne.

'What is that?' I asked.

'The bar at Ballyhackamore?' asked Higgins.

'It's a restaurant too,' said Roxanne.

'That was early,' I said.

'We had breakfast there, didn't we?' said Roxanne.

'Our anniversary meal,' said Drew. 'It's what you do when you have kids. When they're sick and your mother-in-law works evenings. You take breakfast over dinner. So that's where we were when Chloe was done over.' He took his wallet from his kitchen counter and found the receipt. They paid at twenty past eleven.

We left the house quietly and on the way back to the station, outside Stormont, I told Higgins to take a turn. 'Let's call in on Jackie Taylor,' I said.

He greeted us at the door, wringing his hands. 'Any news?' he said abruptly, rubbing his hands with his thumbs linked together.

'No. Not yet,' said Higgins.

'I don't want to come across as a louse,' said Jackie, 'but I'm not interested in having you two here day in day out unless you're bringing news.'

'We have questions,' I told him. 'Can we come in?'

We were invited in but not welcomed. Jackie reluctantly gestured for us to sit while he did the same.

'Where were you yesterday?' I asked him.

'Are you serious with this?' he said. 'I was at work.'

'What is work for you?'

'I repair computers for businesses, largely for banks, so I'm out and about every day.'

'And yesterday morning?'

'I was in Danske Bank, the system was down. I was there from nine-twenty, roughly, for a couple of hours, then went to the drive thru at McDonalds. It wasn't the breakfast menu.'

'So, after ten-thirty?' said Higgins.

'Yes.' Jackie's eyes darted about. 'Then I nipped into the shops to get … what? Milk, cereal and then I got the call about Chloe. The call that ruins your life. That one. The one that makes everything before it insignificant and pretty bloody unmemorable.'

He was hardened. Not that unlike Drew. What is with these men, I wondered, so fucken aggressive, even when you are trying to help them?

'May we talk with Thomas?'

'Hold on,' said Jackie, he took his mobile from his trouser pocket and texted his son. Soon Thomas traipsed down stairs in a clatter.

'Hi, Thomas,' I said. 'How are you?'

'Okay,' he said but he didn't look it. He was as white as a sheet as he clutched his left bicep in his right hand.

'We were speaking with Lewis.'

He raised his eyes as if, is that all? Can I be dismissed, Miss? You could tell he was not long left school; Thomas still saw us as adults, not equals.

'Lewis said to pass on his condolences,' I said, needing to see his reaction. Both boys seemed to have some sort of beef I didn't yet understand.

'Did he?' asked Thomas.

'Yes.'

Jackie was watching his son, concern puckering his face.

'Lewis bombarded Chloe with texts when they split and kept pestering her,' said Thomas in a voice that wouldn't wake a baby. 'Bet he said he didn't mean it. He'll say he was just checking on her. But he didn't care. He'd moved on.'

'Now watch what you're saying, son. I'm sure he still cares for Chloe,' said Jackie.

'Dad, I always see him at the Met,' said Lewis. 'He has a new girlfriend. Well, not exactly new because he was with her before. He had her when Chloe was away, too.'

'Maybe they are friends then,' said Jackie. 'He has friends who are girls? Like you do. Like I do, for God's sake.'

Lewis griped and held his side with both hands.

'What are you studying?' Higgins asked him.

'Foundation studies in Art and Design,' he said monotonously.

'Where were you yesterday?' I asked, feeling Jackie's expression harden and his eyes on my face.

'I had a free study period and was at home.'

'Anyone else here?'

'Like who?' asked Jackie.

'Maybe you study with a friend?' I said.

'No, I was alone.' Thomas now grimaced.

'Are you okay?' I asked him.

'Stomach cramps, is it, son?' said Jackie. 'Gets them when he's anxious.'

'Oh, I'm sorry,' I said. 'None of this is nice for you, for either of you.'

Thomas' face became even whiter. I feared he may throw up on my feet.

'Drew says you called in to his gaff,' said Jackie. 'And obviously you've contacted Lewis …'

'Yes, Mr. Taylor,' I said.

'Then you must have talked to Lizzie?'

'We have. She has called the station.'

'Why did she do that?'

'To see if there was any progress.'

Jackie frowned. 'Maybe you should see if she knows anything. She was very close to Chloe of late.'

'We are planning on going there today.'

'Do you have her address?' he asked.

'I was hoping you would give it to us, or a surname.'

'I'm going to go and lie down, is that okay?' asked Thomas. He was much quicker going up the stairs then he'd been coming down them.

Chapter 7

At five p.m. on Thursday, the day after Chloe was killed, we arrived at Lizzie Donegan-Moat's bungalow. It was at the top of a short steep driveway in a quiet horseshoe off Gilnahirk Road. At the bottom of the drive was a baby blue gate and to the side a large front garden with foliage growing out of control.

Lizzie was in the back garden when we called. She brought us through the side gate, also painted the same shade of blue as the front one. In the back garden, there were patio views of Stormont and some farm land. Horses stood in the distance.

Lizzie had been sunning herself and now she sat back down on a fat, green lounge chair. We sat facing her on the bench.

'Do you think this is our summer?' she asked, holding her arms over her eyes to block out the sun.

'Probably,' I said.

She looked at her painted toenails, curled them over her flip flop. 'You know,' Lizzie said, 'when you just love someone and then, they're gone.'

'It must be hard for you, you said you were close,' said Higgins.

'The closest,' said Lizzie. 'And Chloe was the closest thing I have to a wee sister. I'd call her my wee sister. Just loved the bones of her.'

'I am sorry for your loss,' I said.

'Thanks. *Really*.' She looked at me with apprehension. 'Did you speak to Lewis?'

'Yes, we did. Thanks for pointing us in his direction.'

'Pleasure! What did he say?'

'Lewis sends his condolences.'

'And anything else?'

'I can't really say.'

'What am I asking of you? Did he have an alibi, that's what I mean?'

'He was helpful.'

'Oh, that's a relief,' said Lizzie. 'It's better that it's not him – if it isn't. They had their problems, so ... It's usually the boyfriend in these cases.'

'But he's Chloe's ex,' said Higgins.

'You're right. It's probably nothing to do with Lewis Skelly.'

'Do you know of anybody Chloe was having problems with?' Higgins asked her.

Lizzie bit her bottom lip. 'I did have this vision pop into my head as soon as I heard. After the shock and the ... upset and everything else. Not that I'm *not* shocked and upset now.'

'What was the vision you had?' I asked, trying to fine tune her attention.

'There was this man I remember Chloe telling me about. A gardener. I have this *vision* he killed Chloe. Now I can't get it out of my mind.'

'Do you have any reason to suspect he *actually* hurt Chloe, this man?'

'He was aggressive to her.'

''Allo 'allo,' said a voice coming from indoors, a male voice, English accent. Liverpudlian. He stepped outside to join us; Lizzie's babe. The man who had collected her in his Merc from the Taylor's house the day before. 'Sorry, couldn't resist it when I saw the police car.'

Lizzie looked at him harshly. 'Not funny, Justin.'

'Not trying to be. I was just saying hello.'

'This is Justin,' she said, 'my partner.'

Justin was in overalls, tanned and muscled. Very good looking. Very *conventionally* good looking. Meaning, not my type.

'Nice to meet you,' he said. 'I'm so sorry to hear about Chloe. She was such a beautiful girl.'

'Yeah, I always said that,' said Lizzie. 'She was adorable, actually, if that's a sin.'

Justin sat beside Lizzie on the sun lounger and almost toppled it. Justin stretched his feet out to rebalance it and laughed lightly. He took her hand in his as Lizzie shook her head at him then slowly, sadly smiled.

'I was just telling the police about my vision,' she said.

'Oh, yes,' said Justin. 'The gardener. The word *vision* makes you sound well away.' He tilted his head and wrinkled his sunburnt nose.

'A thought, is more like it,' Lizzie corrected herself.

'Can we hear more about that thought?' Higgins prompted. 'Lizzie, you were about to say …'

'I hope I didn't interrupt,' said Justin.

'No, not all,' said Lizzie, then to Higgins, 'There was one time this man was cutting the grass and Chloe went out to say something to him. And he was inappropriate, like, "Are you not pregnant yet? Do you want to be?" That kind of thing.'

'The gardener really said this to Chloe?' asked Higgins amazed.

'Yes, he really did,' said Lizzie with conviction, as if she felt Higgins was doubting her.

'Did they know each other?' I asked.

'No. This was out of the blue. He saw she was at home on her own. Chloe went out to pay him, and he said that and more, lots of smutty talk. And obviously Chloe told him to swing his hook. He said, something like, "When you pay me you can tell me to sling my hook, love."

49

'And she said, "It is my house," and he was like, "It's hardly your house, wee doll. But if you want to pay me in kind, I have something you can suck here".'

'What the fuck!' said Justin, tensing angrily. 'I didn't know all of that, Lizzie. I'd like to have a chat to this guy now.'

The look of shock on Carl Higgins' face was palpable. Sadly, I'm past all that.

'I knew you would be protective if you knew the most of it, Just,' Lizzie said. 'But don't you worry, Chloe unleashed all fury on him. Sexist pig.'

'Is right!' said Justin, his face serious. He stared off into the field.

'The gardener stood firm, said he wasn't leaving. Chloe told me later, see.' Lizzie looked at me now as she explained that Chloe was intimidated by him. 'Chloe said he started becoming physically aggressive toward her. And he was like, more than twice her age. Twice her size!'

'Would you have a name for this gardener?' I asked.

'Might be wise to ask Chloe's dad,' said Justin.

'No need. I have it,' said Lizzie. 'Because I took heed. He's not someone I'd ever use if that's how he speaks to customers. He goes under *Bushwhacked*. That's his business.'

'You're thinking of the gardener we had in Coleraine,' said Justin.

'So I am! *Clipped and Trimmed*, that's him.'

'Thank you,' Higgins said. 'We'll make a point to talk to him.'

'Mister Clipped and Trimmed is lucky I didn't know about this,' said Justin, still acting the tough guy. 'Sorry, folks, I've to get on to work now.' He stood and Lizzie stood to kiss him goodbye, she in flip flops slightly taller than him. She sniffed his neck. 'Good,' she said, 'you've got sunscreen on, though your nose has got a bit of sun.'

'See, told you I listen.'

'He works on the building site,' she explained to Higgins and me.

'Yeah, good to meet you both. Ta-ra, and good luck finding that gardener,' he said.

*

By six p.m. I called Sylvia to say Paul would collect the boys, and to do the handover; expecting they would be too distracted in person.

'They miss you, Harriet,' Sylvia said. 'I showed them your photo and they reached for it. Next thing they started crying for you. Jared was saying, "Mama, Mama," over and over.'

'Pets!' I said. 'But maybe don't show them a photo of me in future. Just an idea …'

After she'd told me all about their day, mostly negative, Sylvia said, 'Have you thought of going part-time? It's just that it is a long shift for them to put in. They've had you all to themselves this last year.'

'Do you not want to do this, Sylvia? Do you not want to help me?' I asked her, because she had said often enough that she wanted to mind them. Since they were tiny.

Before the twins were born she'd been dropping hints. Now it looked like the sheen had worn off real fast. Reality had set in and they were too active for her, able to pull themselves up to stand, about to walk any day.

'No, I'm not saying that … don't put words in my mouth,' said Sylvia.

'Good,' I said, 'because a girl has been murdered here.'

'I know, I'm sorry for her family. But family should be with family.'

I was sure she meant that I should be at home with my children and that I should screw the career I had lived for all those years before; the service no longer mattered in my life. Neither did I.

But there were two pulling horses in my life; motherhood and career. And my career was – more than ever – my remedy for restlessness. I had decided that you were not a mother until you started to avoid the act of mothering. I had earned my badge in that respect.

Sylvia and my brother could not have children. Not that they were open to discuss things like that, but I had always pictured them like *The Waltons*: with a big God-fearing brood of kids at the table. Low ponytails, dungarees and prayers.

They were going through the process of trying to adopt a child. Now the words *family should be with family* made me think I could have been rude back, said that my children were more family to her than the child they planned to adopt, and that they were willing to sacrifice every belief, and dole out every platitude, to suit their own agenda.

But I stopped myself, because we are all guilty of doing the same.

I gave Paul the evening off and I collected the boys to save any fuss. The whole time Sylvia stood on her doorstep in her too-short jeans, shaking her head, her teardrop earrings vibrating, annoying me even more.

We said nothing.

*

At home, I left the boys with Paul and swung by the Lisburn Road into Bawnmore Road, to Bethany Nursing Home to see Mother.

I had not been guilted by my sister-in-law, I had planned to go anyway. Our family had a rota. Not that I could always make my time, now I was working again. Tonight I could.

It was shortly after seven p.m., and although it was technically my time, Father was still there.

'I didn't think you'd come tonight,' he said.

'I have some time,' I said. 'Not much though. Paul has the boys so I'm good for a while.'

'What do you mean you're *good*? That's how they talk on the TV. When did everyone become so Americanised? You're not *good*, Harriet, you're *fine*. Fine for time,' he grumbled.

Father was doing a crossword, tapping his pen on the page. I had ruined his concentration. I looked over his shoulder; there was one space left.

'What's the clue?' I asked.

'To exercise one's power of reason in order to make decisions, solutions or judgements.'

'How many letters?'

'Eleven,' said Father.

'Beginning with which letter?'

'E.'

I stared at it for a while but he was sighing and scratching his head, so I went to the bedside.

'Hi, Mummy,' I said. 'I'm only nipping in for a while. I'm back at work now. Paul has the babies,' I told her too; I said it as if she knew who Paul was.

He had been in to see her a couple of times, and being medically minded he was very good with her, but he was also too clinical. She was a case study for him, and I was fed up of him asking about her medical history and talking to the staff at the home using all that jargon of his that pushed me out of my own existence.

53

Paul didn't know the woman Mother once was, and she didn't know him. Maybe I was mentioning Paul and the babies for my father's ears, to see if he would say: *That's great. You've got a good one there! A fine one!* Me, wanting his approval for the man I was now sharing my life with. It made me think Jackie had been kinder about Lewis.

But my ex-husband Jason, Father had liked immensely. All the Sloanes had been suckered in.

'Harry,' said Dad. 'This is the last one. Eleven letters. *Excuse* is all I can think, but that's too short … oh, I don't know.'

I went to look at it again. 'No, Daddy, it can't start with an *e*. Look at this one, 4 across: a saline fluid secreted by the sweat glands, twelve letters.'

'Perspiration,' he said.

'Yes. But you've misspelt it. You have *pres*piration. That's not a word.'

'Alright, Harriet,' he snapped defensively.

'Clue, eleven letters, starts with an r … not an e.'

'Alright!' He turned the paper over and slammed down his pen.

'It's going alright at work … now I'm back,' I said. He was silent. 'I'm working on the Taylor case.' Still silent. 'Chloe Taylor: young woman; she was murdered in the PACT offices on the Upper Newtownards Road. You probably heard.'

No doubt he had. He had a special interest in all things Belfast and all things crime, especially in my district. But Father said nothing. He was distracted, when usually he was all for hearing about my cases, being the ex-Chief Constable during the RUC days. Always helpful, usually overstepping by telling me how to do my job.

But that evening in the nursing home, nothing. He almost reminded me of when I married Jason and he said, 'I've always been good to you' – and he had – 'but I can't pay for this and that anymore. Time you and your man look after yourselves.'

Father was handing me over and then I felt like he was almost punishing me, and we'd always been so close. We had a bond he didn't have with his other four children, and I was leaving that bond to have another one with another man.

Needless to say it didn't last, after what happened with Jason and me. Father still doesn't know the half of it and probably never will. But Paul really *was* a good guy, less charming, granted, and definitely less psychotic than Jason. But a good guy. And it felt as if having him in my life – and my sons – had pushed Father aside. He had little time for me, and I – really, and especially now I was working – had little time for him. Sad fact.

'I must get back,' I said. I kissed Mother twice. Once on the border of her brow, once on the crest of her nose.

Father was embarrassed and tetchy, but he was still as sharp as a pin. Although he'd always had his quirks: corrupted barbed wire with *bob wire*, and misspelt things all the time: excited was *exited*, and especially, *expecially*. He never appreciated correction. Though who would? He was a man whose pride could be easily hurt, and that hurt me, because he was old and suddenly a bit silly, and certainly not invincible or powerful anymore. Just another one of those fading men you see everywhere you look.

He seemed like a little boy and I felt towards him how I did for Jared and Rowan. Protective, but also terrified of my potential to damage him.

Father grumbled as I left and just sat staring out of the window. I don't think he actually looked me in the eye the whole time I was there.

Driving home I went past my old house with the apple tree in the garden and I thought of Jason some more. That poison in my mind was waning now, thankfully.

When I was early on in my pregnancy with the twins, I got an email from him reminding me that we were still married and he would try to get custody. Who had given that bastard my email and who had told him I was pregnant? My stomach turned to lava all night.

But now, as I passed the old house where he kept me prisoner in fear for my life, I was thankful for how he had become less significant with the growing of this new life I found myself living, so far removed from everything I ever wanted, but suddenly all I wanted.

There was a new clearness and I could rationalise.

'Rationalise,' I said aloud. Then I counted the letters. Eleven letters.

To exercise one's power of reason in order to make decisions, solutions or judgements.

I knew it would bug Father all day, and although I was tempted to let it, I could not do that to him. So I pulled over and texted him the last answer but I never received a reply, even though his mobile phone was right beside him.

Chapter 8

You only really have bad moments when you remember them. The good moments are just the ones you have forgotten.

I quickly remembered that when I was standing in the kitchen of my house and he came from behind, wrapping his arms over my shoulder, asking me if I was tense and in need of a massage – I think – but I elbowed him in the stomach before he got to finish the offer. Good thing he wasn't holding one of the babies.

'Paul! Sorry, it's just instinct,' I said as I turned. 'It's the job.'

'It's okay,' he said, just about, getting his breath back.

'It's the job, Paul,' I repeated.

'I don't think it is,' he said. 'You're just highly strung like no one I know.'

Then you haven't met someone who has been held hostage for days ... and the rest, I thought. But why ruin a perfectly good relationship with sad facts? Paul was right, it was not the job. The facts were that Jason would have murdered me, only he didn't want to go down for it. I was not worth his life, because one thing I know is that he is a bully, but even more than that I know he is a coward. I couldn't have cared if it was a stranger on a job who attacked me, but this man was supposed to love me, supposed to protect me, in sickness ... and the rest.

'I'm so sorry, Paul. It's my mother,' I lied.

He looked sad, a fake sad. 'How was your mum?'

'Is she ever anything but what she is?' I paused but he did not speak. 'When she was a judge,' I said, 'and, Paul, I've been thinking about this a lot. It's this case I'm working, I suppose ... and the Belfast Rape Trial last month.'

I said all of this as a distraction for my reflexive attack on him and as a distraction for myself, *and* to get my ex-husband out my mind. I could not go back to fearing him or fearing life like that again. And I suppose I had been triggered, as Americans say.

'What is on your mind?' asked Paul.

'Mother would always have let the man walk in cases of domestic abuse.'

'She was working at a certain time, Harry.'

'I can't get my head around it,' I said. 'My mother didn't really like or believe women. She didn't …' I thought aloud, forgetting myself. I was worried I was like her. I'd had my eyes opened by life, mine and those I saw intimately. Mother worked in a courtroom, and in an office, she did not go into people's homes and see the devastation.

'But she was one of the first judges here who was female,' said Paul, as if to convince me I was wrong, as seemed to be his job here.

'And yet …' I said, 'she always believed the men. Or discredited the women they abused. It was like those rugby players …'

Paul looked disinterested. 'It's just a job, at the end of the day.'

It was after eight and I was starving. I put my plate in the microwave.

'The boys went over quickly, didn't they?' said Paul, glad to change the subject from how men like him were suddenly the bogeymen they never knew they were.

'They never slept for Sylvia,' I said. 'She looked absolutely beat.'

'That's just a taste of what we've been going through,' he said, and we were back on side again, on the same side. 'Not that I'd change a thing,' he quickly added and added on a smile for me.

After I ate, we sat in front of the telly and returned to a boxset we started watching before Florida. I lifted my phone and looked up the gardener service, Clipped and Trimmed, and got a name – Dan Hamilton. I asked Paul to pause the TV while I nipped to the loo. I went into the hall, bringing my phone with me.

'Why have you got that?' Paul asked.

'Are you my father now?'

'You're coming back, right?'

'I'm going to take a peek at the babies.'

'Don't wake them, Harry.'

I went and called Sarge Simon. 'Run this name for me,' I told him.

'I don't have to,' he said, 'I've worked in the area for a long time. Hamilton's a convicted murderer, I can tell you that now.'

'Who did he murder?'

'A young woman. I remember the case, she was coming out of a bar on the Woodstock Road. I see Hamilton about from time to time, you know.'

'Do you know the details of the case?'

'Not off the top of my noggin. Let me check, I'll send them through to you.'

'Great. Put it all in an email.'

I went to the nursery door and stood looking at the babies, I was trying to hold my breath when they squirmed. Then I went back to sit beside Paul.

'I could hear you on the phone,' he said and I side-glanced him. 'On the monitor.'

'The boys are sleeping well,' I said.

He pressed play and began our show but I started to fiddle with my phone again, trying to see if there was anything in my inbox yet.

'Are you too distracted to watch this?' Paul asked, pausing the TV.

'No, no, unpause it.' My phone pinged. 'Sorry,' I said and got up. I went into the kitchen. 'I'll catch up. You go on.'

'But you're going to miss who the murderer is,' Paul said.

'I get enough of that.'

'Maybe we'll stop watching crime now. You just like to show off that you can work it out, anyway.'

'You know me so well,' I said, closing over the door.

The email from Simon read:

Dan Hamilton has a conviction. He did time – eight years – in the 90s (he was in his twenties then) for killing a woman, Darleen Boyle, aged twenty-two. A single mother, she was stabbed on the Woodstock Road. It was at night. She was walking home from Speedy's bar and it was completely unprovoked. But it was the only time he was ever in trouble with the law, before or after.

I came back and trained myself to stare at the screen for Paul's sake; going through the motions, but behind my eyes my brain was buzzing, putting together pieces and taking them away, my mind back to how it always was on the job. I just hoped Paul wouldn't give me a pop quiz at the end of the programme, because I hadn't taken in a thing of the episode.

Chapter 9

That night I couldn't stop seeing Jason, especially when I thought about Lewis. I had been swept up by this boy's charm, thinking he could not have done anything wrong. I had thought that because he didn't *look* the type. Now I was disappointed in myself because I knew personally that appearances mean nothing. I woke up wanting to talk with Lewis again.

'Thomas said that Lewis was bombarding Chloe with messages,' I said to Higgins as soon as I spied him in the office that Friday morning.

'Then we need to see him,' Higgins replied.

'Yes, we do. And Lizzie seemed adamant that there was something off.'

'Okay, whatever you say, boss,' said Higgins.

'But I want an alibi for Chloe's dad first. Jackie was shopping around the time Chloe was killed. He couldn't have spent all that time buying milk. I want receipts.'

'I'll get onto it.'

I was sparking my fingers off the computer keyboard, trying to locate Dan Hamilton, researching more about his case back in the 90s, when Higgins told me that Jackie Taylor's alibi had checked out. The manager of Danske Bank in Donegall Square West said Jackie was sorting out their computer system. In fact, the manager said Jackie was there until half past eleven. That fit – McDonalds, shopping, a call from us.

'That's one less person to look into right now,' I said and I relayed the information Sarge Simon had given me about the gardener and showed Higgins what I'd found out.

'Woodstock Road,' he said.

My mobile went. It was Lewis Skelly. 'I was trying to call you earlier,' I told him.

'I was in class. I had my phone silenced.'

'Do you think you could meet us today to talk some more?'

'I don't know what else I can tell you, but sure. That's fine. Where are you?'

'At the police station.'

'I'm on the bus home now, I'm not far. You're based at Strandtown, aren't you?'

'Yes. That's the one.'

'I can be there in fifteen.'

'See you then, Lewis. Just report to reception when you arrive.'

When he arrived at Strandtown he looked nervous. 'Would you take a seat?' I asked him.

'I'm not being interviewed, am I?'

'You're helping us with enquiries.'

'That's okay. Happy to. I just wondered if I needed a solicitor.' Lewis sat down.

'You're not under arrest and you can leave at any time,' said Higgins.

'I get you.'

'We were talking to Thomas,' I said.

'Yeah? How is he?'

'Much the same, really.'

'Okay.'

'Lewis, were you still in correspondence with Chloe?'

'Yes. We were friends.'

'Thomas said that you would have contacted Chloe excessively.'

'He has that wrong.'

'Why would he say that then?'

'Because he doesn't like me?' Lewis said with a note of sarcasm, like we should already know this.

'We got that impression,' said Higgins.

'That doesn't mean I did the killing,' said Lewis. 'That's a ludicrous idea.'

'No one is saying that you did, Lewis,' I tried to reassure him.

'This is so much to get my head around. Yesterday was … I was still in shock, but today is bad. It's bad, man. Really bad. She's really *dead*.' Lewis started to cry, crouching over so his face was in his sleeves, not wanting us to see him be emotional.

'Do you want a tissue?' I asked, sliding the box on the desk toward him.

He shook his head and sniffed then tried to catch a breath. 'I only contacted her, *excessively* – if that's what you want to call it – in the early days of the breakup; I just wanted an answer for why we broke up, why she finished it, then I could move on.'

'Had you already moved on?' I asked.

'No,' his voice went high.

'Thomas seems to think you had another girlfriend.'

'I'm seeing someone now. Seeing … It's not serious. I was with Chloe for years.'

I nodded. 'It's totally okay if you are seeing someone, Lewis,' I said.

'Well, what about Thomas?' Lewis asked, becoming defensive. 'Have you talked to him?'

'We have,' said Higgins. 'He's Chloe's brother, so it's standard practice.'

'He's told you all this? That I have a girlfriend?'

'Yes.'

'What was I supposed to do? Never move on?'

63

'No, not at all,' I said.

'I saw Thomas this morning; he ignored me when I tried to talk to him,' said Lewis. 'He has a display in the Met's summer art show. It's worth seeing.' He looked at us each in turn. 'I really recommend it.'

'Is there anyone we're missing talking with?' I asked him.

'Her cousin. Surely you must know him.'

'Who is that?' asked Higgins, careful not to presume that Lewis was talking about Drew. He was.

'Drew Taylor. He's a well known crim,' said Lewis.

'Would Chloe have been involved in a criminal activity, that you would have known of?'

'Chloe? She's ethical to a fault. Look, I'm not saying this to get anybody into trouble, but I know she and Thomas are not expected to have part-time jobs, their dad gives them pocket money still, just, I think she might owe Drew money. She was never good at paying people back what she owed them. Just don't tell him it came from me. Please.'

'Who else did she owe money to?'

'No one,' said Lewis.

'You said she was *never good at* …'

'Me. She owed me. But I've written that off. I think if you lend something to someone you shouldn't expect to get it back.'

'Really?' asked Higgins.

'It's what life has taught me,' said Lewis.

I looked at him thoughtfully. Gosh, he was a sweetie. I felt bad for him – and Chloe, too, above all – to have been embroiled in such a tragedy, especially when there were vicious bastards like my ex-husband walking the street, untouchable.

'Would Drew have loaned Chloe money?' I asked.

'Hmm, yeah. He did.'

'We'll look into it, won't we?' said Higgins.

'Good.' Lewis lingered. 'You can look at my phone if you want. You can see what the messages between Chloe and me were. I've nothing to hide. Here.' He opened the page and scrolled through, held it to face us. 'There; a few *hope you're wells, please answer your phone, I want to know what I did wrong*, then going back to when we were dating.' He pulled the phone away.

*

'He could have deleted the bad messages,' said Higgins after Lewis had left. We were in the service car. 'That's what anybody sane would do.'

We passed Lewis outside the PACT office. He looked like a zombie.

'Pull in,' I told Higgins. 'Lewis, you okay?' I asked him out of the window. He was staring through me. 'Are you okay?' I repeated.

He broke into tears and hid his face in his sleeves again.

'Are you headed home?'

He wiped his nose on his sleeve.

'C'mon, get in. We'll give you a lift.'

'No,' he said but he came over.

People walking by had slowed down and were watching, especially as he got into the back of the service vehicle.

'That's what hit me today,' said Lewis, leaning forward to tell us. 'I took the bus in past the … scene, and saw all the flowers outside and then it was real. I can't pretend it didn't happen now. Chloe,' he cried. Really cried.

We dropped Lewis home to Orangefield. His mother came to the door.

'What's happened?' she asked. She wrapped her arms around him. 'What's happened?' she asked me. 'Is it about Chloe?'

'I think it's just properly hit him,' I said.

'Oh,' she said. 'Oh, son.' Then she was in tears too. 'I am so very sorry.'

'Let's go to Chloe's mother's house,' I said to Higgins.

We knew that she lived in Ballyhalbert. So we travelled out through Dundonald and towards Newtownards, cut down along the peninsula, along Strangford Lough. Crossed inland to a beaded string of villages. Small communities, self-contained. No need to leave if your needs were modest.

In Ballyhalbert there was a pub, a chippy, a pharmacy. Chloe's mother lived in a terraced house a short walk from shops and a sea that shone like it was made of sequins – at least it did that day. The smell did something good for the soul, it felt great to be out of the city.

An old man approached and asked us how we were keeping. As soon as we said we were well he asked if he could bum a lift home, assuming we knew him and knew where he lived.

Higgins got rid of him for us, and the old drunk stumbled on. I filled my lungs with fresh air and courage before I knocked on the door. Instantly I knew that the woman who opened the door had to be Chloe's mother, I had stared at Chloe's poor lifeless face for long enough that Wednesday. And for two days since, in photographs in her folder which every now and then I consulted for inspiration.

This woman was small with the same green eyes as her daughter's. They looked just as empty. She wore thick kohl eyeliner and had dyed her hair jet black and cut it bluntly into a bob with a thick fringe.

'Glynis Taylor?'

'You're speaking to her.'

I introduced myself and Higgins. 'I don't know if anyone has told you, but we have some sad news to report.'

'I already know,' she said.

'You've heard about Chloe?'

'I have,' she said staunchly.

'How are you bearing up?' asked Higgins.

'Not very surprised, to be honest,' said Glynis.

'Really?' Higgins asked, surprised by her response.

'I knew I'd never see her again,' said Glynis.

'May we come in?' I asked.

Glynis shrugged, then went into her oppressively red living room.

'When did you last see Chloe?' I asked.

'Years ago, now.'

'When?' asked Higgins, taking a seat.

'A couple of years ago.'

'Do you mind telling us why you hadn't seen her in so long?'

'I hope you're not judging me, Detective. I made my peace with what happened to my family long ago.' Glynis ran her bare toes through the mossy green rug on the floor.

'Nobody is judging you,' I said, 'relationships don't always work out; we understand that. We just want to find the perpetrator of this crime and get justice for your daughter.'

'I understand that part of it. End of the day your child's your child. You'd die for them. But I can't catch the culprit. It has nothing to do with me.'

'There are just people we need to talk to,' I explained, 'to get pointers, and you *are* Chloe's mother, after all.'

She looked downcast. 'I did cry yesterday. I thought about her as a wee girl, as a baby, and pictured her wee back, like velvet it was, and somebody putting a knife in it. I pictured that and I cried. But I'm feeling better.'

'Good,' I said.

There was not one photo that I could see anywhere, just one picture, of three flowers, two of them were cream, the middle one burgeoning and blood red. Burnt out candles remained on almost every surface in the room. I lost myself for a moment, looking around the room, trying not to take in what she had just said, the sorrow of it, the callousness.

'I *am* sad,' Glynis blurted out, 'sad in the way I'd be sad for any young one losing their life. I can't say much more than that.'

I thought it had yet to hit her, regardless of their estrangement. I thought about Lewis.

'So, there was a feud …' I started.

'Saying that there was a *feud* in the family is giving the whole thing too much importance,' she said discernibly irritated. 'Talk to Jackie; even he'll tell you it wasn't a feud, just abandonment. He didn't want to know when I was sick.'

'Sorry to hear you were sick,' said Higgins.

'Thank you, that's sweet.'

'May I ask in what way were you sick?' I asked.

'I still am. I have bipolar disorder. Jackie had no time for sickness. We split and he took the kids. Well, not that he took them anywhere. He pushed me aside. Spiteful man.' Her head shook. Glynis became innocent, frail before my eyes.

'That's how the split began?' asked Higgins.

'I suppose it does look like a feud,' said Glynis, 'but a feud is heated and passionate and this was ... cold and heartless. He has no heart, that man. I just had to try to forget about them, since he'd taken my home from me. That house, I'm sure you've seen it, that was mine. I was the one who decorated it, who picked out every stitch and every swatch.

'And I worked. I worked hard. I was a paramedic, I have a brain. Then I got sick and lost everything, so I can't. I'm sorry but I just can't do *this*; I can't go through this kind of pain. It's not good for me. I've already been through it. I can't lose Chloe twice. I've grieved them all already, you see. Thomas too. He's gone to me. It's already done.'

'I am so sorry,' I said. I felt a sob wrack through me that I'd never experienced on the job before. I blamed it on being a mother now. I blamed it on thinking of my own mother and having already lost her to illness.

I never allowed myself to think about it. To feel anything about it.

'Do you work now?' Higgins asked.

'No. I don't, son. I can't.'

'Are you on any form of social media?' I asked her.

'No. I want to disconnect from people. Why do you ask that?'

'That's fine,' I said, lifting my hand to break that branch of conversation.

'Last time I saw Chloe,' Glynis said, 'she was staying overnight and wouldn't do a hand's turn. I asked her to tidy up after herself and she snapped at me, called me "pathetic and lazy". Said all I did was sit around, while she worked and studied and volunteered. She forgot I once had a very good career.

'There was no respect left. I told her I wasn't running a guest house and she could leave. Then she never called me again. And Thomas … well, he does everything she tells him. He thinks the sun shines out of Chloe's backside.' Glynis jumped up. 'Okay, I'm done.'

I could feel my phone buzzing in my pocket.

'Excuse me, a moment.' I went outside and called Sylvia. 'Everything, okay?'

'I can't settle Rowan,' she said.

I sighed. 'Have you read to him? Fed him?'

'He's upset. His cheeks are piping hot.'

'Take a layer off him and give him his teething ring out of the fridge.'

'I don't have it in the fridge.'

'But I said earlier to put it in the fridge.'

'You said a lot of things, it's a lot to take on board.'

Charly, my twin, would know, I thought, only she had done her time with five kids and now was getting her youngest into a special school. These days Charly spent lunching with friends, and I felt a surge of bitterness. For her, motherhood started earlier and she was reaping the rewards by having something of a break now.

But I was also bitter at Sylvia. She had begged me to let her look after the babies, and before that she had a life of swanning about, being a mini celebrity of sorts within their congregation. The First Lady of the Church. Now she was stopping me from working too. But my boys, would they have no respect for me if I was to stay at home, like Glynis had to?

'Give him Calpol,' I said. 'I really have to go back to work.'

But she had already succeeded in guilting me, and the rest of the day a heaviness lay in my heart.

*

Back at the station Higgins asked why I'd brought up social media to Glynis.

'Chloe was getting nasty messages, remember? We should really look at them.'

'Could Glynis have been sending her messages? Her own biological daughter?'

'Glad you had a perfect upbringing, lots haven't,' I snapped, stressed.

'Oh ... Sorry if I offended you. I didn't realise ...'

'Not me, Carl! Lots of people we work with. Sorry, I'm just stressed with my childcare arrangement.'

He pursed his lips like, here we go; she's going to start expecting special treatment.

'I'll get it sorted,' I said. 'Teething problems. Literally.' I picked up my phone as it rang again. Sylvia.

'I know I said that I would give you a month,' she simpered, 'a month to see if you were happy, but I'm prepared to do without that notice period.'

'Are you?' I laughed loudly.

'Harriet, they are your boys, not mine.'

'You're right there,' I said then hung up on her.

I told Higgins to wait, that I'd be back ASAP. I gave Greg Dunne the death stare on the way through. It was all so easy for him. Beyond fucken easy.

I called my sisters while driving. Charly was at an appointment with Timothy, which made me feel bad for thinking she had things easier, when she didn't and might never. She'll always have Timothy to care for, even when her other four children have grown and left home.

Then I phoned my older sister, Coral. Her phone kept going to voicemail, so I called her partner Rose.

'We're in London,' Rose said, 'on a surprise getaway for our anniversary.' She promised she would get Coral to call me back when she came back from the hotel lobby. I told her not to worry, to enjoy herself and not to tell Coral I called.

I stared at the driftwood heart Sylvia had hanging from a nail on the front door. I ignored the jingly church-sounding doorbell and thumped the glass panel beside it, waited for her to appear. With her nose in the air. Like I knew it would be. She was trying to give me an authoritative look. I noticed she was shaking.

'The best place for them is with their mother,' she tried twice to convince me, once for each baby.

I had to bite my tongue to stop myself asking if she would give up on her potential adopted child so easily. I'd been their character witness for the adoption agency even though I'd always found her characterless, standing there with her frazzled grey hair in a low ponytail. I rarely colour my hair, or do anything with it, but her premature old lady style drove me mad.

I said nothing. I carried the babies out of hers while she stood limply holding their bags.

Inside the car I blasted the air conditioner and again had to bite my tongue when she came to the car, saying, 'They're your kids, Harriet, they're not my responsibility.' Bit my tongue to stop me saying, 'I'm only trying to do my job, why are you punishing me?' and to stop myself from saying, 'Maybe your god won't give you a baby because you don't deserve one.' I muttered it under my breath instead, I don't think she heard. If she did she never brought it up after. Which I'm glad of. It was a cruel thing to mutter.

Chagrined, Sylvia went inside and I tried to phone Paul. He was in theatre with a patient so his phone went straight to voicemail. I left him a shitty message.

Then I remembered there was a day nursery in the street beside the police station, so I drove there and parked around the corner. I could not bring the babies into work, I just couldn't. I cried in the car for a minute. It is not often I cry and I wasn't sad, just frustrated as hell.

I went into the nursery, a boy on each hip.

'Usually there is a waiting list of months, but two babies have just left,' said one member of staff excitedly, the one who had greeted me at the locked door I'd been struggling to open.

'Great, can you take them?' I asked.

'Yes, from Monday. And that is very lucky.'

'No, now,' I said, not feeling very lucky, but I knew under it all I was lucky to have the boys, lucky to have children that were healthy and who were in my life at all.

She left to get the manager, Joanne, a tall willowy woman with a bowl haircut.

'May I speak to you in confidence?' I said to Joanne, as I saw her poise herself to give me bad news, to rescind her colleague's offer of starting the boys from Monday. 'I'm a Detective Inspector,' I said quickly, fixing Jared higher on my hip. 'I'm working on that case, Chloe Taylor, the young woman who was murdered in the PACT office.'

'Oh,' said Joanne.

'Joanne, my family can't help and my sitter has let me down.'

'I'm sorry, but ...'

'I'm trying to help a family that has lost their daughter and sister. She was murdered, not far from here, in broad daylight.'

There was nothing coming back to me from Joanne's expression. She was stone cold.

'Glad to see you have the doors locked,' I reached for scare tactics.

'They are always locked. It's our policy,' said Joanne.

'Well, I'm still glad to see it, for everyone's safety,' I said. 'I need to find the perpetrator as soon as I can. I'm in charge of the case. The buck stops with me, Joanne.'

'I thought that murder was random,' she said, 'are you saying that it could happen again, in this area?' She pointed at her feet.

I was stuck; to say yes would mean that she and her staff might refuse to work there for a time. But Jared saved me from answering anyway, he smiled at stone-faced, bowl haircutted Joanne and she smiled, melted and said, 'Okay. But I am breaking all the rules.'

'You're the boss,' I said, then, fearing I had gone too far, 'thank you, I am really indebted.'

'One of the babies is off sick, and it's all down to room ratios, you see. There are guidelines; I didn't make them up. I can take one of the boys up to the toddler room, just this once. Anyway, they *are* probably walking by this age.' She lifted her head and I realised it was a question.

'Yes. Practically,' I said. 'Thank you, thank you.' I worried about them being separated for the first time in their short lives but I'd been gone from work for an hour already. 'I should have just come here in the first place, instead of letting that sitter keep them,' I said, 'she's a flake.'

Joanne took the boys from me and I zoomed through the numerous paperwork, then went out and wept in the car with relief. I tapped face powder over the red blotches that had appeared high up on my cheeks.

I put on my engine and the window down. Lizzie, Chloe's best friend, was walking past my car.

'Hi! Did you find that gardener?' she asked me through the window. She wasn't as glam now, but in blue striped trackie bottoms and grubby grey trainers with fluorescent pink laces.

'Look,' I said, 'you go over to the station, and I'll be with you in ten.'

I drove into the car park, past the high metal sheet fencing. Had a moment to calm down in the loo, then came out to meet her.

'Jackie doesn't care,' Lizzie threw at me, 'that's what it looks like, but I want to make sure someone goes down for this.'

'But it can't be just *anybody*,' I said. 'That's not how it works. It takes time to find the culprit.'

'Obviously,' she said. 'That's not what I mean.'

'Would you like a glass of water?' I asked.

'No.'

'A coffee?'

'No. You look like you could do with one, though.'

'Yes, Lizzie. Let me get one and we'll get back to this.'

'In that case I will join you. Milk, no sugar.'

I left to make them and watched her in the monitor, Lizzie was looking around the room. She rested her chin in her hand and propped her elbow on the table.

'Here you go,' I said, and put the cup in front of her.

'Thank you,' Lizzie said, flicking her hair. 'I have helmet hair,' she said.

I smiled at her. 'Cyclist's burden,' I said, but then remembered she'd been on foot at the top of the hill outside the day nursery.

'Oh, yeah,' she replied with a slight laugh. 'I went for a ride today, but on a horse, not a bike.'

'Do you own the horses out the back of your house?'

'I wish I had that land, or any land. I wish! The owner lets me go riding for free, if I help out mucking out the horses in return.'

'How many do they have? Two?' I asked with curiosity. I have always loved horses. Such beautiful, intuitive creatures. How nice would it be for my boys to have horses, to live in the country, I thought.

'Two.' Lizzie nodded. 'There were three until recently. One of them died. He'd had seizures for a long time. It was shocking to see the dead corpse of an animal, so much bigger than a human. It seemed more tragic.'

'Well, nice day to be out for a ride.'

'Sorry, I'm getting off subject.'

'No problem,' I said, sipping my coffee. I was glad to talk about something normal for a minute. Not murder. Not the murder that finding adequate childcare was proving to be.

'The gardener …' Lizzie prompted.

'Yes, the gardener. He has previous,' I said then kicked myself for being too open. I took another sip of my drink.

'Oh, what previous has he?' said Lizzie, all wide-eyed, wrapping one hand around her cup.

'He has served a prison term,' I said then I stopped. 'I shouldn't have said that. He is known to the police, we'll just say.'

'Has he hurt a woman before?'

I refused to speak.

'Oh my god.' Lizzie took my silence for a yes.

'Lizzie, I … I presume you have something to tell us.'

'Not really. I like to check how investigations are progressing.'

'I appreciate that but I can't say very much and I will keep the family informed.'

'I was much closer to her than they were,' she said looking bruised.

'I appreciate that, too. I'll let you know when we make progress.'

'Thanks so much, Detective Sloane. Harriet, isn't it?'

'Yes.'

'Thank you, Harriet. *Have* you spoken to that gardener yet?'

'I can't give out information on the case.'

'I just want to know that things are moving.'

'They're moving.'

'You're doing a great job.' She smiled at me.

'Just give us time, and take time for yourself. This has been a massive shock.' I knocked back my coffee, Lizzie didn't touch hers. 'If that's all …'

'Before I go, can I just say … Maybe it's something and maybe it's nothing, but Drew …'

Now she had my full attention.

'Drew Taylor,' Lizzie said, 'Chloe's cousin. He's a bad lot.'

'We've been acquainted.'

'There isn't a pie he doesn't have a finger in.' She pulled a face. 'Oh, that sounds filthy.'

'What about Drew?' I asked.

'Well, he's dodgy, isn't he?'

'Lizzie, I'd like to run something past you.'

'Anything.'

'Lewis said that he would lend Chloe money.'

'Oh, I'm so glad you got speaking to Lewis!'

'Twice,' I said.

'And what did you think?'

'About?'

'*Lewis.*'

'I'm mentioning that, Lizzie, because I wonder if you know of any debts Chloe had to anyone?'

She looked disappointed. 'So you must think Lewis had nothing to do with it? You like him.'

'Lizzie …'

'You're on it ... You can't divulge. Fine.' She smiled at me. 'But you'll look into Drew? Drew and that gardener?'

'Look, Lizzie, leave it to us,' I said. 'Just let us do our jobs.'

'Before I go, can I just say that I wouldn't expect much from Drew in the way of truth? He was standing there telling bare-faced lies in the house.'

'Which house do you mean?'

'Chloe's, *that* night. The night of the day she died. You were there,' she said.

'What did he lie about?'

'Drew made out that he hadn't seen Chloe in months.'

'Had he seen Chloe recently?'

'Very recently. She called him and he came to my house that last night.'

'When?'

'The night before. Tuesday just past.'

'Really?' I said. 'Why did Chloe call Drew?'

'For one of his pies. Drew's a dealer.'

'Drug dealer?'

'Come on!' Lizzie said, ribbing me. 'Everyone knows that.'

'Do you know if *he* ever lent Chloe money?'

'Not that I know of, he brought some weed though.'

'Did Chloe have a problem? An addiction?'

'She did like it a lot. I'd have my chardonnay and she'd have a smoke to calm her. She lived on her nerves. Everyone knows someone like that.'

'Would Drew stay, or would he drop and dash?'

'He'd sit and have a smoke, yeah.'

'How about the night in question? Tuesday just past?'

'He didn't hang around.' Lizzie shook her head meaningfully.

'Was there bad blood between them?'

'There always was.'

'Why?'

'Oh God, I have no idea, but does Drew Taylor have good blood with anyone? He scares the shit out of me.'

I let the picture reconfigure.

'Are they yours?' Lizzie asked.

'What?' I looked around the desk.

'The babies?' she asked with a great big grin.

I was surprised she'd seen them. I had been inside the nursery for ages.

'They look young.'

'They are.'

'You need time to be you, too.'

'Yes.' I stood up. 'Well, thanks, Lizzie, for coming in.'

'You'll speak to Drew again?'

'I will speak to everyone I can, me and my partner, Sergeant Higgins.'

'I know you will now, Harriet, because you and I are mothers. We'll get justice for Chloe.'

When Lizzie left I had time to breathe again. My boys were in a safe spot, one where I wouldn't have to worry about them. And I liked the look of that manager Joanne, she was not the type to flap. Unlike Sylvia.

Chapter 10

By mid-afternoon that Friday, I called the mobile phone listed for Dan Hamilton of the gardening company. A man answered and when I introduced myself as a DI and asked to speak with him in person, he hung up.

When Higgins, a little later, called him pretending to be a customer, Hamilton told him he wasn't taking on many more customers.

'It's just for a small job,' Higgins said, 'a little yard.'

To which Hamilton reluctantly told him he would be working in the Kings Road area the next day; Saturday. And if he wanted to, he could call and see the flower bed Hamilton was putting in there. As for a home address, we had no luck in finding out where he lived.

*

Higgins and I had spoken about Lizzie's information some more and decided she couldn't have been her only friend, that Chloe must have had a broader social circle than just one person. What about friends from university? What about the girls she joined on her gap year travelling? Where were they now?

Around six p.m. we went to meet Beatrice Carnduff from Feminist Complex, Belfast in a café beside Castle Court Shopping Centre. Beatrice sat over a stack of syrupy pancakes. She had perfectly spidery eyelashes and an emerald nose stud.

'I believe Chloe was an active member of FCB,' I said.

'She would dip in and out,' said Beatrice. 'But when she was involved she was very involved.'

'Chloe liked to protest?'

'Is *like* the right word? She protested in April, after the Belfast Rape Trial, and the awful treatment of the victim.'

Beatrice was referring to the case against two local rugby players who were on trial for the rape of a young woman. In court her alcohol levels, choice of clothing, language and much more were called into question. Although the rugby players were ultimately acquitted, their stories were questionable and well-aligned.

No one could claim they hadn't acted disgracefully, even in the way they spoke about the young woman in their WhatsApp groups.

Beatrice had used the word *victim*, and I didn't think that anyone who had followed the nine-week trial, as it was hard to miss – and the media still used it as clickbait – could realistically not think that she had been victimised, if even by the legal process.

It led to 'I Believe Her' rallies around Ireland.

'What else can you tell me about Chloe? It seems as if she didn't have a large group around her.'

'I knew Chloe only as an acquaintance,' said Beatrice. 'I don't know much about her personal life.'

'What *can* you tell me?' I asked.

'That she was sensitive. Nice. Feisty when she needed to be. Sensitive.'

'You came back to sensitive.'

'She was easily hurt. But aren't we all: all of us who fight for better things? We have to be pissed off about something to get us to this point.'

'What was Chloe annoyed about?'

'She wanted people to be treated equally, respectfully.'

'How long had you known her?'

'Three years. It galls me, a young woman, is just *disposable*. And after what happened to Erica McClelland.'

'Did you know Erica?' Higgins asked.

'No. Violence against women peeks my interest. Young women in Northern Ireland are the most invisible demographic. Did you know that?'

'But Erica ...' I started.

'Yes, Erica,' said Beatrice, 'her death has garnered more media coverage than Chloe's. And call me cynical, but maybe that's because there were all those photos of Erica looking beautiful on nights out. Whereas Chloe was beautiful too, but she didn't subscribe to this *Instagram perfection*. Or what we are taught by advertisers, and airbrushing, and Photoshop, to think is *perfection*. Erica was that perfectly groomed ideal. People are still talking about her. As they should be! Yet Chloe's killing was really recent, and yet it's as if she is already forgotten about. But she won't be, we're holding a vigil outside PACT.'

'Let us know when.'

'We will.'

'Would *you* have any idea of someone who would do this?' asked Higgins.

'My brain doesn't work like that, fortunately.'

'How do you mean?' he asked.

'I can't think why anyone would physically harm anyone,' Beatrice said. 'There is nothing that would ever make me act that way.'

'Beatrice,' I said, remembering Jackie mentioning a Beatrice before. 'Didn't you go travelling with Chloe?'

'Me?' she said slowly. 'No.'

'I thought your name was brought up in relation to Chloe travelling.'

'When she worked for Amnesty International?' Beatrice said.

Higgins and I looked at each other. 'When she went travelling around Europe,' he replied.

'I don't know about that. She didn't go with me.'

'Maybe another Beatrice,' said Higgins.

'Chloe worked with Amnesty International?' I asked.

'Chloe worked with girls who'd had FGM.'

'What's FGM?' asked Higgins.

'Female genital mutilation.'

'In Europe?' I said.

'No, not in Europe,' said Beatrice. 'Actually, Chloe talked very little about it, like it was something she wanted to forget. I didn't ask too much. I think she just wanted to show me, look, I've earned my stripes, here's what I've seen, something bigger and even more rotten than girls here are going through.' Beatrice linked her fingers together. 'The wider group didn't know.'

'Okay,' I said, taking some notes. This was completely new to us. 'Did Chloe have a friend called Jane, or June?'

'There is a lecturer of hers. Professor June Lundy.'

'At Queens?'

'Yes,' said Beatrice.

'Thank you,' I told Beatrice. 'That was more helpful than you know.'

'Good!' she said with the mix of a smile and frown, pushing the pancakes away from her and lifting her phone instead, starting what looked like a text.

Chapter 11

'It's your day off,' Paul said on Saturday morning, 'and mine, too.' But still I got dressed for work.

'I know,' I said. 'I just need to go to Bangor.' That, and I wanted to see the gardener with Higgins.

'Why Bangor?' asked Paul.

'Because Chloe Taylor was stabbed three times and so was Erica McClelland.'

'Oh, yes, Erica McClelland. I've seen her photos.'

'I'm sure you have,' I said.

'What's that?'

'She was only a kid,' I said. 'Won't be long.'

'But it's the wedding, thought you'd want to watch it.'

'Erm, no thanks.'

The boys were in their playpen, I kissed them on my way out.

*

I stood in the office hurrying Higgins along. Fleur Hewitt looked surprised to see me.

'Aren't you supposed to be at home, putting your feet up?' she asked me.

'Putting my feet up!' I got touchy.

'They can't get rid of you here.'

'Who wants to get rid of me?' I asked and she looked baffled.

Higgins came over. 'DI Sloane,' he greeted me professionally for Hewitt's benefit. 'I heard on the grapevine that last night Drew was dragged out of The Bell while having a drink. He was pulled into an alleyway and dealt a punishment beating.'

'Any lasting damage?' I asked.

'His leg is broken.'

'Social control,' said Hewitt. 'They want him to keep quiet about something.'

'Probably a drugs thing,' I said. I didn't like how she was explaining a good old Northern Irish tradition to us. 'The organisation doesn't like dealers,' I told her.

'No shit, hen,' said Hewitt. She walked away, letting herself straight into the chief's room without knocking.

'What a bitch,' I said quietly.

Higgins was laughing. 'She can be.'

'How in the world did she get that job?'

'Sour grapes?' he said.

'Something's sour and it isn't me.'

'Don't let her annoy you.'

'Easy for you to say, Carl.'

'What do you mean?' asked Higgins. 'I put up with you; I don't let you annoy me, do I?'

*

It was sunny on the way to Bangor, so sunny Higgins put his shades on and sang *Didn't we have a lovely time the day we went to Bangor*.

'Stick to the drums,' I told him. After a minute I had second thoughts. 'Sorry, Carl. Let's go and speak with Drew instead.'

'You sure?' he asked me.

'Sure,' I said.

'Are you sure that's okay though?'

'Carl, if you ask me if it's okay and I say it's okay with me, then it's okay.'

'Can't believe you're in here on your day off anyway,' he said, 'and with a royal wedding on.'

'I really wish people would stop saying that to me,' I said.

'Not a fan?'

'Are you?'

'I liked the last wedding.' Higgins looked in the mirror and fixed his fringe.

'You liked Pippa Middleton's arse,' I said.

'How do you know that?' He laughed.

'You talked about it for weeks.'

He only laughed harder.

'Good that you can laugh at yourself,' I said, 'anyway, it's media propaganda: she has no arse. They just can't let a royal girl have a day to herself.'

'I like a conspiracy theory!' he said.

'It's the Daily Mail I blame,' I said.

Higgins laughed 'Let's hear it, Harry.'

'Google these words: *Daily Mail, royal* and *steals the show*. Honestly, they love it. 'Pippa steals the show at Kate's wedding', 'Prince George steals the show at Charlotte's christening', 'Tindall's little daughter steals the show at the Queen's birthday'. Bullshit!'

'You know a lot about them. Their names, anyway,' he said. 'I only know about Pippa.'

'And she isn't even a royal.'

'Meghan's a babe, too,' he said. 'I liked watching her in that show *Suits*. Looks like Pippa a bit.'

'Does she?' I frowned. 'Does Meghan have an arse?'

'Ooh, Harry. You are hard.'

I laughed as he pulled up in front of Drew's house. I didn't know if Higgins was growing on me or if I was just comparing him to Fleur Hewitt.

Maybe I was just delighted to get out of the house on a long structureless Saturday.

Saturdays had become the bane of my life since having the boys. If Paul was off work it was even worse. He liked days out; making the most of *time as a family*.

I couldn't do my own thing, put the boys in the double buggy and go out for a run. Then get them to nap so I could put on a movie, pour a glass of wine. Paul just wanted to talk. We had so little in common, and he wasn't the funniest person I'd ever met.

Higgins, dear help me, was my adult conversation. Mindless and amusing.

At Drew's house Roxanne answered the door. She was holding the little girl whose pox were less angry.

'You heard the news,' she said.

'We heard that Drew was …' I looked at the girl, certain she could understand some things at her age.

'Come in,' Roxanne said. She shooed the little girl upstairs to play in her bedroom and on the sofa Drew was lying with his leg elevated and in plaster. His face was scuffed. A pair of crutches leaned against the wall. The baby was tottering about; he came over and held onto my knees and smiled.

'What age is he?' I asked.

'Ten months,' said Roxanne.

'And he's walking?' I asked, unable to hide my shock.

'Harrison's been walking since he was nine months,' said Drew.

I felt kind of resentful, my two were still uncommitted to getting up on their feet.

'Are you feeling better now?' I asked Harrison. But when Drew looked at me I turned my attention back to him. 'I hear *this* happened to you, where was it?'

'I've already been asked to give a statement, but thanks for your concern,' Drew said.

'And you gave a statement?'

'Yes.'

'Are you sure?'

'He refused, didn't he!' said Roxanne.

'Why was that?' I asked.

'Do I look like a tout.'

'It's okay for someone to do this to you, to break your leg?' said Higgins.

'What do you think, mate?'

'Mr. Taylor,' I started.

'There's no getting justice on some people …' Drew interrupted me. 'It's nothing to do with Chloe, if that's why you're really here.'

'How would you know that for sure?' I asked.

'It stands to reason,' he said.

'Does it?'

'*I've* pissed somebody off. Nothing to do with Chloe.'

'They can't be allowed to get away with this, Andrew,' said Roxanne.

Drew tutted at her.

'Maybe someone has decided that your cousin had it coming, too,' said Higgins.

'No,' Drew said strongly.

'So, you know who killed Chloe?'

'The fuck I do.'

'How can you be sure it's not the same people?' I pushed him.

'She doesn't know these ones and they don't know her.'

'Who?'

'Nice try.' He chortled, then clutched his ribs.

'Sore?'

'What do you think? After they set on me I was lying there, busted open.'

'This can't be easy for you,' I said to Roxanne and she looked back at me with an emptiness in her eyes that gave me a chill.

'What are your thoughts on this attack?' Higgins asked her.

'Keep her out of it,' said Drew with more than a hint of a warning in his tone.

I looked at Roxanne for a few moments. 'Oh, I give up,' she said, sweeping Harrison up and leaving the room. 'I'm not allowed an opinion on anything.' Soon Roxy was upstairs, talking loudly to the little girl.

She was saying, 'You are three, Ella, you know how to use the potty.'

'Drew,' I said quietly. 'Chloe owed you money.'

'That's alright,' he said. 'She's my kid cousin, and not much money for that matter.'

'What did she owe you money for?' asked Higgins.

'Nothing.'

'Was it drugs?' I asked, in an almost-whisper.

'Chores,' he said.

'Okay ... when did you last see her? The truth this time.'

'A fortnight or so. Could have been a month.'

'So *not* Christmas?' said Higgins.

'Wasn't it Tuesday?' I said. 'The night before she was murdered?'

'Who's been filling your head with that shite?' Drew asked.

'You saw Chloe then, at Lizzie's house.'

'If she says so.'

'Do you say so?'

'You ever let a man rest in peace?'

'No,' I said. 'Never.'

Drew raised an eyebrow at me and half-smiled.

'Who was there, at Lizzie's house?' asked Higgins.

'Mad Lizzie, as you know. Our Chlo, and that's it.'

'And you?' I said.

'For half a second.'

'Delivering drugs?'

'Nah, just saying hi.'

'You and Lizzie are friendly, then?'

He said nothing.

'And no one else was there?' asked Higgins.

'Your man with the budgie smugglers came home,' said Drew, 'and that was that, I was on my way out anyway.'

'You mean Lizzie's partner?'

'Yeah, the English twat. He came in briefly.'

'Justin?'

'Yeah. Him.'

'Do you want to tell us why *this* happened to you?' I tried to coax Drew again.

'Because some people are sore.'

'What about?'

'Are you here re: me or re: Chloe?'

'Re: you pressing charges,' I said. 'I think you should.'

'Who against?'

'Whoever did this to you?'

He grimaced. He was a brick wall, but I sensed he could be pushed over.

Chapter 12

'Will we forget Bangor?' asked Higgins looking at the time as he drove. He was due to meet with Dan Hamilton soon.

'I'm not sure,' I said feeling my phone buzz in my pocket. It was Father. 'I have to take this.'

'Harry,' Father said, 'I've had a call from Bethany.' He meant Mother's nursing home but made it sound like a person, another woman, or the chippy on the Newtownards Road.

'Yes?' My heart sank but instantly there was relief, all in a couple of seconds. I thought my mother might have died, and would no longer be in limbo. We would have an end, finally, to the routine that pulled our lives away from us. 'Is Mummy okay?' I asked.

'Oh, she's great.'

'Great?'

'The same as usual, Harriet,' he sounded impatient. 'It's not about your mother, it's something else, alright?'

'Yes?'

'Someone has threatened the nursing home. They received a letter to say they know where Adelinde is and that someone is going to come and ... the staff were reluctant to let me see it.'

'What did it say?'

'The letter?'

'*Yes*,' I said, almost losing my cool.

'You don't want to know,' said Father. 'It could be someone she put away in the past. It could be anyone.'

'Not really,' I said.

'How do you know! It could be someone who visits here and they recognise your mother, or they recognise me, and are still holding a grudge about some legal issue.'

'Oh, fuck sake,' I said.

Higgins glanced at me and frowned. I shooed him away, as if, don't listen, it's not your business.

'How can we cope with this now, knowing someone might harm your mother?' said Father.

'I don't think it's likely,' I said, trying to calm him.

'She is lying here unresponsive. What if someone was to molest her?'

'Daddy!'

'Things like this happen, Harry, as we well know in our line of work.'

'But why say it now? She's been like this for years.'

'Well, I've told you,' Father said, 'so on your head be it if something happens.' He hung up the phone.

'Fuck sake!' I said, maybe too loud.

Higgins turned fast to look at me. 'God, what's wrong?'

'It's personal.'

'You shouldn't be in today,' he said.

'I know, and I'm going home. We'll go to Bangor later.'

Usually Higgins would joke but he didn't. He turned the car and we went back to the station.

Back at Strandtown Lewis, Chloe's ex, called. Hewitt put him on the phone to me.

'I'm out of the loop,' Lewis said. 'Any news?'

'None,' I said.

'Will someone let me know if you get the culprit?'

'Believe me,' I said, 'everyone will know when we get him.'

Chapter 13

Hamilton was working at a house on Kings Road like he'd said he would be. He wore beige khakis and a red fleece. The garden was beautiful, spring was crackling. I could see why he'd be proud of the flower bed he was grafting on. Around it laburnum hung like crayon-yellow grapes, the clematis in full flower, red tulips reached upward like thirsty tongues.

'Are you Daniel Hamilton?' I asked him.

'No,' he said.

He had a long face. Long ears and nose. He looked like an e-fit in person. But I had a photo, I located it from my pocket. It was him.

'I go by Terry. My middle name,' he said. It was a done-to-death ploy, by certain types. Thank god for middle names.

'We would like a word with you, if you please.'

Hamilton said, 'I'll be with you in a minute.'

'I won't take a minute.'

He gave me a look I knew; a look that made me angry. We directed him over beside the car and he sullenly followed.

'I called you before and you hung up. Detective Inspector Sloane,' I introduced myself.

'Must have been a bad connection.'

Hamilton was looking over my shoulder for this potential customer he was waiting for.

'We want to speak to you about whatever you were doing on Wednesday of this week.'

'What time?' he said impatiently, to get shot of us sooner.

'Between ten and twelve, morning to noon.'

'If you want to ask me something you can take me to the station.'

'Fine, *Terry*, would you accompany us the station?' I asked.

'Am I being arrested for something?'

'You are not, but we would like your assistance.'

'I'm not in the mood for assisting anyone today,' Hamilton said.

'Do you cut grass in the Summerhill area?'

'It seems that answering that would be assisting you.'

'Need I remind you of the name Darleen Boyle, who you were convicted of murdering in 1994?'

He glared at me. 'Fine, what is it? Do I cut grass in the Stormont area? Yeah, I do and I have done. Is that illegal now?'

'Mr. Hamilton, refusing to answer simple questions makes you look very suspicious.'

'To you, maybe.'

'Mr. Hamilton,' said Higgins, 'you may have heard of the death of a young woman in East Belfast? Chloe Taylor, aged twenty-one, she was attacked in the office of PACT.'

'So I heard.'

'When did you hear about the incident?'

'I heard on the news that night. Okay, are you done?'

'I believe you were her gardener,' I said.

'Was I? That's new information to me.'

'I have been informed that you had an altercation with Chloe at one point.'

'Where did she live?' Hamilton asked.

'Summerhill Park.'

'Rings a bell.' His face broke into a smile. 'I know that wee girl now.' He laughed. 'It's nothing.'

'Tell us about it. It must be funny.'

'It was. Her new next door neighbours were having a flap because they needed to turn the water off but they couldn't find the mains. I went in and turned it off under their sink and it didn't help.'

'That was nice of you.'

'They were potential new customers.' Now he looked at Higgins. He slid his tongue up under his top lip.

I nodded. 'Go on, Dan ... Or Terry, is it?'

Hamilton gave me a double take, then said, 'I went out looking and there was no manhole in their garden – there was, actually, I'm their gardener now and know the place better, it was just grown over with grass – but I explained that sometimes it's in someone else's garden. I turned the water off in their house ... Jackie, that's the fella's name, he let his wee girl run the show.'

I didn't know why he'd stopped. 'Keep going,' I directed him.

'The wee girl came out in a towel and went, "Hello, what's going on?" and the woman in that next house, it's the Gormans that live there ... well, the Gorman woman told her the craic and the wee girl said she was in the shower and, on and on it went, anyway.' Hamilton clapped his hands. 'Time wore on and we couldn't get the water stopped. She, the wee girl, was ringing the doorbell, and – all dressed now – was ... just bitching at me, you know.'

'She was annoyed that you turned her water off.'

'That's the length and breadth of it.'

'Did you ask if you could turn it off?' I asked.

'It was only for a minute. I did ring the doorbell and she wasn't answering.'

'Because she was in the shower and couldn't hear you?' said Higgins.

'Fuck! We know whose side you're on!'

'We're just trying to understand the altercation,' I told Hamilton; Dan, Terry, whatever he needed to call himself to strip himself of his past, and the unprovoked murder of a young single mother.

'This wee girl at Summerhill was just going daft and I was saying, like, "Keep your knickers on".'

'Were you aggressive towards Chloe?'

'No,' Hamilton said. 'Ask the Gormans, they were looking at her like she was mental, too.'

'What was Chloe saying?' I asked.

Hamilton exhaled heavily.

'We're just trying to find out how she was acting *mental*, as you put it.'

'She was just saying, it didn't matter how many times I had to ring the doorbell, I had to get her permission. She was a kid, like, telling me I needed permission. I was only trying to help people.'

'That is a funny story,' said Higgins, dryly.

'Where were you on Wednesday morning?' I asked now he was speaking freely.

'The Ulster Hospital, on dialysis,' Hamilton said. 'I have kidney failure.'

Higgins took notes. 'We'll have to check that up.'

'Oh, I'm sure you will and all.'

'Great, we're all on the same page,' I said.

'Can just about do the odd job these days, like I told you when you called pretending to be a potential customer.' Hamilton looked at Higgins. 'I don't have it in me to go stabbing people to death.'

'Nope, but you did. You did before,' I said walking towards the car, watching him lug the lawn mower out of the trailer. He kept looking back.

'Was young and fit then,' he shouted over. 'Was a mad bastard with a lot of problems.'

'And now just a mad old bastard,' I said quietly as I got into the car.

'Active though, for a man on dialysis,' said Higgins as he drove off, on up Kings Road. 'That's much more than a flower bed he's working on.'

'He's a fucken liar,' I said.

We wasted no time and by four p.m. were at the hospital. The staff was finished for the week. Nobody knew anything, even when I said my partner was Dr. Paul Coulter and even when I told them what we were there for. A murder, and a suspect. A potential alibi, or lack of one. The receptionist was as much of a gatekeeper as I'd ever seen.

'Sorry,' she said, but she didn't seem sorry. 'Someone will be back there on Monday. Why don't you try then?'

*

I thought of Chloe's mother Glynis when I washed the boys in the bath that night, and after I stroked their backs. I felt weepy again and if I wasn't on my period I'd have worried I was pregnant, but then, despite Paul claiming to be sterile, I still took precautions. And hadn't we only slept together five times in our fifteen-month relationship? To think that any of those times could have made a baby would be another huge disappointment. I couldn't keep letting my fertility hang over me like that. I resolved to get sterilised, but how could I explain that to Paul? I could say it was because my periods were a pain, but he had surely already garnered that they were not. I'd never complained about them to him. Plus, he would know the person putting me under for the op. It is a small world in anaesthesia.

Since Jason, my fertility felt like it belonged to others and not to me, but to men who tried to own it or did not even know that they did.

I fed the babies with Paul and put them to bed, and decided I was just emotional because the love I had for them eclipsed everything. Which is not to say that I wanted to extend that year at home with them. It was work, too. Harder in some ways because it was newest to me.

That night I got into bed and watched the highlights of the wedding.

'It is lovely,' said Paul. 'Look at the way he is looking at her, and her at him.'

'You're an old romantic at heart,' I said.

'Very much so.'

'It is lovely,' I said looking at Prince Harry and Meghan looking at each other, looking beautiful.

'I don't know why you've been fighting it,' said Paul. 'It's only love.'

'I'm just waiting for someone else to walk in and steal her show,' I said.

Chapter 14

On Sunday afternoon we got on the road to Bangor. There we met with Detective Reynolds who I had trained with all those years ago at Garnerville.

'Hey, I heard you were back,' he said.

'With a vengeance,' I said.

'How are the kids?'

'Good,' I said. 'And yours?'

I'd never asked a colleague that question before, but I made sure to ask him. No one spoke about kids or family when they mentioned the men in the service. It was alright for a man. It *was* alright for a man. They escaped the *how do you juggle* question; they were not talked to as if they were clowns.

'I've three now,' Reynolds told me.

'Good-o,' I said. 'Times have changed since training days.'

'We all have to grow up sometime.'

I tried to get off the topic, I did not want to be known as *that detective with twin babies*. 'It's a bad time in East Belfast, at the moment. You've had it bad in Bangor, too,' I said.

'Yes, with Erica,' said Reynolds. 'There are similarities, I suppose.' But he was pulling a face like he was not convinced the similarities were strong enough to warrant a half-hour drive to Bangor.

'So tell me about Erica McClelland.'

'You mean tell you what you haven't already been able to read online,' he said.

'They've had a field day with her.'

Reynolds agreed.

'Tell me.'

'The victim wasn't found until six a.m., that was a busy night for us.'

'Why?' I asked.

'Between teenage girls beating up their own at Pickie on the seafront, and vandalism …'

'Was it kids doing the vandalism?'

'No, the vandalism was done by someone in a car, at Bexley. They … actually, Sloane, do you remember Officer Kinahan?'

'Kinahan,' I wrung the name out.

'The firearms officer,' said Reynolds, 'he did the training at Garnerville.'

'Oh, yeah. Pat; Pat Kinahan?'

Reynolds said, 'Yes.'

'I do now.'

'There was vandalism and damage to personal property at Pat's house. His wife woke to someone putting his car windows in at three a.m.'

'Was that the same house the handgun went missing from?' I asked.

'It was. You heard about that?'

'I tried to stay in the loop when I was off. I don't recall anything super specific, I just heard a gun went missing. Any more details on the car?'

'Yes … don't you worry about it. We have our ears to the ground in Bangor.'

'Are you sure?' I teased him.

'What are you saying?' Reynolds acted offended.

'This is a cushy number, compared to Strandtown.'

'You reckon!' he exclaimed. 'There's plenty of rough in with the smooth out here, and sometimes the smooth ain't the smoothest.'

'Yeah, well, you don't catch us closing over lunchtime in East Belfast.'

'We have to.'

'Well for you!'

'Like a village shop,' said Higgins out of nowhere, but his joke landed badly with Reynolds who gave him a death stare. I offered Higgins a smile for taking the trouble to back me up.

'So that makes sense,' I said, 'that the house was Kinahan's. That the gun was Kinahan's.'

'So, the victim ...' said Higgins.

'Yes ... getting back to Erica McClelland ... that's why it was a busy time for us anyway, that day.'

'The vic was stabbed,' I said.

'Yes, but McClelland's cause of death was drowning, in the end.'

'She was found in the water,' said Higgins.

'It was shallow,' said Reynolds, 'but she was weak, had lost a lot of blood by then.'

'Wow!' I said.

'But yes, she was stabbed three times.'

'So was Chloe Taylor,' I said.

'With the utmost of respect ...' started Reynolds.

'I know what that means,' I interrupted him.

'What?' he asked, trying to look innocuous.

'Usually the opposite. Contempt, right?'

'No ... I don't see why you think it is linked, Sloane. I get that you're looking into it, and there *are* some similarities. Well, one.'

'Tell me more about Erica, something that isn't in the public domain, if there is anything,' I said.

'She was found at Ballyholme beach.'

'That's public,' said Higgins.

'There was a bite mark on Erica's arm,' said Reynolds.

'That isn't,' said Higgins glancing hopefully at me.

'We surmise that at one point the victim must have had the perpetrator in a headlock. It didn't match the DNA profile of anyone in her family, friends, colleagues.

We took swabs of fifty taxi drivers who were working in the area, because she was obviously driven there. Imprints were made of the bite.'

'So they know about the bite mark, family, friends?'

'No. No one does.'

'Erica was conscious, to a point, then?'

'Yes, she fought alright. But ... she was drugged.'

*

'There's the link,' said Higgins as we drove along Abbey Street.

'What with?' I asked.

'Erica was drugged,' he said.

'But Chloe wasn't.'

'Maybe not a link to Chloe but to those other girls who claimed they were drugged in bars and nightclubs.'

'What girls?'

'You'd have missed it, being on holiday.'

'Maternity leave!'

'Weren't you in Florida?'

'Not the whole time! Go on,' I said and he told me.

The next day Higgins was gone.

Chapter 15

It began raining just before ten on Sunday night. It lasted hours. The tyres of cars clopped like hooves down Mount Eden, but we needed that rain. I lay in bed listening to it and the crackle of the baby monitor and was happy. The next morning was cooler, cloudy and dull, perfect for a Monday. Perfect for my mood.

Superintendent Fleur Hewitt met me at the gates as I came into the station.

'You and me,' Hewitt said. 'Your wee pal is suspended.' She walked towards the main door.

'Carl?' I asked in disbelief.

'Aye. Higgins is being investigated for cheating in his sarge exams, the whole lot of them are.'

'He'd already taken that exam twice,' I said. He'd been trying desperately and failing completely. And now, this.

'It's third time the charm,' said Hewitt, 'or, he cheated his way in, man.'

'Shit,' I said. 'I've really been starting to warm to him.' I was thinking how conscientious he seemed now.

'Maybe you'll warm to me,' said Hewitt. 'I've spent the last few hours playing catch-up, and we're going to Queens University to talk to Chloe's lecturer, Prof. June Lundy.'

We drove there in silence along the bridge, right beside my old apartment. We went past St George's Market and through Ormeau, then through Botanic until we got to Queens and parked up. Then we walked through the stony grey grounds of the university arse-about-face, until we landed in the front entrance. A woman in a bright yellow shirt came down the stairs and walked towards us.

'Are you here to see Professor Lundy?' she asked us.

'Yes,' Hewitt told her. The woman asked that we follow her to a room on our right.

June met us there with a plate of biscuits and a pot of tea. 'Chloe was doing great,' she said.

'Did you have *any* concerns about her?' asked Hewitt, stamping herself on the case like she was in charge. I suppose now she was.

'She was very quiet,' said Prof. Lundy, 'and then she had problems at the end of year one Law, and deferred for a year.'

'She was unwell?' asked Hewitt.

'Depressed, somewhat.'

'And after?'

'She went travelling, came back and started a new course. Chloe transferred to year 1 of a BA in Social Anthropology, then she was like a new person.'

'Happier?' I asked and Hewitt looked at me.

'Happy and vivacious, much more vocal, she was taking part in debates all the time.'

'But you say she was quiet lately?'

'Just very lately. But when I think about it, she was restless when she came back from Pakistan …'

'When did she go there?' Hewitt looked confused.

'August 2016, till March 2017.'

'Before or after she travelled Europe?' I said. That journey was still a possibility in my mind.

'I don't recall her travelling in Europe. She went to Pakistan, it was after the Quetta attacks. Fifty-four lawyers were killed, if you remember.'

Hewitt stared on; I couldn't remember either. Far away tragedies didn't cut me the same.

'Chloe wanted to go and she did,' said the prof. 'Her father might have tried to talk her out of it, but when she returned she talked about it in such detail ... I have no doubt that was where she went.'

'What did she do in Pakistan?' asked Hewitt.

'Chloe volunteered with Amnesty International.'

'I have heard this from another source,' I said.

'What did she do, work-wise?' asked Hewitt.

'She worked in the office. Sometimes she helped support girls who had been through female circumcision. Chloe found herself in danger once or twice. When she came home we met for a coffee. She looked lead tired and fragile. I said to her, "You can save someone but not everyone".'

Prof. Lundy's comment brought me to think of Higgins and how, when he brought up the girls who believed they had been drugged, and told me all he knew, I'd said that we couldn't solve every crime but that we could solve Chloe's. I had resolved to hone in on it, but now I felt I understood Chloe, and her passion, her resolve. And I was determined to look at the cases of these other girls, too.

Five days had passed. We'd had no huge breakthrough with finding her killer and we possibly never would have that breakthrough. Parents of murdered children die waiting for justice. Hadn't Chloe died before she got to right all the things she perceived to be wrong with the world? I wouldn't let it happen to her case.

'When I said that to her, "You can save someone but not everyone," Chloe was uncharacteristically angry at me,' Prof. Lundy told us. 'Chloe said she had as much right to help as girls in Pakistan have to read and learn. I told her she was no good to anyone dead.' June sighed.

'Before the Quetta attacks, Chloe was upset about the veils. We talked about that before she left, I pointed out that world leaders wear veils and they are not the most oppressed; that women who have never seen the light of education, they need help and there are plenty here, on her doorstep. It was important Chloe got her own education sorted before she went off fighting for other women's rights.'

'Fabulous things you told her,' said Hewitt, sounding insincere.

'Chloe was determined to go back some day.' Professor Lundy looked me dead in the eye. 'I know she would have carried on and made a difference, she was an agent of change. Oh, I am sorry you never got to know her. You would have loved her. She was what this world needs more of.'

'These times correspond with when Chloe's family say she was travelling in Europe,' I said, flicking back through my notes.

'She didn't tell them?' asked Hewitt, not looking so caught-up on events now.

'Possibly not,' I said. 'Professor Lundy, did Chloe ever say much about her dad?'

'Only to say he didn't like that she'd taken this detour in her studies, he wanted Chloe to get her shit together.'

'Her brother?'

'I've never heard of any siblings.'

'Mother?' I ventured.

'I'm sorry, Detective, I have nothing more to add on the personal side.'

'Boyfriend or girlfriend?' asked Hewitt.

'Again, no. I'm here for my students but I set clear boundaries. Unless there are problems, which there were a couple of years back with Chloe, then we don't get into the personal. And she was an adult, entitled to a private life.'

*

Hewitt said, 'Everyone has something different to say about Chloe.'

'That means she had good interpersonal skills,' I said. I had started to feel this huge warmth for Chloe.

I could not protect her now, no one could, but I could stand up for her. She did it for strangers, didn't she? 'Don't we all change who we are depending on who we are with?' I asked Fleur.

'I don't,' she said.

Maybe you should, I thought, but I knew Fleur already did whether she could see it herself or not. She had treated Prof. Lundy with respect, even if it was sycophantic respect; she spoke to our Chief with respect, warmly, verging on unprofessional; and Fleur disliked me, and couldn't help but be a bitch, and I had been to an all-girls school. I understood it well.

Chief Dunne called Superintendent Hewitt and told her to head to the Taylors' house. They were quite the little team. He had barely acknowledged me since I'd returned and now I had to put up with their closeness.

I was driving as I heard his instruction and headed towards Stormont direction, to Chloe's home. I noticed a missed call from Mike Birch, so I called him back once I'd parked up. He was mine, I decided, not giving Fleur the chance.

Birch began to tell me that a letter addressed to Chloe had been left at the PACT office and that he had given it to her father.

'Maybe I should have given it straight to you, or binned it,' Mike said down the line. 'But Jackie opened it in front of me.'

'Yes?' I looked at the door, there Jackie was waiting for us.

'It was vile. Hate mail, if you like,' said Mike.

'We're at Jackie's house now,' I said. 'He'll show us the letter.'

'Do you think I should have binned it?' Mike asked me.

'No, you did the right thing.'

'Jackie was upset, and rightfully so.'

'If any more letters for Chloe arrive,' I said, 'bring them to us, or we can pick them up. We're always passing by the office.'

Mike thanked me, swore at himself and ended the call.

Inside the house, the letter sat on the dining table for us. Jackie stayed away from it and from us. I sensed now was not the time to tell him about Chloe's secret trip to Pakistan.

The envelope read: Chloe Taylor DRIP, PACT offices, Upper Newtownards Road, Belfast.

'Drip?' asked Hewitt, like maybe it was a local saying she was not familiar with.

As far as I knew drip meant a soppy, overly-sentimental or weak character flaw. I could only shrug. I opened the envelope, the letter read:

Bye Chloe,

This is what you get when you want to behave like a man. Women are put on this earth to be soft, sensual and sexy. I'm sick of seeing men being oppressed and victimised. Well, look who is oppressed now. You've made yourself the victim. Too bad!
DRIP (Don't rest in peace)

'Drip?' said Hewitt, 'That's a new one on me.'

'What sicko fuck sends this kind of thing to a dead girl,' Jackie said.

'You're quite right,' said Hewitt. 'We just need to locate said sicko fuck.'

A tight smile registered on Jackie's face. He prefers her to me, I thought.

We took the letter with us. Outside Daniel 'Terry' Hamilton was pulling up. He took his mower from his trailer and started pulling it over next door's grass, all the time looking our way. If it had been up to me I'd have gone straight back to the Renal Unit at the Ulster Hospital to check out his dialysis alibi, but Hewitt palmed me off when I suggested it. I had a feeling that if I said the sky was full of clouds, she'd have said it was the hottest, clearest day on record.

'We're heading back to the station,' she said. 'I want a word with the chief, then I'll decide where we go after that.'

I started the car and thought, come back Carl Higgins, all is forgiven.

Chapter 16

Fleur was looking cosy with the chief again by lunch, so I called the renal unit. They were reluctant to give out any details over the phone, data protection, GDPR, and similar shite. Then Fleur eventually came out of his office and the chief soon after. Dunne told us to get to Belfast Met, where Thomas' art teacher, Cyn Dockrill, had reported receiving hate mail because of Thomas' art.

'I want to see a copy of the Irish News,' he said. 'Grab one on your travels.'

I went online as he spoke and saw the front page. The paper read, *Slain Activist's Brother's Sick Art Capitalises on Murder*. The image was too small to make out. I knew that Chief Dunne's eyesight was failing and he wasn't a lover of glasses.

'Cyn Dockrill says that Thomas' work has caused a stir,' he said and paused. 'She wants someone to come and take the hate mail away. Get a copy of the Irish News while you're at it.' His repetition was my cue to leave, followed by his impatient cough.

'Yes, Chief. You said,' I told him.

'Let's go,' said Fleur.

*

Cyn had curly blond hair and a gap in her front teeth that showed when she smiled. The smile soon faded when she produced the letter and set it out on her desk among dried paint and a mess of papers and materials.

'Hold on,' I said, getting a glove from my bag and putting it on, then holding the letter up to the light.

'Apologies,' said Cyn. 'Typical artist's desk.'

I smiled past the letter at her, then went back to read it, it said:

Bye Chloe,
Can't even let sleeping dogs lie now, you still must be shoved down our throats with your exploits. You are sick in the head, my dear, and I am disgusted that people are allowing your damaging agenda to get out there. You deserved everything you got.
DRIP (Don't rest in peace!)

I gave Hewitt 'the look' that said, here we go again. Same person.

'Can you show us this artwork?' asked Hewitt.

'Sure,' said Cyn, 'follow me through to the hall.'

She walked slightly ahead of us and led us to a long rectangular room where there was an exhibition set up. The exhibit she stopped at was intricate, a cluster of artwork, all oversized. Paintings and drawings, all different kinds of media and materials.

First was the heading of this exhibition.

By Thomas Taylor.

'I'll let you look, and then I can tell what I know, how does that sound?' asked Cyn.

'Spot on,' said Hewitt.

One shot or two

The first painting was a charcoal drawing of a girl lying dead on the ground. The girl looked a lot like Chloe. The hair stood up on the back of my neck.

Fridge

The second certainly looked like Chloe's face on the body of a small girl. The girl was holding a smaller girl with a younger version of Chloe's face. They were in a trailer that was attached to the back of a bicycle, the ground around them covered with rubbish.

The trailer instantly made me think of Hamilton the gardener heaving his mower away and the look he had given us.

Shower

The third was a mixed-media collage. The subject in it was a girl with blue hair, she was wrapped in a sarong and holding a jug of water on her head, a line of women behind her, all of them were Chloe, getting steadily younger and smaller. Russian dolls.

The name *Shower* made me think of Hamilton too, him and Chloe having words when he turned off her water. Her in a towel instead of a sarong.

Man-flu

The fourth piece of art was a shaded drawing of a pregnant woman lying on a hospital bed, the veins in her skeletal arms protruding. Her eyes closed. That face was Chloe's again. I was starting to feel quite ill, taking a visceral reaction to the artwork.

Slow as Hell

The fifth image was a print of a girl writing at her desk by candlelight. The face was recognisable again as being that of the artist's sister.

Below it flowers, lots of them, little notes tagged on: *R.I.P.; sleep tight.*

As we were looking, three young people came into the room, ignored all the other displays and stood beside us. They whispered about Thomas' art.

Hewitt turned and asked everyone to clear out. She asked that Cyn not let anyone else into the hall. Cyn guided the young people out as I took photos on my phone of the art work individually, and of the whole scene.

'That title,' said Hewitt. 'First what, hen? First born?'

'Is he obsessed with her?' I asked, not expecting an answer, knowing Hewitt did not have one.

Glynis had hinted he was. Then I remembered Thomas bringing a large board upstairs the night I first went to the house. The night of the day Chloe died.

I had not seen the other side of the board. He was holding it facing away, so I would not. I did not know if it already contained a picture of his dead sister then. Or which one of these pieces it was. Or if it was simply another board, perhaps blank, waiting to capture her image again. To immortalise his sister.

Cyn sidled up to us. 'I've locked the door to give you some privacy,' she said. 'Do you have any questions for me, because like all art, this lacks meaning without context?' She held her hand sideways, her fingers splayed like a crab about to jump on the boards. 'I had suggested putting up cards to explain but Thomas was against it.'

'So that title,' said Hewitt. '*First?*'

'First World Problems,' said Cyn. 'Thomas liked First, alone. He wanted his exhibit to be obscure, foggy, thought-provoking. He wanted people to question what they were looking at.'

'These are not the questions he wanted, surely,' said Hewitt, 'to add to the discomfort?'

'He wanted a dialogue,' said Cyn. 'Well, maybe not to be part of it, but to hear it, at least.'

'Why choose his sister?' I asked.

'He chose Chloe as a subject because of her activism. Thomas wanted to show everyone about privilege and birthright. They can't see themselves in people's shoes until they *see* themselves in other peoples' shoes, in the literal. At one point he wanted to have a pair of Chloe's shoes there. He thought his sister wouldn't approve of that part. She needed them then.'

I watched Hewitt eye the boards as Cyn spoke, she looked at each piece and I had to say they were entrancing, unsettling.

But the detail and his skill made them beautiful. And maybe if his subject was not Chloe – Chloe dead or ill or suffering – and if I had not only seen her dead, I would not have had the same reaction. Cyn was right about context.

'It made sense to Thomas to use Chloe as his model and muse,' said Cyn. 'Here is a reasonably well off white girl carrying water on her head. That visual jars for the onlooker, doesn't it?'

'The titles are provocative,' I voiced. '*One shot or two?*'

'Yes, initially this was called: *My Starbucks latte came with one shot instead of two*,' said Cyn. 'Then *Fridge*: this one shows street kids, it's about how kids in the first world whine to their parents, "There's nothing in the fridge". These kids in other parts of the world have no fridge.'

'The others?'

'*Man flu*, is more than a nod to the HIV/AIDS epidemic in the developing world. And in relation to first world problems, you know how we joke about man flu. First world problems, see? I think it's clever and socially conscious.'

'Yeah,' said Hewitt, almost sleepily.

'The women carrying water, *Shower ... there's no hot water left for a shower*. They are a dialogue about suffering set against simple complaints that seem hideous when you look at what is going on in the world.'

'And *Slow as Hell?*' Hewitt asked.

'*This download is show as hell*. A girl doing homework by candlelight because she has no electricity.'

'It's really deep stuff,' said Hewitt.

'Thomas is a deep kind of kid,' said Cyn. 'But that's artists for you. That's teenagers for you. Put them both together, what have you got?'

'A bit of a mess,' said Hewitt.

'Okay, we'll talk to him,' I said.

'He'll clam up,' Cyn warned us. 'Thomas is extremely introverted, so I wanted to let you know what the meanings are. He has it all up here.' She pointed to her head. 'But he isn't an articulator. And I know how it looks, how the papers and the hate mail make it look. Thomas isn't *capitalising* in a financial sense. These aren't for sale. They will be graded, that's all. That reaction is the danger with provocative art. Once it's made it no longer belongs to the artist. The viewer makes of it what they will. They bring their own prejudices, experiences …'

'Jackie didn't mention the paper,' said Hewitt when we were going to buy a copy.

'I doubt he buys the Irish News,' I said.

'Is this a catholic/protestant thing?' she asked.

'It is. It was …'

'People probably feel uncomfortable to tell him, too.'

We went into a Centra facing the Grand Opera House for a takeaway coffee. 'Oh fuck,' I said under my breath when I saw her: the chief's wife, Jocelyn Dunne. I was trying to escape when Hewitt shouted, 'Ah, of all the places.'

'You know her?' I asked in a low voice. Was she that much a part of Greg's world?

'Who, Jocelyn?' Hewitt said. They chatted while I tried to walk away.

'Harriet,' Jocelyn said. 'How are things?'

'Good,' I said, feeling an unfamiliar blush on me that I never feel, only in anger. Maybe seeing Jocelyn made me angry. Or that she and Fleur seemed so comfortable together. Or that I was put on the spot. I grabbed a copy of the Irish News and folded it over.

'Hey, I believe there was the pitter-patter of tiny feet, times two,' said Jocelyn.

'Yes yes,' I said. 'Busy busy. We probably need to be on our way,' I said to Fleur. 'Lovely to see you … ah,' I pretended to have forgotten Jocelyn's name.

'I suppose you are busy,' she replied warmly. 'I wanted to chat to you at Christmas but we were at different tables, and Greg tells me so little. Before you head off, quickly, show me a photo.'

'A photo of?'

'The babies!' She smiled fully.

'Oh. I …'

I could feel Hewitt analysing my face as she relieved me off the paper and paid for it and our coffees.

I quickly showed Jocelyn the screen saver on my mobile. 'They're precious, Harriet,' she said. 'Names?'

'Jared and Rowan.'

'Gorgeous. We have a Jared, too.'

'You do?' I asked; I hadn't known. Her husband must have said at some point. Then I wondered if he knew our babies' names; he had never asked me the question. Did Greg know that he had two sons with the same name? Had I known? Had I done that subconsciously? How ridiculous. How embarrassing.

'My Jared's thirty. You've good taste in names.'

But bad taste in men, I thought, we have that in common too.

'We must head on,' I said.

116

'They don't look like you.' Jocelyn still held the phone. 'They must be their daddy's double.'

'Hmm, not really,' I said. 'Paul is blond. I think they have that black shiny hair like the men in my family. My eldest brother especially.'

Now I remembered the Christmas do, and Greg and Jocelyn dancing together. How I had managed to dodge her all night, and how I had forgotten who I was too, long enough to stick the lips on Carl after he and his band played their session.

'How do you juggle everything? You're like Wonder Woman!' said Jocelyn smiling again.

Then Hewitt and I left the shop. My face was on fire. Hewitt was enjoying my discomfort.

'Are you overheating?' she asked in the car. 'You're beetroot, even though the air con's on.'

'I'm fine,' I said.

Sarge Simon texted to say I'd had a call from the hospital, and I was thankful I could read it out and we didn't have to talk about what had just happened.

But all I could think was, they know each other. Hewitt is new but to Jocelyn *I* am the strange and interesting one. Hewitt hummed the Wonder Woman theme tune while sipping her coffee and looking at the front page of the paper.

I called Simon, who said we finally got a call back from a senior ranking member doctor who confirmed that Daniel Terence Hamilton, the gardener, *was* undergoing dialysis and had been treated by him between ten-thirty and twelve-thirty on Wednesday, five days prior. By which time Chloe would have been killed and found.

'Ah, that's a pity,' said Hewitt condescendingly. 'That would have been nice to have an answer. And a nice neat bow.'

Chapter 17

All day I was trying to phone Thomas to ask him to meet up with us. There was still no reply. But we did have a call or two from Lizzie Donegan-Moat, who was an articulator. Lizzie had some information she thought might help us and help Chloe's case.

By three p.m. we were at hers. She met us in the porch way, and I don't know why, but I was surprised to see how rundown the bungalow was inside. The décor was cheap and in red and black; everything felt neglected. There were pictures everywhere of her and Justin wrapped up in each other.

'We haven't met. Superintendent Hewitt,' said Fleur.

'Where is Sergeant Higgins?' Lizzie asked, she was all dolled up in a frilly dress and a scarf around her hair, she looked like an Instagram picture. I could see her on that bicycle of hers with the basket, that dress, á la Bardot. A little grey kitten. A stiff French stick.

'Higgins is on leave … holiday,' Hewitt snuck in before I had a chance to respond.

'Is this a good time to take himself off?' asked Lizzie.

'It's never a good time. But we need holidays, too,' I said, still sporting my tan and pissed off that everyone back here in Belfast was just as brown.

'More than most, I'd say,' said Lizzie.

Justin entered the room. There was a light sweat on him and he was wearing sports gear; a tight long-sleeved T-shirt and short shorts.

'Going for a run, babe?' Lizzie asked him.

'Meeting a client,' he replied. Nodded his hello to us.

'So early?' asked Lizzie.

'What kind of client?' asked Hewitt. I read into her tone 'what kind of client do you service in that attire?' I remembered Drew referring to his shorts as budgie smugglers. He wasn't wrong.

'Aren't you a building constructor?' I said, trying to show that I knew more about him and the case overall than Fleur Hewitt did, and still reeling from my pleasant run-in with Jocelyn Dunne.

'Justin's a personal trainer by night, usually by night,' said Lizzie. 'Isn't he gorgeous?'

'He's a good-looking guy,' said Fleur dryly.

'You're both making me blush now,' said Justin.

If you could roll your eyes without rolling them that's what I did. I was embarrassed for the lot of them, Fleur included; she was being unprofessional. If that was what got you the job of Super, I didn't want it.

Lizzie looked at me for an answer, I looked back at her. All I was interested in was this information she had for us that warranted us calling out when we had important things to do.

'I start early on the building site,' said Justin, 'go out with clients in the afternoons, evenings, and weekends. Here and there.'

'Good earner,' said Hewitt.

'Mainly women,' said Lizzie. 'It's no surprise why they'd take up his services, none of them are lookers. He takes a 'before' photo of them.'

'Don't mind her.' Justin looked at Hewitt. 'Liz just likes to see me squirm.'

Lizzie laughed and there was an awkward silence.

'And what do you do, Lizzie?' asked Hewitt.

'I work in a care residence for disabled adults.'

'Which one?' I asked.

'Just down the road,' said Lizzie.

'Which road?

'Kings Road, Dundonald. I love it.'

'You're a nurse?' said Hewitt.

'I'm an activities planner. Art, bingo, you name it. It's good craic.'

'Go on yerself! Worked there long?'

'After I got my Psychology Master's I worked in the Regional College as a Psychology tutor but I hated it. I much prefer this. I'm made for planning and I love a challenge. You need a strong stomach and a good sense of humour.'

'Like in this job,' said Hewitt.

I hated the way she was bonding with these two. There was rapport building and there was rapport building. This was a joke. Had they all forgotten about Chloe?

'You have children, don't you?' I said, looking around. Lizzie stared at me. 'You said you're a mother … at the station,' I reminded Lizzie and watched her clam up. Maybe Hewitt had something in her friendly ladette routine that I hadn't got. Patience, humour, time to waste.

'I lost my babies,' said Lizzie, 'two little boys, but I still think of myself as a mother.'

'Oh, I'm sorry,' I said. My stomach lurched.

'You weren't to know. I'm trying to talk Justin into having a baby. He's steadfast, aren't you, babe? Unlike any of my exes. I'd love to see my genes in a little girl.'

'Mixed with mine, Queen,' said Justin before he kissed her and they got a bit intense having a snog before he left.

'I know they won't have told you about Chloe,' said Lizzie.

'Who?' Hewitt asked.

'Her family, they won't have told you everything.'

'What about?'

'That she spent time in a mental patient's facility.'

'We know Chloe had some issues, everyone has been open about that,' I said.

'There is still this stigma. They'll dance around it, people like Jackie,' said Lizzie.

I shrugged.

'Chloe had bipolar disorder,' said Lizzie. 'She was seeing a psychiatrist. They had this *relationship*. She talked about Martin all the time.'

'Could it be innocent?' I asked.

'I don't think so.'

'Why didn't you say this sooner, Lizzie?'

'Because there are more obvious people who would hurt her, like Lewis Skelly, or that gardener.'

'Was Chloe having a sexual relationship with the psychiatrist?' Hewitt got to it.

'She was in love with him.'

'But was it reciprocated?'

'I think so, but she was secretive lately. Let's not gloss over it,' said Lizzie. 'Chloe had issues and she was seeing him *a lot*. And he liked her, too. I could tell.'

'How do you know?' I asked her.

'I saw them together once.'

We let her witter on and then Hewitt said we had to go.

'She is a time-waster,' I said to Hewitt after. 'If Lizzie doesn't have one idea who it is, it's the next one: Drew; Jackie; Terry Hamilton; Lewis Skelly; and now this Martin guy.'

'She's alright,' said Hewitt. 'See all those pictures on the wall of them two, and her eating his face off? Although, you wouldn't say no, would you? Isn't he gorgeous?'

'Fleur, why did you say yes when she asked you?'

'No point saying no, hen. I'm not a good liar.'

I rolled my eyes properly this time.

'He is a piece of prime real estate, I'm not going to deny it, Harriet.'

I was tired. It was no joke working full-time with two babies. They weren't bad sleepers, thank God. I adjusted the air conditioning and Fleur turned it off on her side, the passenger side.

'We should have asked if Lizzie knew about Amnesty International and Pakistan,' I said.

'Let's give LDM a wide berth,' Hewitt said. 'You and your wee pal Carl have wasted enough time on her and her attention seeking. It's the artist we need to get a hold of, if he would ever answer his fucken phone.'

Chapter 18

That evening there was a call from Bethany Nursing Home's manager to say that another letter had come.

'Take a photo of it and text it to me,' I said.

The hate mail that had been coming for Chloe was still in my mind. I wanted to see if it was set out the same. This was what it said:

> *Adelinde Sloane, you bitch, you should have died. I am going to make sure you suffer, expecially for everything you put me and my family through.*

So it wasn't the same. And *expecially*? I knew the person who had sent it. I just didn't understand his reason.

I called him straight away. 'About this new letter to the home,' I said.

'So, you care now?' he said. 'What are you going to do about it? Have you informed the police?'

'No.'

'Then I will,' he threatened.

'Good.'

'We can't let someone come and harm her.'

'What do you suggest?' I asked him but he was silent. 'Informing the PSNI is all we *can* do.'

'No, it's not,' he argued.

'What do you want me to say, Daddy? People who send warnings are cowards, they won't do anything.'

He hung up on me.

Chapter 19

The next morning I dropped off the boys and went into work. 'I've just been talking to Thomas,' said Hewitt without looking in my direction. 'He has class then he will meet us at three p.m.'

After a whole day of trying to speak with Thomas the day before, we'd almost given up on him.

'Can't we get him sooner?' I said. 'It feels like he's messing us around.'

'There's no hurry,' said Hewitt.

Shortly after, Cyn Dockrill the art tutor phoned me to say that the original letter of the hate mail she had received, had been left in the library photocopier. The librarian found it and took it to the head of the college.

'We know who it was,' Cyn said.

'Who?' I asked, expecting her to say Thomas, or any other student. Even Lewis, or a friend of his at that campus. I was surprised when Cyn told me there was a woman, a *big* woman, she liked using that detail, 'A big Yorkshire woman called Lucinda Press who works as a cleaner here in Belfast Met. I'm astounded,' Cyn continued. 'I finish up my work in the afternoons and Lucinda is always outside in the corridor, mopping, singing operatic tunes. I've often said to her, "You're wasted here." If you could only hear her voice! Nothing like her talking voice. It is beautiful, really.'

'People surprise you,' I said. It was my mantra.

'They most certainly do,' Cyn agreed.

'How can you be certain it was her?' I asked.

'Lucinda was in work first thing; the librarian can vouch that it was her. The students don't leave originals behind. It was weird to see the cleaner in the library at all, and she is so big and tall, so she stands out, *and* she's always singing.'

Cyn had a Newtownabbey address for Lucinda that had been given to her from the college director. He wanted everything done away from his door. The annual art show had drawn enough bad attention. More police visits were not what the director wanted.

We paid the letter writer a visit. Lucinda was at home in Newtownabbey, not expecting us. She was in her dressing gown and fluffy slippers. And she *was* tall, far taller than me and I'm tall. And she was broad. And warm, surprisingly. Extremely warm to begin with, for someone who had just been caught trolling a dead girl.

She had small eyes and short sandy-coloured hair. A single mother to three grown up sons, the youngest lived at home and was eating his breakfast in the kitchen. A big-boned boy, he had black hair that hung down his back and when he stood his T-shirt proved too short. A little roll of belly fat hung over the top of his pyjama bottoms.

Lucinda brought us through to the living room. A huge dreamcatcher on the wall split the windows in two. We asked her about her work and before we could quiz Lucinda on anything, she said, 'I don't think that young man should be exploiting the situation like that. The media has put their own spin on my letters and made my intentions something altogether different.'

'Why did you do it?' I asked.

'Like I said, I thought that brother of hers was exploiting the girl's death.'

'Is that really the reason?' asked Hewitt.

Lucinda refused to reply.

'Your original letter was found in the Met's library photocopier,' I said. 'Why send it?'

'I sent two,' said Lucinda, smiling, 'one to the politician at the PACT office.' She was melting into one of the seats that was covered in throws and cushions.

'Mike Birch?'

Lucinda nodded. 'Him.'

'Okay, and the other was for the college?'

'Yes, because I was appalled that they let that revolting dog muck get displayed like that.'

'What was revolting about it?' I asked, pissed off.

'That I have to go into a job I love and have those images rammed down my throat.' She became angry.

'I think that if you knew the story behind it …' I started.

'I know what you'll say,' said Lucinda, 'I know that you'll say that it's art and that it's open to interpretation.'

'Yes, I believe so.'

'But he was trying to get a reaction and all I did was react.'

Hewitt looked at me as if Lucinda had a point.

'I'm not here to argue about the art display, Ms. Press,' I said.

'No, and I won't argue either,' she replied. 'I know I'm right.'

'I just want to see if you were sending the letters.'

'I was,' she said. 'I'll stop the whole thing, I promise. It's very embarrassing, you calling like this.'

'Why did you do it, harass the family of a dead girl?' I asked.

'I wasn't harassing anybody, she's dead.'

'Ms. Press …'

'Lucinda, please,' she said to me.

'Lucinda,' Hewitt jumped in. 'You have got to know that this type of behaviour is not acceptable.'

'Chloe's father doesn't need this stress, not after everything else,' I said.

'I'm ashamed. I'll tell him so. Can you put me in touch?' Lucinda blinked her tiny eyes.

'I don't think that's a good idea, not right now.'

'Tell him then, please, that I'm sorry,' said Lucinda. 'It's just that I was always taught to not draw attention to yourself.'

'Unlike Thomas?' I asked.

'Unlike Chloe,' she edited me. 'It's how girls were brought up in my family. Just traditional.'

'I heard you have a wonderful voice,' I said.

Lucinda waved the compliment away.

'Maybe you should have drawn attention,' I said, feeling grumpier than usual, thinking, catch yourself on, woman; you are too old, too smart to act like this.

'Draw attention to my voice? But then I wouldn't be a cleaner,' she said.

I said nothing. I was done. We had caught her at least.

'I enjoy cleaning,' she said, still on the defensive. 'Everybody cleans their own loo; I'm not doing anything that's beneath anybody.'

'Fair enough,' said Hewitt.

'That's not me,' said Lucinda, 'to be the centre of attention, but thank you.'

I had really pissed her off.

'Maybe it's yourself you should be angry with, not me,' I said.

'I'm not angry.'

'Not to worry.' I stood up and stretched.

'Oh, I'm not worried, my dear,' she said.

'Okay,' said Fleur, 'we'll be seeing you again, Lucinda, no doubt.'

'I'll let you out.'

'Don't worry, we can do that ourselves,' I said.

'Oh, I'm not worried,' she said again, in madness, there was more than a glint of it. It made sense now; I often mistake madness for warmth.

I felt the door brush my back ever so slightly as I left, I turned to look at her. Any harder and I'd have had her.

'I'm not worried,' she said again, barely audible through the door.

'Not to worry, Ms. Press,' I had to say again, for badness.

'Jesus Christ,' muttered Hewitt as she walked to the car.

'She'll be the centre of attention now,' I said.

'Only if the media gets wind of it,' said Hewitt.

'She brought the media into it.'

'She was alright, I thought,' said Hewitt. 'Humble, like.'

'A whack-job more like,' I said as I cut back towards the motorway.

'Was she suitably embarrassed for you, Sloane?'

'For me?' I asked.

'Yeah. I liked your little life coaching moment. "You could have been a professional singer."' Hewitt put on a posh Northern Irish voice.

'Shut up,' I said. 'That sounds English.'

Fleur laughed for the first time. 'I'm pulling your chain, Harriet. I think you don't get my sense of humour. Don't worry, you're not alone in that.'

'Do you clean your own toilet?' I asked her.

She laughed again. 'What? I'm a lady. I don't even shit.'

'Good, nice and ladylike. Lucinda would approve. What do you think she means by Chloe drawing attention herself?' I pictured Erica McClelland as I said it. Drawing attention by being stabbed to death? Was that crime acceptable to Lucinda because Erica liked to take care of her appearance, because she, unlike Lucinda, made the most of what she had.

'Who knows? She's crazy,' said Hewitt.

'Who?' I asked.

'*Ms. Press*,' she made fun of how I had addressed her, showing Lucinda the respect she had not shown any of the Taylors. 'Lucinda wants to live in a world where she only sees what she wants to see. Sounds nice, huh?'

'Sounds boring,' I said.

Sensing that Fleur Hewitt was warming to me I asked her about Janet Ward.

'Come again?' she said.

'The woman who came from London asking you to reopen her sister's case.'

'Oh, yeah … *Your* pal.'

'I just sat beside her on a flight.'

'So, you're practically related.'

'She's a nice person,' I said.

'Aren't most people?'

'I don't know about that. Lucinda turned pretty quickly.'

'Don't worry,' said Hewitt, 'I'll be sure to tell *Ms. Ward* that it was your push that got the ball rolling again.'

'Really?'

Hewitt shrugged. 'I think it's a good time to look again and Greg agrees. I couldn't give Janet a date there and then, but I will. I don't want to get her hopes up until we get a budget allocation. It costs hundreds of thousands. It could take a year too.'

'I know,' I said. 'Thank you.'

Hewitt nodded. 'I'm not doing this for you, Ms. Harriet Sloane.'

'I know that, too.'

It was still a thorn in my side that she had the post and I did not. But I had a heap of responsibility already. Almost too much.

*

At noon Paul texted me:

Your dad was just here.
Where, in the hospital?
Yes. He was looking for me.
Why?
I got paged to go and see him, thought something had happened to one of the boys, or you.
No, I'm fine. They are too … I hope.
He wanted the lowdown on my job. Talk about timing!
Do you want to just call me?
I'm about to go into theatre.
Why was he there in the first place?
Says he was seeing a friend
He doesn't have any
Like father like daughter!
FU!
Could he have been here for an appointment he doesn't want to worry you about? Dementia?
Not his style, not worrying people. He would say, believe me!
He was saying he hasn't seen you
That's a joke, no one comes near when I'm on maternity for a year, suddenly he wants to talk now I'm back to work. He was a right grump last time
Okay, I am finished my break now. Kiss the kids from me.
I'm gonna stay on late and catch up.
Okay, I'll give the kids a kiss from you then xx
Thanks, mate!

Chapter 20

That afternoon we waited for Thomas but he didn't show. Then we tried to call him to no reply, so we called at his house.

'I haven't seen him, he didn't come home last night,' said Jackie.

'Where could he be?' I asked him.

'He fucken better be okay,' said his father, 'after that shite in the papers. He's sensitive.'

'Has he stayed out before?'

'He's stayed at a mate's a couple of times without saying. I'm hoping that's what it is. He's not a kid.'

'Are you worried about him?' I asked.

'I swear, if I get my hands on the person who put that shite in the paper.' Jackie clenched his fists.

I couldn't tell Jackie about Lucinda there and then, not when he was threatening her like that. And neither did Fleur. We'd tell him later, when he seemed to calm down.

'How is Thomas' mental health?' I asked Jackie.

'Fine,' he said.

I knew Jackie had not dealt with Chloe's mental health issues well, or Glynis', and I didn't know how honest he was being now.

'Has Thomas ever been to the doctor's or the hospital about anxiety or depression, or self-harm?'

'No. Don't start going down that line. He'll be at a mate's.'

'Do you have the numbers for any of them?'

'No,' Jackie said. He did not want to help us, I suspected Thomas had been at home and Jackie was covering for him, and had to make it look convincing. Concerning enough, but not overly so. Jackie had to stop us calling a search party.

'Look,' I said, 'while we have you here, Mr. Taylor, we want to speak to you about Chloe.'

'What else would you want to speak to me about?' he asked abruptly.

'Lewis talked about Chloe taking a gap year and travelling. He said she went to France, Spain, and that region of Europe.'

'Correct.'

'We have spoken …' I looked at Fleur. 'Well, Sergeant Higgins and I, we spoke to peers of Chloe's who said she didn't go to Europe.'

Jackie's nose scrunched up. 'What are you getting at?'

'Mr. Taylor, we have good reason to believe that Chloe was working for Amnesty International for a few months, from August 2016 to March of last year.'

'Where are you going to tell me she was doing this?'

'Pakistan.'

'Get the hell out of here. Are you fucken mad! As if she would be in Pakistan and not tell me.'

'We've heard it a few times now, Mr. Taylor,' I said.

'Why would she have been *there*?'

'Helping girls, getting them away from gender mutilation, and that kind of danger,' said Fleur, 'helping them be safe.'

Jackie refused to believe it. 'She called me from her mobile, not all the time, but every now and then.'

'There are ways to find out if it's true,' said Hewitt.

Jackie phoned Thomas. This time he answered his phone right away.

'Did you know that Chloe went to Pakistan? The police are here saying that.' There was a pause. 'Are you lying to me, boy?' Jackie hung up on him. 'There you go, he's fine and answering his phone now.'

'That's a relief,' said Hewitt.

Jackie took off into the kitchen and took a red box out of the cupboard, it was full of tapes and letters, certificates, medical cards and passports. He took Chloe's red passport out and skimmed the pages, and there it was, a stamp from Pakistan.

'Now, this!' He jabbed his finger at the stamp. 'This here, it looks like she didn't trust me.' Jackie searched my face, then Hewitt's.

'What young woman, or man, doesn't have secrets from their parents?' she asked him.

'I'd never let her go there,' shouted Jackie. 'And Chloe knew that, surely. I know she did when she lied about it. How dangerous would that have been? What must she've seen out there?'

'Chloe did it for the right reasons, Jackie,' said Hewitt, 'she was an activist. Must have had a strong calling.'

'Well, let people who have some life behind them be the activists and let them fight wars too,' he snapped.

'Is there anything we can do?' I asked.

'You can take off, please, and leave me to digest this.'

'Maybe we shouldn't have told him,' I said to Hewitt, fanning myself in the car. It was a pleasant day, weather-wise, not too humid, but Jackie's anger had got me hot under the collar.

'I wonder what it was really like out there. She probably kept a diary,' said Hewitt.

'Why would she?'

'Wouldn't you want some sort of account?'

'Do you think someone from over there did this?' I asked. 'That's what Jackie will be thinking now, that his girl got involved in something over in Pakistan and it followed her back to Belfast.'

'No,' said Fleur, 'that would have happened in Pakistan; Chloe Taylor wouldn't have been deemed important enough to follow to a wee office on the Newtownards Road, and certainly not a year later. She was only a *wee girl*.'

'Look at Malala Yousafzai,' I said, 'she was shot for blogging, for wanting an education.'

Hewitt shrugged. 'I'm thinking Chloe *will* have written about this.'

'Why? She wasn't much of a writer that I could see.'

'Wasn't she? What about Facebook? What is that, if not a diary? Making an account of a life and being read.'

'Never looked at it that way,' I admitted.

'We're going to have to start looking at everything differently. This is not our usual day-to-day.'

Chapter 21

Late afternoon Greg called me into his office.

'Yes, Chief, just a minute,' I said. It was the most he had acknowledged me one-on-one since I'd returned to work. By the time I went into his room he was standing by a filing cabinet looking at papers. 'Everything going well?' he asked.

I wondered if Jocelyn had mentioned seeing me in the Centra.

'We have a few leads,' I said, 'the brother, Thomas Taylor, didn't show today. We need to track him down. We've left messages but he hasn't replied to us. Though he spoke to his dad, and we know he's alright. I'll get him into a tight corner.'

'Good,' he said. 'And you? Personally. Everything okay with you, Sloane?'

'Yes,' I said and stopped holding my breath, allowed myself to properly look at him. 'Everything okay with you?' I asked in return.

He ignored my question, watching the door. Greg Dunne is one of these people who make you think they are not entirely interested in you but always waiting to hear from someone else, always having to leave rooms urgently, like a bodyguard protecting a president under threat.

Or something equally ridiculous.

No: correction!

Making *you* feel that you are the something ridiculous. And by *you*, of course, I mean, *me*.

'Good, I'm glad to hear that,' he finally said. 'Harriet, I wonder if you would kindly relieve me of something.' His eyes were still on the door.

Sounds ominous, I thought. 'What would that be, Chief?'

He looked surprised at me addressing him this way. He coughed, unearthed a thick brown jiffy bag and handed it to me. I held it, turning it over. It had no markings.

'Do me favour,' he said, 'if you can, and take that.'

'What for?'

I watched him look at it, then he finally made eye contact with me. I peeled the side back and saw that it was full of money. 'This looks suspect,' I said.

'Believe me, it's legitimate. We sold the villa in Portugal. All the kids got the same amount.'

'What is …'

'It's for you and …'

'*Oh!*' I said. 'Thanks.'

I should have set it on the table and walked out, acted offended, but some rude curiosity got the better of me. I went into an empty office, locked the door behind me and counted it out. Forty grand for the twins. Twenty each. I closed the jiffy bag again and went to my locker but I'd forgotten my key. Hadn't needed it in so long. God only knew where it was.

'We're going to Lizzie Donegan-Moat's,' said Hewitt, coming up behind me. 'She's remembered something she thinks will be helpful.'

'Again with LDM?' I asked. 'I thought we could try to corner Thomas, preferably away from Jackie.'

'Leave Tommy boy for now,' said Hewitt. 'And I'll be with you in a minute.' She eyed me dubiously.

Outside I stuffed the jiffy bag into a plastic bag. The glove box was full, so I put it on the backseat of the service car and waited for her to join me.

'Mind if I drive?' Hewitt said. 'I get car sick.'

I got out and into the passenger seat.

'And you're a dreadful driver,' she added.

'You better be an excellent one,' I said, 'after a remark like that.'

'Ah, Harriet, lighten up,' she said, 'I told you, you don't get my humour.'

On the Newtownards Road someone passed by in a Boxster just like Paul had until the kids came along. He sold it to prove he was serious, came home with a people carrier for us. I thought about Greg's money in the back seat: the boys' money. They were well provided for. Disney holidays. Every toy under the sun. I thought I might surprise Paul with a fun little Boxster instead. Was forty grand enough? Probably not. But he deserved something nice.

We arrived at Lizzie's house and parked at the bottom of her driveway, she was standing on her doorstep as we walked up towards her. 'Sorry to have you coming out again,' she said.

'We were in the neighbourhood,' said Hewitt. 'It's no trouble.'

'Did you look at the papers?' she asked us.

'Yes.' We tailed her indoors.

'And they've been sending hate mail?' she said.

'How do you know about that?' I asked her.

'I work with someone whose partner works with Jackie.'

'Okay.'

'They sent Mike Birch hate mail?'

'It was for Chloe,' said Hewitt.

'How sick!'

'Yes, indeed,' said Hewitt. 'Sick is the word.'

Lizzie got her laptop and set it on her knee and unlocked the screen. One screen was Chloe's Facebook page. We looked at it together.

Lizzie went into the message and scrolled back to ages ago, April 2016.

'Two years ago,' Lizzie said.

I saw you on TV, who do you think you are asking world leaders stupid questions. Bit cheeky if you ask me, and with that mad green hair! Someone above everyone else, that's who you think you are. But you are nothing. A wannabe. Take my advice: forget feminism and get back to femininity. Bumptious little bitch. Nobody likes you.

'Well, I liked her,' said Lizzie. 'And who uses the word *bumptious*! I don't think it's a word I've ever heard anyone say in real life.'

'Who sent that?' I asked.

'It was an account just set up to send those messages. It isn't linked to an email address.'

I took a note of it. 'May I see?' I stood and moved to the table, asked if it was better to sit there. Lizzie agreed it was. So there we sat as I scrolled through the messages. 'There are no messages from Lewis,' I noted.

'There were. Tonnes of them. Chloe deleted them.'

'How do you have access to this account?' asked Hewitt.

'Chloe signed over custody of Facebook to me in case of her death. I did the same to her. We were having a drink one night – a smoke for her – and talking shit, as you do.'

'As you do,' said Hewitt dryly.

'We agreed that's what we would do.'

Lizzie walked across the parquet wood block floor, her flip flops clopping at her heels, she looked out of the window and said, 'There is the newspaper now. I'll be right back.'

'Don't you already have it?'

'No, my colleague just told me. I get the afternoon edition delivered.'

Lizzie went outside, I could hear her talking and then a man's voice.

I looked into Lizzie's messages to Chloe, they seemed caring, supportive. The most recent were: *Haven't heard from you in a few days*, and; *Everything okay, hun?*

Then I clicked on Lizzie's 'wall', only slightly wary of her looking at the search history afterwards. Her page was full of inspirational memes and quotes. One meme that said: We only fight because we love each other. And another: Only passionate relationships have ups and downs, mainly in the bedroom. She had tagged Justin in these.

'Did you have a visitor?' Hewitt asked Lizzie, to alert me to go back into Chloe's account.

'Chatting to the paperboy,' Lizzie said, flushed. 'Our delivery boy is a man, and he drives a car. You couldn't make it up!'

'Can I have the details of Chloe's account, to have a better look at the station?' said Hewitt.

Lizzie wrote them down. 'Did you see the photo on Facebook?' she asked.

'Which one?' I asked.

'The psychiatrist.'

'No.'

She showed it to us, Chloe with her arms around him, and his arm around her. He was not very tall and had short, tidy brown hair.

'This looks like they are socialising together.'

'She was in love with him,' said Lizzie.

'He looks older than her,' I said.

'He is. A lot.'

'Married?' Hewitt asked.

'I think so,' said Lizzie.

'Do you know that she was having an affair and are afraid to break your friend's confidence?' I asked.

'What can I say to that.'

'So, they *were* in a relationship?'

'Chloe was harbouring a secret in the last while,' said Lizzie. 'At the very least she had a huge crush on Martin, was always talking about him.'

Lizzie held the newspaper out. The front cover featured Lucinda Press. *Grandmother of seven still trolling dead girl activist.*

'Wow!' said Lizzie. 'You knew and you didn't say?'

'Don't worry about the hate mail, we have our person for that,' said Hewitt.

Chapter 22

In the car, in a panic, Hewitt called Jackie and explained that we had our person for the hate mail.

'A woman,' she said, 'an older woman, harmless, just not quite right, has some funny ideas.'

He had already heard and wasn't happy. I could hear him reply. But to be honest, I'd heard him angrier.

Around five we stopped at the garage to buy our own copy.

'It says that we have been getting taunting letters too,' I told Hewitt.

'We?' she asked.

'We at the service.'

'Have we? I don't think so, or I'd know about it.'

'Ha,' I said, 'and the paper has been getting mail of their own.'

'What?' She pulled the newspaper toward her.

We, here at the paper, have been getting taunting letters saying that our coverage is 'rubbish' and that the PSNI is doing a 'pathetic job'.

'True enough.' Hewitt laughed. 'Their coverage has been rubbish … compared to the ink they spilled over Erica McClelland.'

'What do you mean?' I asked. I just wanted to hear Fleur say it.

'They loved Erica and her nightclub photos, showing plenty of tit. And leg.'

'That's awful,' I said.

'Awful but true. Admit it.'

I couldn't, even though Fleur Hewitt was one hundred percent correct. Even the paper's Nights Out section was as bad.

There was never a bunch of lads snapped or an average-looking girl. It was just tit, fake tan and more tit.

Page 3 may have been done, lonely old lads of Belfast had the Nights Out section.

'Who is doing this?' I mused. 'Probably Lucinda Press.'

'Maybe not,' said Hewitt. 'Everyone has an opinion on everything these days.'

*

At Strandtown there was mail addressed to Chief Dunne. He read it out to us.

This is a confession: I drowned Erica McClelland.

'Was that sent here?' I asked.

'No, Bangor,' he said. 'Is it Lucinda Press' style?'

'I'd know it if I saw it,' I said. I looked at the photocopy, cut and stuck letters. 'No, not at all.'

'This is getting crazy, does no one just say what they think anymore?' the chief asked.

'Cowards, an age of cowards these days,' said Sarge Simon.

'And a world full of banana peels,' said Hewitt.

'Poetic,' Chief Dunne said.

'I do try.' She winked at him and he smiled back.

My stomach plunged.

*

At six p.m. we arrived at the psychiatrist's office on the Upper Newtownards Road. 'We were just closing up,' his secretary said.

'We just need a word with Martin Walsh.'

'I'll get Dr. Walsh now,' she said.

She tried to phone him but he was coming out of the room with his briefcase in hand, sorting out car keys. 'Hello,' he said, alarmed.

'I'm DI Harriet Sloane,' I said, 'and this is …'

'Superintendent Fleur Hewitt.'

'What has happened?' Martin asked.

'We're here to speak with you about a patient who as murdered.'

'Chloe Taylor?' he said.

'Yes.'

'You go on home and I'll lock up,' he told the secretary.

'You sure?' she said.

'Yes, thank you.'

She gathered her belongings and left.

'Come through,' he said and went into his room and sat.

'This is making me uncomfortable,' said Hewitt, 'I'll just move my chair.' I watched her bring her chair close to his. Martin was smiling with amusement and confusion. 'Now I'll not feel like I'm being analysed,' Hewitt said.

I tried to keep a straight face. 'We are here to ask you about your knowledge of Chloe Taylor.'

'Chloe was my patient,' said Martin, 'as you've already gathered.'

'How long were you treating Chloe?' I asked him.

'A while. Not very long.'

'How did you meet her?'

'She self-referred. A private patient. She had some feelings she wanted to work through.'

'She had mental health problems?' asked Hewitt.

'That is not uncommon,' said Martin. 'Most of us will at some stage in our lives.

'Chloe was proactive, because of her family history of mental health problems, she was great at noticing the signs and getting help.'

'How often did you see her?'

'Anything between once a month to once a week.'

'When did she last see you?'

'A fortnight before the incident.'

'Her murder, or some other incident?'

'Her murder. I didn't like to say the word,' he explained.

'How did she seem, then?' I asked.

'Manic.'

'I'm not an expert like you,' said Hewitt. 'What does that word mean, *manic*?'

'She said she'd been spending money she didn't have, she was excitable, and with her disorder there are lows. And when she didn't show on the Tuesday night, the night before the murder, I assumed she was feeling low.'

'She would cancel often?' asked Hewitt.

'At times,' he said, cocking his head to the side.

'Was there anything inappropriate in your relationship or with her outlook toward you?'

'There was *nothing* inappropriate. How do you mean?'

'Did she have a crush on you, perhaps?' I asked.

'Not that I'm aware of.'

'We have been told that there seemed to be a relationship between you two,' Hewitt announced.

'Me and Chloe?' Martin Walsh laughed. 'A relationship. Hmm …'

I locked eyes with him.

'That's just ridiculous,' Martin said.

'But you saw her socially?'

'No. Never.'

'Yet there is a photo of you and her together. It's on Facebook.'

He looked confused. 'I can't think what photo that would be. There are none.'

'You are at a bar and you have your arms around her,' said Hewitt.

'And she with you, Dr. Walsh,' I added.

'I do. I know now. That was at The Bell.'

'The bar in Ballyhackamore?'

'Yes, Ballyhack. I was there eating and she was there, heavily intoxicated. She was acting *silly* when she saw me – I suppose because it was out of context from when we would normally see each other, in our therapist-patient capacity. She was saying to her friends, "Look, it's Martin," you know?'

'And so you went and had a photo taken with her?'

'There was nothing in it, if that's the angle you're taking. Which, I appreciate, seeing the circumstances. The *tragic* circumstances. But, for goodness sake, my wife was there. It was Rebecca who said, "Go make a sad girl happy".' Martin paused. 'Chloe had just recently split up from her boyfriend, I remember thinking that that was why she was drunk. So as not to feel the pain of that relationship ending.'

'You never discussed it again after?' I asked.

'The next time I saw Chloe after seeing her in The Bell, I said, "Did you have a good night?" and Chloe couldn't remember a thing about it ... or so she said. I thought she was embarrassed about her behaviour. Not that there was anything untoward about her behaviour, she was a little tipsy, so I dropped it. Because I'm not in the habit of making people feel worse about themselves. That's the opposite of what I'm about.'

'That's nice to hear,' I said. 'So ... the photo?'

'Maybe putting the photo on Facebook was Chloe's way of trying to make her ex jealous?' He shrugged. 'You know how these relationships are with younger people these days and social media's part in it.'

'Martin, where do you live, if we need to speak to you again?'

'You can call here. I usually take lunch at one p.m.'

'I'll take a note of your home address and phone number anyway,' said Hewitt.

Martin lifted a business card and wrote his address on the back of it, Leathem Square, Dundonald.

'Would you put a mobile number or home phone on there for me, thank you kindly,' said Hewitt.

'I'm at work more often than not.'

'But you are heading home now, aren't you?'

'Yes,' he said. 'I am.' I could see him tense up.

*

'She was a smart, liked, attractive girl; surely, she would have a relationship,' I mused.

'Yeah,' said Hewitt. 'Surely! If she wanted one. Though some people *can* be on their own.'

'There must be signs of a relationship in her room. A memento. A ticket stub, a love letter,' I said.

We went to Chloe's house at 7p.m. and Thomas eventually opened the door to us.

'Is your dad about?'

'He's at the shops,' he said.

'We want to take a look at Chloe's room, we have a feeling there might be a clue there.'

His lips parted slightly, I thought he might say something to stop us but he held it in.

We walked past him and went upstairs and into a room that was painted white with the built-in furniture also white. The desk, the overhead cupboards, white too. Apart from their glass doors, and inside a row of all the Harry Potter books. Chloe's bedding was pink, gold and white and disarranged; still as she got out of it the morning she was murdered.

Glynis decorated this room when her daughter was much younger, I could sense it.

It was pretty but the real adult Chloe appeared in the ethnic mementos, colourful incense-scented candles. Posters on the wall of Malala Yousafzai, Frida Kahlo, Rosa Parks and other women whose faces I did not know, but really should have.

I shook the books above her bed waiting for a letter to come out, while Hewitt searched under Chloe's mattress for a diary, stopping to smile sadly at the Bagpuss on her pillow. Thomas came and lingered at the door, his mobile phone in his hand.

'Have you found Chloe's tiger coat?' he asked.

'We haven't. We missed you earlier,' I said, trying to block his view of Hewitt as she carried out her search.

'Should you be going through her things?' he asked.

'We are trying to look for anything that would help us, help your family.'

'We missed you earlier, Thomas,' said Hewitt this time.

'I missed my bus. It went earlier than it was supposed to.' He developed a typical teenage stroppiness on his face.

'And you couldn't call us? Your phone was turned off, it seemed.'

'My battery was dead.'

'Missed bus and dead battery,' I said. 'Notice all these USB ports cropping up everywhere for people to charge their phones lately?'

'No excuse these days for a dead battery,' said Hewitt. 'Plus, we were here when you answered the phone to your dad.'

He said nothing. Then he hardened his face like, *I'm not the kid you think I am. I'm not the person you think I am.* I felt a flicker of fear as he blocked the doorway. 'I was on one percent battery when I was talking to Dad. I managed to charge it for a second after borrowing a friend's charger.'

'Is this the friend whose house you stayed at?'

'What?' he asked.

A car flew into the driveway, the engine shut down.

'We wanted to meet you hours ago.' Hewitt looked at her watch. 'Four hours ago. You're not avoiding us, are you?'

The front door opened and Thomas called out for Jackie, who came storming up the stairs.

'We were only wanting to know about your art project,' I told Thomas, putting a photo album back in its place.

Jackie's face was red with rage. 'Fuck off and do it now.' He looked from me to Hewitt and back to me.

'Thomas,' I said, 'why are all the pictures in your display of Chloe?'

'She posed for him,' said Jackie, 'they were close; only siblings. We're a small family who stick together, now fuck off.'

'Okay, we'll leave,' said Hewitt. 'We know this is hard and that you're grieving, Mr. Taylor.'

'Grieving?' asked Jackie. 'I can't start grieving until Chloe's murderer is found.'

We walked out, Jackie coming down the stairs behind us. I sat in the car and texted Thomas:

Do you know Chloe's email address?
Chloe@amnesty.gmail.com
And the password by any chance?

It'll be her date of birth – 2 February 1998 – or mine – 3 September 1999.

'He knew about her trip to Pakistan,' I said, 'he knew and now his dad is angry with him for keeping it secret.'

'Look what I found,' Hewitt said taking a piece of photographic paper from her jacket pocket.

'What is it?'

She turned it face up, it was the same photo that was on Chloe's Facebook of Martin Walsh and her.

'*Thought you might like to frame this copy*, it has written on the back, M and C, and a small x. Oh, an x is a kiss.'

'You took it?' I asked.

'It won't be missed.'

'I can't believe you took it.'

'Oh, grow up,' Hewitt told me.

'Let's go to his house.'

'Martin's?'

'Yes, let's go right now.'

'Alright,' she said. It was the first time she had listened to me and taken my lead. We went to the courtyard of stylish townhouses off East Link Road in Dundonald.

Rebecca, a voluptuous woman with shoulder length brown hair, opened the door and we went through the introductions.

'We were speaking to your husband earlier,' Hewitt said to her, 'and we wanted to ask him a few more questions.'

'My husband doesn't live here; is this the address he gave?'

Hewitt showed her the back of Martin's business card.

'Unbelievable! What do you want to talk to him about?'

'A patient of his.'

'Something's not right,' said Rebecca.

'With what?' I asked.

'That you are calling out here when you say you have just spoken to him. That sounds urgent, and if he is making out that he and I are fine, then he's a liar.'

'We're just following a trail when it's warm, Mrs. Walsh.'

'Martin's having an affair,' Rebecca said. She had sad large brown eyes. She looked close to tears.

'Oh, I'm sorry,' I said.

'When did you find out?' asked Hewitt.

'No big ah-ha moment, a sense … he starts caring more what he looks like, those movie clichés.' She looked around outside and added, 'Come in. This is awkward, speaking like this in the hallway.'

Rebecca had been cutting the stems off flowers that spilled over the kitchen table and sat beside a sheet of cellophane. A large kitchen knife sat across them like a silver boat caught in a shimmering wave.

'And you've fallen out with Martin?' I said, looking out of the two narrow patio doors with their little black balconies, and out onto the main road.

'Spectacularly,' said Rebecca.

'When did you fall out?'

'A couple of weeks ago. He moved in with his friend Bill in the meantime, until we get the house sorted, get it sold.'

'There's no for sale sign.'

'It's out on the road.'

'Where does Bill live?' I asked.

'A flash apartment, it's in Kincora Mews. In one of those big old houses that have been repurposed.'

'You probably heard about a young woman, Chloe Taylor, who was murdered last week. *Almost* a week ago.'

Rebecca savoured her bottom lip.

'She was a patient of your husband,' said Hewitt.

'Soon to be ex-husband,' Rebecca corrected. Hewitt nodded. 'She was Martin's patient?' Rebecca asked for clarification, her mind still clearly on how he had wronged her. She was unable to see beyond it, to see the bigger picture.

'That's right,' I said.

'So she's the one?' said Rebecca.

'Which one?' Hewitt frowned.

'The affair he's been having. That makes sense.' Rebecca looked around the room, and then she frowned too. 'There was a *Chloe*, I remember now. She saw Martin on a night out and couldn't keep her excitement to herself.'

'*You* saw Chloe?'

'Once. That's right. That's who that was ... That dead girl. Oh God!'

'When was it? Was it when this photo was taken?' Hewitt took the photo from her pocket, careful to only show the front of it.

Rebecca's frown deepened as she looked at it, then her face relaxed. 'Yes,' she announced. 'That girl wanted a photo with him. I remember now.'

'Martin was telling the truth about that,' I said. 'That you were there when this photo was taken.'

'Yes, I was. Do you think he's implicated in some sort of way, in her murder?'

'We're not suggesting that,' said Hewitt. 'We are just trying to speak to the main players in Chloe's life, and we're trying to learn whether, or not, there was a connection between Martin and her.'

'Did it seem as if she liked him?' I asked.

'Yes. But as a wife you also think, that's too obvious, the way she was behaving. I mean, asking for a photo? Hugging him. Is that *too* obvious?'

'Do you honestly think that it was reciprocated, say, if Chloe did have a crush?'

'I'll tell you something,' said Rebecca, 'it's not the first time a young woman has fallen for her therapist. People falling for their therapist is very common. People are vulnerable, and here's someone who finally cares.'

'So, there have been other instances?'

'Absolutely. This is the only time I think he has acted. And I know he has because of the signs, and he's a man, for god's sake, if a pretty young woman is putting it on a plate …'

'What makes you think the affair was with a patient, and possibly Chloe? Those allegations could hurt his career.'

'His leaving could hurt our children. It *has* hurt them. Look, I don't know for definite, I'm not alleging this exactly, but am I looking at it as a possibility. I know he's seeing someone. It's only now I'm seeing that this girl and the murdered girl are maybe the same person. I only saw her for a short time that night. But Martin had ample time to come clean. We went for a drive, for hours and hours, we talked. Drove everywhere: Newtownards, Bangor, Crawsfordsburn, pulled up at Helens Bay and talked some more.'

'Talking about?' I asked.

'Me asking him if he wanted another woman, giving him a chance to admit something.'

'Did Martin admit he was having an affair?' asked Hewitt.

'A wife just knows,' Rebecca stated. 'They know. He denied it, like I knew he would, but once you see one lie everything else becomes a lie too. Then – and this is embarrassing; I haven't even told my best friend – I found his bag of tricks.'

'Bag of tricks?' I said. 'What was in that?'

'He had a bag full of stuff: condoms, a black leather G-string, lubricant. It was in the loft. That G-string was not for him — let's put it that way. So that's how I know … After our youngest child was born I had an emergency hysterectomy. Sod's law, because two months before that Martin had a vasectomy. We never used condoms. He came back to get his stuff, and guess what? The bag is missing too.'

Hewitt looked at me and sucked her back teeth.

As we left the townhouse, Justin ran past by on the main road, he was with a woman who had long hair, a brown swishy ponytail. They were both red faced.

'Hello strangers, working hard,' he shouted over, in a flirty, breathless tone.

'You're working hard, I see,' said Hewitt.

'Come join us,' he said running backwards and nearly stumbling onto the road.

Yes, I thought. I wanted to run. My baby belly was still there, a little bit, that dead unshifting tissue of my C-section was the other bane of my life. My brother Addam and I usually did the Belfast Marathon every May, but he had stopped running and I hadn't registered that year. If I couldn't make a good time, I wouldn't do it at all.

'Wow, Justin is a flirt,' said Hewitt, getting into the car.

'I know,' I said. 'Thick as shit though.'

'You can bet it's purely physical between him and Lizzie.'

'I couldn't do that,' I said.

'No? You need a smart one, obviously.'

'What are you on about?' I asked her.

'Isn't your fella a doctor?'

'He is,' I said, 'and I do like brains, but they don't have to have letters after their names for me to like someone, just a common intellect.' Maybe it was job snobbery, but a personal trainer would never interest me.

'Naw,' said Hewitt, 'bit of beefcake would do, quite honestly. That is catnip to me. At this point, a pretty one would do nicely.'

'So you think it's better to be the smarter one in the relationship?'

'Who's talking about a relationship? I wouldn't mind a go on that, that's all.' She elbowed me in the arm.

I pictured Drew. I don't know what had gotten into me but he was the first crush I'd had in forever. It was like a crush you got when you were a teenager. It was hard to explain, I couldn't even stand him.

I normally went for good-on-paper kind of men. Charming, accomplished men who were admired by the people around me.

And Drew wasn't even conventionally good looking. Not preppy rugby boy handsome like Paul, not gym-bunny chavvy gorgeous like Justin, or even mod retro-pretty like Higgins. And he was a complete asshole layabout with no job, or a dubious criminal one. But I had wondered quite a few times what it would be like to kiss him, what Drew would be like in bed. Not that I was going to tell Hewitt.

*

By nine p.m. we were following that warm trail to the apartment in Kincora Mews where Martin Walsh was staying. The old houses were split into apartments. Aside from the large driveways you wouldn't have known.

They still had that classy but crumbling look. The driveway was shaded by a huge cherry blossom tree that snowed pinkly all over the cars.

Martin was standing with a glass of wine in his hand and another guy, Bill, I presumed, was eating his dinner at the white dining table at the end of the room, sitting on one of the stylishly mismatching velvet chairs.

'Sorry to disturb your dinner,' I said. 'But you gave us a false address.'

'Come in,' Martin said.

'Friends of yours, Marty?' Bill asked him, standing up and putting a white cloth napkin on the table.

'It's, erm, the police,' Martin told him, 'they need to speak with me about a matter. That girl I was telling you about.'

'Oh, god yeah,' said Bill, smoothing a fingertip over one eyebrow. 'That was awfully heart-wrenching. Do you need some privacy?'

Martin waivered, he watched Bill, who blew out the candle between the two-place setting, then undimmed the ceiling lights.

'We can microwave dinner later, no problem,' Bill said, then he moved to the black velvety corner sofa under the monochrome prints from obscure movies I'd never heard of, and Martin sat beside him.

'Thanks for staying,' said Martin and instantly it struck me; Bill was his lover.

I became flustered. 'Rebecca,' I said, 'we were speaking with her, obviously. That's why we are here, and she …'

'Are you sure you wouldn't like privacy, Dr. Walsh?' said Hewitt.

'No, I'm sure,' he said. 'And it's Martin, please.'

'Rebecca told us where we might find you,' Hewitt continued, 'and it seemed that she had concerns that you might have had a close relationship with Chloe, because you told her you are possibly seeing someone else.'

A huge rag doll cat with a cream coat and bright blue eyes slunk into the room. Bill lifted her. She lay in his arms like a baby, him nuzzling the top of her head. I panged for my babies and wanted to be home.

'Now,' said Hewitt, 'because we have already received similar information, and we need to speak with people who were close to Chloe Taylor, we don't want to miss out on speaking with you again, Martin.'

'Rebecca is just hurt,' he said, 'she'd say anything. It's embarrassing. But I am *not* having an affair.'

Bill sat further back into the seat, and the cat got to its feet, slunk off to sit by my side, wanting petted.

'I don't like this,' Martin said.

'What is it you don't like?' I asked, petting the cat, but I never was a cat person. This beauty almost had me swayed.

'That there is just no privacy. God knows what she has told you, but I won't stoop to her level.'

'Marty,' said Bill, 'you're not a compassionless man.'

'No, I know I'm not,' Martin said.

'So don't let it sound as if you are. Ladies, the end of a marriage is a painful thing.'

'It is,' I said.

'Can I say something?' Bill asked Martin.

'Can I stop you?' he asked with a small smile turning up one corner of his mouth.

'Can I ask that you don't tell Rebecca anything we say?'

'You can ask,' said Hewitt.

'You aren't blind, ladies. You can tell, and maybe if Rebecca Walsh walked in at the same time, she'd see that we're in a romantic relationship and have been for a while.'

Martin looked at the floor and bit his lip.

'We all went to university together, were all great friends.' Bill held Martin's hand. 'She doesn't know any of this and we didn't, and don't, want to hurt Rebecca. When the dust settles on the divorce, and maybe when she meets someone else, then we'll tell her and the kids. We don't see any reason to hurt her more right now.'

'That's right,' said Martin, easing his hand away from Bill's. 'Can I ask that you don't tell her, or anybody?'

'There's really no reason why we should,' said Hewitt. 'I don't think it's relevant.'

'Thank you,' said Bill.

'Thank you,' echoed Martin. 'I'm sorry to have you running around all night. You understand though, right? It is a delicate time in our lives.'

'Yes,' said Hewitt getting to her feet. 'We understand.'

'And I promise you there was nothing between me and Chloe. Nothing. Maybe wires were crossed somewhere but I can assure you there was nothing on my part and nothing inappropriate ever happened with her or with any of my patients, not ever.'

'Can I just show you one thing, please, Martin?' Hewitt asked. She fetched the photo. He looked at the back of it.

'That's not my handwriting, you have my handwriting on the business card I gave you.'

Fleur was looking uncomfortable for the first time. 'So, who wrote that?' she asked.

'Maybe Chloe did. It was not reciprocated. I'm a professional.'

We got into the car and as soon as we lifted off we each burst into laughter.

'He's gay,' I said, feeling giddy but detached.

'Your face, Harriet!'

'Oh, come on, that was embarrassing.'

'I think we can say without reservation that the G-string *is* his,' said Fleur.

I rolled my eyes. 'Is this worse, for his wife?' I asked.

'No!' said Hewitt.

'But she'll be angrier in the long run, to find out he's gay and to think that she wasted time on a man who couldn't love her properly.'

'There are plenty of people who can't love properly.'

'I know that, Fleur. Regardless of sexual orientation.'

'But, Harriet, you keep saying he's gay and how do you know? Maybe he's bisexual. Maybe it was not a case of choosing Bill *or* Rebecca.'

'Then, in that case, there could have been Chloe,' I said, annoyed at myself. I should have known that the heart does not work like that, telling us who we should and should not love, or at least be attracted to, or even obey its own orders.

'Question for you, Sloane: Do you think they got out the vanilla candles and put on that nice music just to get Martin out of the line of fire?' Hewitt laughed.

'That would be clever.'

'Then we won't dismiss him completely,' said Hewitt, 'though your face, it was a picture.'

'I'm not a prude, you know,' I said. 'Yes, I should have known better than to jump to conclusions and call him gay but my sister calls herself gay, even though she left her husband for a woman, so, she wasn't always gay,' I said. 'Her ex was pretty fucked off when Coral said she'd fallen for Rose, and had only ever liked women. So that's where I'm coming from.'

'Hey, no shit?' asked Hewitt.

'What?' I asked. 'You're going to tell me that your sister did the same?'

'Only child.'
'That makes sense.'
'Cheeky! No, *I* did the same,' she said.
'You?'
'Me. Left my husband for a woman.'
'But you're ...'
'What am I?' she asked me.
'I don't know,' I said. 'A flirt ... around men.'
'Am I?' Fleur almost choked.
'Oh, you absolutely are. Take Justin.'
'Gladly. Just for an hour. But also, Lizzie's not bad. Nice bum. Peachy.'
'So you're in a relationship now?' I asked her.
'No. It didn't last. I left my woman for a man.'

I laughed and she joined in, only Hewitt's laugh was careful and pointed.

'Hurting people is really funny,' she said sarcastically. 'I'm not proud of it, but I'm not ashamed of leaving weak relationships, or of being with women – just to be clear.'

'You really don't know me,' I said. 'I couldn't care less who you are fucking.'

I thought, but it's Greg, right? You're fucking my ex.

'Keep what I just told you under your hat, Harriet.'

'I don't think anyone's interested in people's sexuality anymore.'

'You think so?' she said. 'That's not the point, anyway. It's my private life and I'd appreciate you kept it to yourself and away from big noses at Strandtown.'

'No probs,' I said, but I was lost to curiosity, and something changed with her trusting me with a bit of insight into her life.

And I was glad, finally someone else's love-life looked as messy as mine.

Chapter 23

For years I was unable to sleep, now it's a struggle to stay awake. And I used to dream. But now, if I do, they get stuck in the sleep. That is what having two babies will do to you.

On Wednesday morning I woke early, earlier than the twins or Paul, and remembered the plastic bag with the jiffy bag, with the money inside it. Rattled, I drove straight to work.

'Just here to pick something up,' I told Ted on security. I was to go back for the boys.

I checked the backseat of the car. Nothing.

We had left the service car on the street many times the day before. We'd been so busy I'd forgotten about the money.

'Did someone clear out the car?' I asked the desk sarge.

'No. Why?' he asked.

'Nothing, just baby brain.' First and only time I was happy for that stupid phrase.

Hewitt was already there. 'Fleur,' I said, walking to her, 'I had a plastic bag yesterday.'

'Yeah, that's right.'

'You didn't move it anywhere, did you?'

'Has it gone missing?'

'Well, yeah.'

'What was in it? Booze?'

'Nothing important,' I said.

'Seems important.'

'It's not.'

'Okay. Be secretive,' she said.

'Did you lock the car doors every time? You were the driver,' I said.

Hewitt pulled a face. She didn't reply. She wouldn't have taken it, would she?

I thought about everyone we saw that day. Checked the toilets and the car again.

I went home, was a mother for an hour. Found my locker key, after the horse had bolted. Then I brought my boys to nursery and crossed the road to work. Father had told me in an extremely brief call that it was a bad idea, that people could see me go in. His paranoia was paramount that week.

I, too, was in a spin, thinking about Janet Ward and her poor dead sister. I was itching to get to work on that case, telling myself to wait, don't start, the time would come. But patience is not my strong suit.

I thought about the girls Higgins had told me a little about, who thought they had been spiked. I had detoured away from that vein with his hasty departure.

'Any news on Higgins?' I asked Hewitt.

'If he's found guilty he'll leave.'

'Or be asked to leave?'

'And rightfully so,' she said.

I felt for him a little bit. 'He's not a bad policeman,' I said, 'he has ambition but falls down in exams.'

'He falls down in testing scenarios?' said Hewitt, letting me know that if Higgins was not good under pressure he was not good at all.

The phone rang, it was the press office to say that it was in the media that Lucinda Press had been found dead in a Belfast hotel. 'No foul play suspected.'

'Suicide?' I asked.

'She'd taken an overdose.'

I began spinning even more.

When Thomas had not met us, I briefly worried that he had taken his life. And I had thought, please, no; not over art. Not over what someone has said about it.

I thought that kids, kids like Thomas and his sister, were not resilient and I worried for their generation and how it was impossible to stop bullies.

They didn't leave school, or work, or home, and get respite. The bullies were in their phone, in their pockets, in the papers, always lying in wait.

But with Lucinda that cowardly darkness now had a face, and now it had been revealed in the paper that she had not been resilient either. A strong Yorkshire woman. A grandmother who wanted Chloe to be less strong.

Lucinda was strong enough to harass her and her family only in the dark. Now the spotlight was on her, Lucinda was exposed, vulnerable, and ultimately ashamed. And now, dead. By her own hands. This too was sad.

'These trolls are different when they are unmasked,' I said to Hewitt. 'Let's see if the letters stop now …'

'Was she a troll?' Hewitt asked me.

'What do you mean?'

'Maybe Lucinda believed what she said, in which case it's not trolling.'

'It's still harassment,' I said.

'Yes, but trolls don't care, they don't even believe what they're saying, they just want to cause maximum disruption.'

'Did she not cause maximum disruption?' I asked. 'And how could Lucinda be so against women having rights? It makes absolutely no sense.'

'I didn't say she made sense,' said Hewitt, 'but she had the right to think those thoughts.'

'Well, she obviously regretted the letters … up to a point,' I said.

'Hmm. She doesn't deserve to be heard anyway, she's only a woman.'

'Baffling,' I said.

'We don't have to understand it, fuck sake. Just have to go home at the end of the day and forget about it.'

'Is that all? Easy as that?'

'Yeah,' said Hewitt, 'it's in the beginner's handbook: *How to be a Bad-Ass Copper*.'

'You seem to know a lot about it.'

'It's got crazy, Sloane. You'll have missed it, I suppose, being away.'

'Being *off*.'

'Half our bloody workload is Facebook-related.'

'Abuse and trolling?'

'It's against the law to hurt people's feelings now. It's gone too far.'

'I don't think it's gone far enough,' I said. 'It's more than that, and you can't say it wasn't disgusting; Lucinda said Chloe deserved to be killed.'

'I know. Hundred percent! That was totally uncalled for.'

I nodded, satisfied that I could understand my new partner at last.

'Would she have it in her to stab Chloe though?' Hewitt said in a bruising voice. 'I think not.'

Chapter 24

The reconstruction was at 11.15 a.m. in the PACT office. As it played out Hewitt and I sat in Wee Buns. Lyndsey Matchett had finally given me the list I asked her husband Boyd for a week before. Who was in the bakery that day?

It went like this:
school kids getting sausage rolls,
an elderly woman getting a tea and bun,
mums getting coffees,
two work men getting their late morning coffees.

Justin, a construction worker, went through my mind, and next Dan Hamilton, the gardener. But Dan had his dialysis alibi.

I watched Mike Birch out of the bakery window. Where was he at the time? He seemed sincere. I caught myself on; trust no one, Harry. No one.

'We should find out more about Birch.' I nudged Hewitt.

'It could be somebody completely unknown,' Lyndsey shouted over while buttering bread for sandwiches. 'There *was* that robbery.'

'Yes, at Mayhew's pharmacy,' said Boyd.

'No further on one week later. Fuck this for a game of chess,' said Hewitt in a low voice.

'I want to speak with Justin,' I said to her quietly.

'Why, because Lyndsey said there were workmen?'

'Yeah,' I said.

'How many workmen go through this area?' Hewitt asked louder.

'A lot,' said Lyndsey.

'His building site is not in the vicinity,' Hewitt said. 'He is working on new apartments on the outskirts of Comber. Didn't Lizzie say?'

'Did she?' I asked. Must have missed that.

We stood outside and watched. A lookalike for Mike Birch came and called into the PACT office, while the real Mike was standing with us.

'My God,' he said, 'they even have my outfit down to a tee.'

'You arrived last Wednesday at around midday?' I asked him.

'Yes.'

'After being where?'

'Having a lie in,' he said.

'Until midday?'

'Till eleven.'

'Weren't you supposed to be working?'

'Chloe said she would open up shop.'

'Was this a regular thing? You are the employee and she was just a volunteer.'

'Yes; I mean, no. She was a volunteer and it wasn't regular at all. It was my birthday the day before.'

Hewitt tilted her head and honed her gaze at him.

Mike said, 'I had a heavy night, is what I'm wanting to say. Chloe saw on Facebook that I was out for my dinner and she called me.'

'Where was she?' I asked.

'At home maybe? I could hear people in the background.'

'Male? Female?'

'Both.'

We had already learnt that she was at Lizzie's house.

'Chloe phoned and said, "I didn't realise it was your birthday".'

'Did she usually phone you socially?'

'No, but she said, "Enjoy your night and I'll open up tomorrow".'

'Then she had a key, a volunteer?'

'She didn't,' said Mike. 'She asked how would she get in and I told her that, before I went to bed, I would put a key in the driver's door pocket of my car, and leave my car unlocked.'

'Were you drinking, Mike?'

'On my birthday? Yes, indeed I was.'

'And driving?' asked Hewitt.

'No, no. I snared a cab. Value Cabs, if you want to check.'

'What time?'

'I don't understand why this is important?'

'Every little bit of it's important. You can see the effort put into this reconstruction,' Hewitt said.

The pretend Mike Birch ran out and into the toning beds, and back into the PACT office and out and into the bakery, but he said nothing there, then he ran back out into the street. The actors playing employees from both places came out and stood with him while actor-Mike pretended to call the police on his mobile phone. While a young actress in a pink wig lay on the floor in the office beside scattered sheets.

'I was like a headless chicken, wasn't I?' Mike asked me.

'Chloe knew where you live?' I asked him.

The police, a pretend me and a pretend Higgins, came and I even heard our conversation on the way. I paused and watched, mildly amused but mostly horrified. They both went inside, out of view.

Quite the crowd had gathered, and TV cameras rolled. Hopefully this would jog some memory somewhere.

'Chloe knew where you live?' I asked Mike again.

'Yes. I told her, but she knew.'

'Had she ever been to your house before?'

'Erm, no,' he said, distracted and emotional now. Hewitt gave me a look that told me to ease off.

After the reconstruction, I bought Mike a coffee in the bakery and we sat down for a chat. 'You live alone, Mike?' I asked.

'I live with my elderly mother,' he said.

'She can vouch for you being at home last Wednesday morning?'

'She was at a Slimming World class that morning. She does that then goes out shopping with friends after.'

'Who did you go out with for your birthday? A partner? Friends?'

'My mother took me out. That sounds pathetic.'

'No,' said Hewitt. 'It sounds bloody cute.'

'You said it was a heavy night, though,' I said.

'Underestimate my mother at your peril,' said Mike Birch. 'She can drink me under the table.'

'My kind of woman,' said Hewitt.

Chapter 25

The sun was holding strong and I was in an awful mood. Chloe's killer was no closer to us. She could end up being that one in four who never gets justice.

For a moment I wondered if I was cut out for this game anymore. Maybe it was also the missing cash. I was pissed off someone had taken it, and it wasn't pittance.

I thought about Greg himself, and wondered if he'd watched me take the money out and hide it in plain sight, instead of being sneaky about it, which I'd thought would look more obvious. Had he seen me then gone and taken the money back, maybe to teach me a lesson?

I had to shake all of that from my shoulders and think about the case, but then all I could think of were the young women who were potentially drugged.

It was early afternoon, around two p.m. when I called Sarge Simon over. He only had a vague idea what I was talking about.

'Higgins was telling me,' I explained.

'Call him,' said Simon.

'Give me Higgins' mobile number.'

Simon called it out from his own phone.

'Where are you?' I asked Carl Higgins.

'Home, why? Have you got news for me?'

'Who were the young women who were possibly drugged?'

'Oh,' he said sounding disappointed. 'Maisie Hockley was one. I called out to see her after she wound up in Dee Street.'

I took a note. 'Yes, and?'

'There are two more. Let me think and I'll get back to you.'

He texted me with the names Kayley Molineux and Victoria Black.

I located their files and printed them off to draw on comparisons.

Maisie Hockley.

On Wednesday 4 April, Maisie was partying in Optimo at the Odyssey complex when she got separated from her friends. Maisie admitted that she was drunk already, drinking too much having just split from boyfriend.

Like what Martin said about Chloe.

Can't a woman just have a good time? I thought. Instead there has to be an excuse: a man somewhere taking the blame, taking the credit.

Maisie ended up on Dee Street bridge with no idea how she got there. Her underwear had been removed. She was said to be wearing pink low-rise briefs before.

Kayley Molineux.

Then on Saturday 15 April, Kayley was at Rocky Place, a bar on the Woodstock Road. Kayley was initially alone, then she played a game of pool with a group of men she knew, then she was chatting to locals and drinking, but only a couple. Kayley had considered herself to be sober. Next thing she found herself in the centre of Holywood. She too had her underwear removed. Grey 'boy' shorts this time.

Victoria Black.

Then, on Wednesday 18 April, Victoria, a physically disabled woman, was waiting at The Bell in Ballyhackamore for a friend who ended up cancelling at the last minute. Victoria was drugged with phenobarbital, the results were just back from toxicology after all this time, and her underwear, white pants with a gold heart on the front, were missing when she was discovered by a passer-by in Dee Street.

The overwhelming similarity was that all had been picked up in bars and found later without underwear, but there was never any evidence of sexual assault. All three cases were either dropped or on hold as the details were thought too fuzzy, and there was not enough evidence to proceed.

I showed my findings to Simon. 'Did nobody think to link these?'

'I remember now,' he said. 'We put out a Facebook post to remind women to stick together and not get too drunk.'

'Just women?' I asked.

'Didn't go down well.'

'I'm sure it did not.'

'There were all those rallies in April, hashtag *I Believe Her*. You know, after the furore that followed the Belfast Rape Trial. The timing was poor.'

'It was more than poor timing.' I sniffed. 'It's called victim-blaming.'

'Yeah, wasn't good. Then the following Thursday morning, Erica McClelland is found dead on Ballyholme Beach.'

'But they can't be linked to Chloe, they are completely different,' said Hewitt who I realised then was listening in.

'Still, if anyone has drugged these girls, it *is* sexually motivated,' I said, 'even though they didn't assault them, they took their underwear as a token.'

'Could be building themselves up to assault the next person,' said Simon.

'Two on Dee Street, can't deny a link there,' said Hewitt. 'One a week. If Erica, and let's say, alright, it is linked, then being drugged and transported away … then a kill …'

'But Erica's underwear was not removed,' said Simon. 'Not that I know.'

'You're right,' I said. 'But maybe that was the token in itself, the kill.'

'Could Erica's murder be sexually motived?' he asked.

'It could be any number of things,' said Hewitt, on board. 'Maybe that's why the perp has taken a break now. It's been a month since then, and after one a week.'

'Unless there have been more that no one has reported,' said Simon.

'Well, the Facebook post wouldn't have helped that … the reality of the rape trial too.'

'But Chloe,' said Hewitt, 'no pants removed …' She wrinkled her nose. Seemed to change her mind on the spot.

'No, but it was daytime,' I said, 'in an office, on a busy road. And her coat wasn't found. The one with the tiger face on the back.'

'Not the same effect, is it?' said Simon.

'No,' said Hewitt. 'That's not sexual.'

'So why the break, if it isn't the same perp who then killed Erica?' I asked.

'I get your point,' Hewitt said. 'So, if so, it's only a matter of time before he strikes again.'

'And apart from Kayley Molineux, the rest were out drinking on a Wednesday night,' said Simon. 'Erica was found on a Thursday, but …'

'Chloe Taylor was killed on a Wednesday!' Hewitt said, and I watched the two of them join the cause.

'Exactly,' I said.

Simon went back to his paperwork.

'It's Wednesday today,' I said to Hewitt. 'You want to go out tonight, Fleur? Do a little tour, have a look at barmen, bouncers. There might be one who works around a few places.'

'Okay,' she said. 'Are you that desperate for a night out?'

I felt like making an excuse, acting defensive, but the wall had to come down between us. So I simply said, 'Yes, I am gagging to get out of the house.' And she burst out laughing.

'At least you're honest, hen,' Hewitt said.

I wanted to get into the case, there weren't enough hours in the day, but I was not averse to an excuse to dress up and go to a few bars that the girls had been to.

'I'm going to be looking fucken fabulous,' Hewitt said. 'You had better bring your A game.'

'Don't you worry about me,' I replied. I suggested she could have a drink, and I'd drive. 'Or would you get too car sick?'

'Nah. Not if I've had a few.'

*

When I collected her that night, it was properly hot. Hewitt was wearing white trainers and a lightweight oversized leopard print jacket.

'That's your A game,' I teased her, feeling overdressed in heels and a dress.

We went first to The Bell. The barmaid asked us if we were there to eat and walked off when we said no.

'We should have given her a drinks order,' said Hewitt.

We watched some couples eat for some time. 'Are you always this busy midweek?' I asked a barman with a thick groomed hipster beard who had no interest in serving me let alone answering a question, not when a crowd of younger women had just arrived, all dolled up. After they got their drinks they went upstairs.

He pretended he couldn't see me and watched them climb the stairs. I watched him. I could imagine him lacing a drink with drugs. I kept my eye on him.

After I finally got served, I went to sit down beside Fleur and surveyed the place.

We sat in silence. We needed to look like friends, there for chat and a laugh. I had nothing to say, I wished I had a glass of red wine in my hand.

There was a man at the bar, he was wearing earphones, bobbing his head. Laughing to himself, and trying to ease an errant lick of hair back down onto his head.

'He's enjoying himself,' I said to Fleur. 'Oh, it's Martin.'

'Shit, so it is,' she said.

After a while he noticed us and gave us a nod, removed the earphones.

'In a wee world of your own, there,' said Hewitt.

'Listening to a podcast, a comedy,' he said. 'It's my little come down at the end of a day, podcast and a pint.'

'Good for you,' said Hewitt.

Martin Walsh finished that pint pretty quickly and left.

'It's getting noisy in here,' I said.

'It can only get worse. Live music upstairs on a Wednesday.' Hewitt pointed at the poster.

'Carl Higgins was saying that his band plays here at times,' I said. 'Let's speak to the bouncers.'

They were like twins, both hench and bad, one with a beard and the other without. They were both acting cool and standoffish as we picked up our drinks and approached.

'What was up with Drew Taylor on Friday night?' I asked them.

'Who's he now?' asked the one with the beard.

'Drew Taylor,' I said, 'he was beaten up in that alleyway.' I pointed to my left.

'What are you, a peeler?'

'Is it that obvious, boys?' said Hewitt.

'We're not at liberty to discuss it,' said the clean shaven one.

'Even with a detective inspector and a superintendent?' asked Hewitt.

He looked her up and down. 'Are you two on the clock?'

'Never off it,' she said.

'And you're only investigating this now?' asked the bearded bouncer.

'No,' said the shaven one, 'someone *was* out, asking.'

'Sergeant Simon was out speaking with you,' said Hewitt.

'Yes, Simon,' said the bearded bouncer.

'I didn't see anything,' said the other one.

'You know Drew?' I asked them.

'Him and Roxy come in for a drink and bite to eat most weeks,' said the one with the beard; his colleague didn't disagree.

'But Roxanne wasn't here that night?' I asked.

'No,' said the beard. 'He was with his uncle, the da of that girl who was killed. They were having a quiet drink.'

'And Drew was dragged out of here …' I said.

'He wasn't dragged out of here,' said the beard. 'They must have got him when he was going to his car.'

'Who?'

They both laughed. 'I'm sure Drew could tell you if he wanted,' said Beardless.

'Can't you?' asked Hewitt.

'No. I could not. Sorry, girls, I'm not getting involved.'

'What about the young woman who went missing from here and wound up on Dee Street?' I asked.

'A few weeks ago, another Wednesday,' said Hewitt. 'Have either of you remembered anything else about that day?'

'Victoria,' said the one with the beard, 'that's who you're talking about, isn't it? The girl with the limp?'

'Yes, Victoria Black.'

'She came in on her own. Then there was trouble in here, so I didn't see her leave. But she wasn't drunk when she was sat at the bar.'

'What trouble was there?' asked Hewitt.

'Ah, this old alcie. He's okay till he drinks his fill and then we have to boot him out. Sometimes he kicks off.'

'And you don't bar him?'

'Occasionally,' said Beardless. 'He's barred at the minute.'

'Victoria Black was drugged,' I said.

They looked shocked.

'It was possibly a practice run for a killing. You heard of Erica McClelland; the girl killed on Ballyholme beach in Bangor.' I was pushing it now, giving away too much but we needed something.

Maybe they had daughters or sisters. Sometimes that's what it takes for certain men to humanise women.

They both nodded quietly.

'Fuck, that makes a difference,' said Beardless. I knew it would. 'I'll tell you what I know about anything regarding that, but I'm not getting involved with any business involving Taylor.'

The bouncers looked at each other. The bearded one said, 'It doesn't change that I don't know anything, personally. I wasn't here that night Victoria was in, but we'll jog our memories, sure.'

'Good,' said Hewitt, 'that's all we ask, lads.'

*

We moved on to Optimo nightclub at the SSE arena on the Laganside. Inside was all techno music and teenyboppers. All mostly girls. Mostly with fake tans and long silky dark hair. They could have all been the one person. They could have been me or my sisters at that age.

At Optimo the bouncers were even less of a help. We showed them a photo of Maisie Hockley, and reminded them of the date she had been there.

'I don't have a clue,' said one.

'Never seen her,' said another. 'Your daughter?' he asked me.

I was livid. I'd have had to have been a school girl to have a child her age; an adult child. I suppose that happens, young girls become mothers. Half of them probably do a better job at it than I'm doing now.

'She does look like you,' said Fleur after.

'Invisible,' I said, to quote Beatrice from Feminist Complex, Belfast as more girls tottered into the nightclub only to not be seen. Any wonder they were trying so hard to be noticed.

Chapter 26

'Do you want to go to Rocky Place?' I asked Hewitt.

'I want my bed. Aren't your feet burning?' she asked.

'No,' I said. But they were. So we called it a night. When I got home Paul was up, sitting in the kitchen.

'Boys go down to sleep, okay?' I asked him.

'Eventually, they were overtired. Jared especially.'

'I'm sorry.'

'No, don't be. You deserve a night out.'

'It was work.'

'It's okay to just go out and have fun,' he said.

'Really?' I said; I hadn't liked it, I didn't want nightclubs, my life was a fucken nightclub. Noisy with sensory overload. Who would be young and go out partying these days? Drinking, I definitely didn't mind. But not with all the noise attached.

I sat down beside him and Paul got up.

'I'm going to hit the hay,' he said.

'Are you not happy to see me dressed up?' I was flirting, or so I thought, but his response worried me. We were never very physical and now when I wanted to be he was shrugging me off. I noticed his face was grey. 'Paul,' I said, 'you look unwell.'

'The kids have probably picked something up from the day nursery and given it to me.'

My first thought was, please no, what would I do with the boys without his help, what if he was to get sick? Really sick. For the first time Paul's old battle with cancer seemed real.

He went to bed and I followed.

'What's wrong?' I pushed.

'It's stress. There's an audit at the hospital.'

'Oh?' I said, relieved it was only a mental thing; a worry about work.

'There's an investigation,' he said. 'It will be fine, I'm sure.'

'It will. You're great at your job.'

'Go to sleep,' he said but I couldn't. The faces of five girls shuffled in and out of my head all night. The words, 'Your daughter?' going through my head too. I was a tiny bit glad I was a mother of sons.

Chapter 27

The next morning was warm but cloudy. It was also Chloe's funeral. The first funeral I'd been to that the rain stayed away. Being that the family were humanists there was no church involvement. They had a service in the house, which I stood outside for.

There were readings and everyone had been asked to wear bright colours. And after, when the traffic moved again, I went inside.

Drew and Roxy were not brightly dressed. Upholding tradition, she wore a black dress and he wore a black suit. She kept her children there for a while, who were dressed in dark blues.

'Not contagious anymore, not now there are scabs,' I heard her say when people commented on the little ones' spotty faces. But soon she put them in the double buggy that was stacked upright by the door and left.

Everyone else was dressed as if they were going to a rave: girls from Feminist Complex, Belfast; Mike Birch; Prof. Lundy; and a sea of young people, possibly old school friends, possibly friends of Thomas'.

The door to the dining room was open, there Lizzie chatted with Thomas, they were dressed brightly too, him in a Hawaiian shirt and shorts, she in capri pants and a red top with bright orange flowers on the front that I saw when she turned to see us and gave me a little wave.

They were looking at photos on the far wall.

Out of nowhere Jackie appeared between us.

'Sorry, Mr. Taylor, do you want us to leave?' I said when I saw his face catch me and falter.

'No, it's okay.' He sighed.

I walked over to look at the photos on the wall, they were of both Taylor kids together.

The posture and face in the top photo was that of the street kid in the trailer as depicted in Thomas' art piece, *Fridge*.

He walked off to grab a sandwich from the table behind him and I followed, despite Lizzie trying to talk to me.

'Chloe never posed for you, did she, Thomas?' I asked him.

'No,' he said, 'I used these photos of Chloe ... at different ages.'

I looked over at the other photos, they were either of both siblings together, Thomas on his own, or Chloe alone. I felt like I recognised every expression from his exhibition. Thomas had simply looked at that wall for inspiration while he worked at the dining table.

'I took her photos from there,' he said, 'well, what I mean is I copied them from there, and I only did it so I wouldn't have to ask anyone to pose. I know it sounds soft but it's embarrassing to ask in case people say no.'

'I totally get that, Thomas,' I said.

'I didn't ask her either because it was going to be a surprise. If anyone would get what I was trying to do, it would be Chloe.'

'You're right,' I said. 'From what I've learnt about her. It's clever, your art work. Your dad has two very socially conscious kids. If my children grow up to be as good as you and Chloe, I'll be proud. I can see that Jackie's as proud of you both as he is protective.'

But I could sense the divide between them, and I reckoned it came from Chloe's secret travels and Thomas knowing about them.

'You don't think I have anything to do with Chloe's murder, do you?' Thomas asked me.

'If we thought that you'd be in custody. And you're not, are you?'

He gave me a goofy smile. 'Chloe was my inspiration for my art project. I thought, if she can be brave like that ... when she travelled, you know?'

'I do,' I said and touched his arm.

What was happening to me? First Lewis, then Thomas. I just wanted to wrap my arms around them and give them a hug. I had to walk away before I did something stupid like that.

Superintendent Hewitt came in the door looking for me, she found me and beckoned me into the utility room. 'Look what came for me.' She took a letter from a pocket in her bag.

You keep being pathetic at your job, Fleur Hewitt, while Chloe doesn't rest in peace.

'They've taken Lucinda's phrase from the paper,' I said. 'After the letter was sent to Belfast Met they showed it in the media.'

'Could have been Mike Birch,' said Hewitt. 'He got that letter and it said the same thing.'

Hewitt was rattled. She didn't like that her name was on there. So much for her dismissiveness over so-called trolls. It didn't feel as painless as Fleur had thought, I could tell by her face.

'So, it's not Lucinda,' I said.

'Was it ever, though?' asked Hewitt. 'Maybe she was taking the fall for someone. That son who was at home ... He seemed proper weird.'

'Then why suicide?'

'It's her funeral today, too,' Hewitt told me.

'I hope she rests in peace,' I said and it jarred for me. Apparently that's a Protestant thing, but I don't know, it's not an expression I have ever used. I just hate the acronym. R.I.P. *Rip*.

We snuck out of the utility room and found Jackie crying in the kitchen, trying to take a moment to himself. He didn't acknowledge us but Lizzie was watching him from the living room dabbing at her eyes, she couldn't stop looking at Jackie trying to hold it together. Lizzie didn't try to talk to me now, probably to look loyal to the family and not to us.

'That is killing me,' she said to the woman beside her. 'I have to go.'

Lizzie thumbed at her phone then brought it to her ear, then thumbed again and looked at the screen, then turned her phone off and popped it into her bag.

Drew hobbled over to her. 'What's up with your bake?' I heard him ask her.

'I need to get out of here. I can't …' She gestured at Jackie who was now hugging Thomas and crying, while Thomas was standing there with a blank broken expression, holding his father up. 'Justin isn't picking up,' said Lizzie.

'Come on and I'll drive you home.'

'Aren't you going to the crematorium?'

'No,' Drew said. 'Come on.'

'Can you drive with your leg like that?' said Lizzie.

'It's automatic,' said Drew. 'So, yes.'

'Your leg's automatic,' she said smiling and dabbing her eyes.

'You want a lift or not?' he asked her, not unkindly.

'Yeah. I do. Thanks, Drew.'

They left together and that old friend of mine reared its ugly head. Envy. Does she like him? I thought. Does he like her? Is that what this show is all about? Him slagging her and her slagging him, so we don't add up the equation and see that he would visit her house under the pretence of seeing Chloe. But he timed it for when Justin was out training a client. And Drew seemed jealous of him too.

I imagined all this passion and envy and lust I hadn't had since Greg, and I was sorry Paul and I had never had that chance. We didn't have years of it in the bank before babies. We were just straight into babies. In fact, they were there first. It was like they all came as a package deal, the three of them.

Even Drew and Roxanne had breakfast dates, Lizzie and Justin had date nights, Martin and Bill had candlelit dinners. Martin and Rebecca had long drives alone to talk over their problems. Paul and I were a family straight away. I knew I should have been grateful.

I watched Lizzie and Drew leave in his car and I should have been thinking about Chloe but I was thinking about myself.

Chapter 28

By lunchtime, and with the Taylors gone to say goodbye to Chloe their own way, we were at a loose end, when Hewitt said, 'Let's do this the proper way.'

We went to the Woodstock Road and to Rocky Place: a 'working man's' pub with wine-coloured walls and dodgy boys in corners. There was a beer garden out the back and a rowdy game of darts going on as we arrived.

There were plaques on the wall for Best Kept Pub, only it had a different name: Speedy's. Where Darleen Boyle had been drinking back in 1994, before she was stabbed to death by Dan Hamilton further down the road.

Wilson Morrow, the manager, was in the office eating his lunch. He came out and spoke to us at a corner table.

'Yes, I know Kayley,' Wilson said. 'She's a regular here.'

'Are you aware that she was drinking here when she woke up somewhere else?' I asked him.

'I bet I know the night that was,' he said. 'She was comatose, Kayley. I saw this woman and told her to keep an eye while I got a bucket … in case she was sick.'

'Had she been sick?'

'It was only a matter of time,' said Wilson.

'And the woman?' I said.

'You see, thing is, when I came back with the bucket they were both gone.'

'Oh,' I said flatly.

'But I went looking, and she was helping Kayley into her car. Shouted over to me to say she knew how to get her home.'

'Did you get the impression she knew Kayley?'

'She didn't say. But there wasn't much time for talking. I presumed she looked at Kayley's ID for an address.'

'So you believed that Kayley was being looked after?'

'Yes. Only, when they drove off I noticed there was a someone in the driver's seat. I've thought about that a bit since.'

'Do you have a description of that someone?'

'No, it was just a shadow. But I think it was a man.'

'And the woman? What else can you tell us about her?'

'Young. Long dark hair.'

'What kind of car?' I asked Wilson.

'I didn't take that in.' He kissed his teeth. 'A wee boxy number. I was busy. Have you spoken to Kayley?'

'She has given a statement already,' I said.

*

Kayley's foster mother welcomed us into her home. Kayley was getting ready to go to work. Her face was orange-brown and her hands pale and freckled. What a shame, I thought, she was probably covering a face full of beautiful freckles.

'I remember a game of darts and having a drink but it's all hazy to me,' Kayley said.

'The manager at Rocky Place said you left with a woman,' said Hewitt, 'he had left her with you while he went to get a bucket. He thought you were about to be unwell. And then you left with her.'

'I don't remember any of this,' Kayley said, pushing her silver hairband back and forth, raking her hair into a quiff. 'I don't even think the police went there to ask anything after I reported this. I thought no one was taking me serious, that they thought I was just pissed, and what? Removing my own pants to take a piss, or something? And waking up embarrassed? I'm not embarrassed.'

'We are taking it seriously, Kayley,' said Hewitt. 'And we suspect that the person, or people, who did this to you, have done it to others.'

'Who?' she asked.

'Other young women have reported similar things,' I said. 'We know that one of them had her drink spiked.'

Kayley drew her arms around herself.

'Wilson from Rocky Place told us that the woman said she knew how to get you home.'

'I can't remember any of this. I can't remember anyone.'

'He thought that she'd checked your ID for your address.'

'I didn't have ID on me that night, never for the Rocky Place. I don't need it because they know me there. They know I'm not underage. And they're strict, like. I can't understand that remark about ID,' Kayley said. 'I can only think that I said "Holywood", or she thought I said Holywood and that I wandered off. That's all I can think. I have no idea when my underwear was removed or who removed it. It makes me feel sick.'

Her foster mother rubbed Kayley's shoulder. 'I just want to see Kayley out and about, being social again,' she said. 'She hasn't been herself since.'

*

We visited Maisie, the young woman who had been at the SSE Arena. She told us all she could remember, and she noted a man with dark hair in Optimo who kept smiling at her down the bar.

'And that's all I can think,' she said, 'next thing I go into the toilets and then, I don't know. Lights out.'

'Is there a chance your drink was spiked when you went into the toilets?'

'I brought it in and set it beside the sink when I was in the cubicle. That's what I always do. Terrible you have to think like that, but it's a habit I have.'

'Did you talk to anyone in the toilet?' I asked her.

'Girls always chat in the toilets, don't they?'

'Can you remember anyone that night?'

'Not really.'

'And you had broken up with your boyfriend?' I asked.

'No,' she said. 'I've never had a boyfriend.'

I wondered how this boyfriend breakup myth had made it into her statement.

'How much did you have to drink, Maisie?' asked Hewitt.

'Two drinks, one shot. Nothing, hardly,' she said pushing her veil of brown hair from her face. You do look like me, a younger me, I thought. 'I'm glad someone is finally speaking to me about this,' she said. 'I thought I was being laughed at when I reported it.'

'I don't want you to worry,' I told her, 'but there seems to be a spate of such things.'

'I's not just me?'

'It's not just you.'

'That means I was drugged?'

'You weren't tested at the time?'

'No,' said Maisie. 'No one suggested that I should. It wasn't really an option. I was so embarrassed; my sister came and collected me after I went into a shop and asked to use their phone, because my phone had gone missing. I've tried using the *Find my iPhone* app since and it says it's at the SSE.

'So I went there but no one had handed it in. Anyway, when my sister brought me home, she said, "This is totally out of character for you," and she phoned the police and they came out, but they didn't say a lot.

'I knew they were looking at me as if I was lying, like, I don't know … I was doing something I shouldn't have been. I mean, it was *humiliating*, so I saw them to the door and said, "Forget about it," but then one nice one, he said, "I'm filing this so it's in the system."'

'I suppose if he hadn't done that you wouldn't have been able to contact me.'

Good old Higgins!

I texted him to thank him for the names of the girls when I got back to my desk. I was about to call Victoria Black, the woman who had been tested and had definitely been drugged while drinking at The Bell. I wanted to arrange to go and see her, but Chief Dunne came crashing out of his office.

'Complete carnage in Dundonald,' he said. 'We're sending support.'

'What's happened?' I asked.

'There has been a mass shooting,' he said. 'It looks like there are a few fatalities.'

Chapter 29

It happened on a Thursday at two-thirty p.m. On the most beautiful day you're likely to encounter in Belfast. Half way along Comber Road, as Chief Dunne said, was 'complete carnage'.

A man in a car had been shot twice and, unbelted, had fallen face first onto the shoulder of the woman in the driver's seat. Whose seatbelt could not save her from the bullet in the centre of her forehead.

She was still there, slumped back in her seat, eyes open, mouth too, still in shock as the sun shone down on her, and onto the kerb, where she must have parked up before the attack.

Now she was shaded from the sun while men and women worked in white coats, with powders and cameras and cordons. The overgrown grass beside the kerb shook in the light breeze. The air was thick with pollen. Everything swelled, every fibre, every lash, every drop of blood.

Blood had wept from both their heads where the bullets entered. It smeared the headrest behind the woman. The exit wound.

More blood – his – had run down her shoulder. An iPhone lay in the footwell.

Up the road lay another body. Up the road that took you to the central crossroads, that took you to Belfast or Comber, or to the hills that sat over the village, or to the hospital, where the man from the car, whose light breathing was almost missed, had been rushed.

Up from that lay the body of a boy.

He could not have been more than twelve. He received one bullet in the back of his head. He lay now in his school uniform, in among the dandelions and overgrown grass.

The sun was moving slowly away from him and the traffic lights still arrogantly changed in sequence. Traffic was diverted. White tents were put up over the car and over the boy. And his mother, at the traffic lights, cried hysterically about being kept away from the body of her boy.

Chapter 30

Two private ambulances took the bodies away: the woman from the car, and the boy from the street. Brian Quinn came over to me in his white suit.

'Male vic in the front seat was lucky this happened so close to the hospital,' he said.

'What happened?'

'They were shot through the car window, from the path.'

'Someone on foot,' I said. I just had a feeling in my stomach it had to do with my case.

'And the boy,' he said. 'He was on foot, and he was shot, and unfortunately he didn't make it.'

The Dundonald branch was there, this was their district but I couldn't leave until I saw for myself.

'Any IDs?'

'The man doesn't have any ID on him, but the woman did have hers. She was called Mary Heaney. We presume, until we learn otherwise, that he was Mr. Heaney.'

'And the boy?'

'He was called Ince Ross. He went to the local secondary school. He had an appointment card in his blazer, must have got out early for an orthodontist appointment.'

'So the booster seat in the back of the Punto is not his,' I said. 'No kid in the car?'

'No.'

Kate Stile was at the other side of the car, holding a camera in her hand.

'No breakage on this window,' she said.

I told her Quinn had already told me. 'A killer on foot,' I said.

She skimmed through the photos. 'Shot the boy once,' said Kate. 'It was quite a skilled shot.'

Kate showed me the photo of the deceased woman slumped back in her chair. She had a bullet wound in the middle of her forehead.

'She must have looked at her killer straight on,' I said.

'And this guy's in surgery at the moment,' said Kate. 'He was shot twice, once in the chest and once in the head, neither one was a perfect shot. He would have been looking at Mrs. Heaney, the driver.'

'I know him,' I said when I saw the photo. 'That is not her husband.'

Chapter 31

Justin was on life support in his own private room in ICU. I saw Lizzie's back as we approached. She was sitting by his side staring at him.

'Are you okay?' I asked her and she turned around and hugged me. Maybe she thought I was someone else.

'I'm so very sorry,' said Hewitt and Lizzie reached out and hugged her too.

'And on the day of Chloe's funeral, as if I'm not hurting enough,' Lizzie said.

'What is the prognosis?' asked Hewitt.

'You mean, is he going to die?' asked Lizzie.

Hewitt said yes rather coldly and Lizzie took in a giant breath. 'He'll be alright,' Lizzie said.

The nurses had already told us there was a very slim chance Justin would pull through, but I understood why Lizzie wanted to believe that he would be fine.

'Have you let his family know?' I asked.

'He has no family,' she said. 'Just me.'

I looked closer at his face.

'Have you any idea what happened?' Lizzie asked me before I had the chance to ask her.

'The other people didn't survive,' I told her.

'I know,' she said. 'Do you know why he was in that car?'

'I don't, Lizzie.'

'Wasn't she a client?' asked Hewitt.

Lizzie and I both looked at her.

'The other victim in the car, the driver, I think I saw her out running with Justin before. Remember, DI Sloane?'

It dawned on me, outside Rebecca Walsh's Leathem Square townhouse.

'Oh, maybe ...' I said and watched Lizzie.

She frowned and asked, 'Why would he be in her car?'

'Maybe to chat?' I asked.

'Or maybe they drove to where they ran,' said Hewitt.

But this was just around the corner from where Martin Walsh's wife lived, this *was* where they ran. Lizzie was jealous and I understood it. It was also not far from where Drew lived, and equally close to where Justin lived himself. Why *were* they in the car? It wasn't the worst question.

'Maybe Mary was giving Justin a lift home,' I said.

'Dundonald PSNI will find out. It's their area,' said Hewitt.

'I want you on it,' Lizzie said. 'You, Harriet.'

'She's busy working on Chloe Taylor's case at the moment,' said Hewitt, pulling rank.

Lizzie blinked away a tear. 'Where's Drew Taylor right now?'

'Last time I saw him was at the funeral,' said Hewitt.

'He left with you, Lizzie,' I said.

'He gave me a lift,' she said, 'I thought he was being kind but all he did was slander Justin. And now ... look.'

She clutched Justin's hand and squeezed it as his machine beeped slowly.

Chapter 32

Dundonald branch dealt with the Ross family. We called in briefly and sat with the detective concerned, DI Lowry. He told us how he had visited the boy's parents.

'They were distraught.'

Well, naturally.

'Leah and Kelvin Ross are originally from Luton, they moved here with their four children, after the eldest got injured in a knife crime incident. They thought it would be safer here. The young boy, second youngest in the family, little Ince, needed his dental braces corrected and was out of St Pat's school early to go to the orthodontist. He was to meet his mother at the Spar. He never got there. He wasn't caught in the crossfire though, that we can tell, he was purposefully hit and killed with one bullet in his brain, and it wasn't a stray. It was intended, that young boy's death. How can you tell that to the parents? An innocent kid.'

I looked at Ince's photo, a cute boy with an impish smile. His face was on my mind when we went to question Drew.

'Hey, are we two bad cops here?' I asked as we pulled into Tullycarnet.

Hewitt said, 'No. You're going to have to go in softer.'

'Why me?'

'He knows you, and hates you.'

'Thanks a bunch,' I said.

'Well, he hates us all, but he is more suspicious of me, the *outsider*,' said Hewitt.

'You think?'

'Not from here, am I? I'll be that loud Scottish bitch. You go in and bat your lashes.'

'If the shoe fits,' I said. 'Loud and Scottish, I mean.'

'Here, forgot I had this for you,' she said.

Hewitt put her hand in her pocket. When I looked she was giving me the finger. I had to laugh, it eased the tension, then I remembered Ince Ross' smiling face and I hardened mine again.

'You are well known to have links, *and* you were hurt lately,' I said to Drew across his dining table.

Roxy was dishing their dinner on to plates, potato waffles, burnt sausages, congealed beans. She had her back to us, her long dark hair sat on her back like a glossy saddle. She had changed from her funeral clothes into jeans and a T-shirt. Drew had not; he was still in his black suit, sans jacket and tie.

'Tit for tat?' said Hewitt.

'Don't be ridiculous,' said Drew. 'If you think that I would waste my time …'

'Why do you hate Justin so much?' I asked.

'Look at Roxy's phone and you'll see why,' said Drew.

'Tell us.'

'He was sending her sleazy messages. Okay, want to know the truth? The night before Chloe was killed I *was* at the bungalow. He came in like a big bollocks, asking me if I was trying it on with his bird. He was wearing next to fucken nothing. Next thing he's friended Roxy on Facebook, hasn't he! She accepted him because of Chloe and everything … which I'm not delighted about; then he was commenting on all her photos. She deleted them first thing in the morning before anyone saw. I'm not on there so I don't know. And she waits for days to tell me.'

'When was this?'

'Tuesday,' said Roxanne turning to face us. Which was when I noticed her black eye.

'This Tuesday?' asked Hewitt.

'How did you get that shiner?' I asked her.

'The wee man headbutted her,' said Drew.

'I was asking Roxanne,' I said.

'It's true,' she said. 'He nutted me. Harrison was tired and throwing himself about when I was bringing him up to his cot for a nap. That's all that happened.'

I could not trust Drew and it worried me that I felt such an attraction to him. He looked even better in that suit than I'd seen him look. And dishevelled. Post-fuck lovely. Or was it post-shooting? That would be like me, married a psycho kidnapper and rapist, now I fantasised about a possible killer and definite drug dealer.

'Chloe is dead,' he said, 'and that fucker's more worried about sending my missus messages about how he wants to eat her pussy, and shite like that.'

'So these messages were this Tuesday,' I said.

'Any reason your wife took her time telling you?' Hewitt asked Drew.

'Knew I'd be livid. We've had two sick kids to deal with, a murder in the family, and I've been bust up.'

'Livid, you say? Livid enough to shoot Mr. Nicholson?' asked Hewitt.

'What!' Drew protested. 'And two innocent people who *didn't* send Roxy messages? Livid enough to shower them with bullets? Fuck sake, man. Wise up.' He gave an unbelieving laugh.

But this was no bullet shower, this was precise.

'I had the impression that you and Lizzie didn't like each other,' I said.

'We don't.'

'But you left together after the funeral.'

Roxanne stared at him.

'She couldn't get Justin to answer to her,' said Drew, 'she needed a lift, *and* she doesn't drive. That's all, before you go trying to make anything bigger from it.'

Roxanne stormed out.

'Thanks a fucken lot,' said Drew. 'Did you really have to go there?'

'You have a lot of friends, Drew,' I said. 'If you think Justin had something to do with you getting beaten up, or Chloe's murder, then you should have told us. We would have put him behind bars. It's our job, not yours.'

'Really?' he said sarcastically. 'You wouldn't know what your job is half the time. Lot of progress you've made finding my cousin's killer!'

'You were given the chance to speak up,' said Hewitt.

'Even if, for instance, I thought Justin was responsible for Chloe, or anything else, he's no good to me in jail, is he?'

'You *were* planning something?' I asked.

'I'm not saying that,' stated Drew. 'That sex chat on Facebook doesn't annoy me. Honestly. Couldn't give a fuck, mate.'

'It seems very much like it does annoy you,' said Hewitt.

'Me and Roxy have been together since the age of fourteen, some poseur twat isn't gonna come in and ruin anything.'

'You didn't hit her, Drew, did you?' I asked him.

'I'm not dignifying that with an answer.'

'It wouldn't have been Roxanne's fault if Justin was sending messages,' I said.

'I know that,' said Drew. 'I trust that girl with my life, alright.'

'Okay,' I said, kind of convinced. 'Do you think Justin had something to do with Chloe's death?'

Drew stayed quiet for a while. 'Nah,' he said.

'Are you just saying that?' Hewitt asked.

'Fuck sake, arrest me or go.'

He knew there would unlikely be a conviction, not for these paramilitary activities, and nor did he want one.

A tout Drew was not.

He said he was with Roxanne and the kids all day too. Just as they came into the kitchen for their dinner, and Roxanne set out the plates around us and then tried to put the baby into his highchair. Harrison struggled and bucked against her. She strapped him in and sighed.

'You're going to give your mummy another black eye,' Drew shouted at him.

'I don't like these sausages,' said the little girl.

Roxanne looked about ready to burst.

We stood up and got ready to leave.

'You were together all day?' I asked Roxanne.

'Yes,' she said, 'except that I left the funeral after the service. An hour or so later, by midday, he was at home. He's never out of my hair, though I wish he was, because sometimes it's bloody claustrophobic.' She gave him a dirty look. 'And sorry – desperately sorry – for what happened to that boy … and that woman, and even to Justin, and I know you're only doing your job but this is a waste of time. Eat up, kids.' She looked at me. 'So sorry to disappoint you. Kids, eat up before your dinner goes cold.'

Ella cried again that she didn't like the sausages and after we left Drew walked out behind us and disappeared up an entry in the estate.

'Where are you going now?' Roxanne called after him from the door, then she used all her strength to slam it shut.

Chapter 33

We had nothing on Justin in our system, but he wasn't Belfast born and bred. He had grown up in Liverpool, and I remembered he had lived in Coleraine.

Early evening, I got a reply from Merseyside Police. They had more details about Justin Nicholson. I took the call and watched out of the window as I listened. 'Does he have any record?' I asked.

'He had cautions alright, I've a file here as thick as a loaf,' said Sergeant Moreland from over the water, 'before he went private as a fitness instructor Justin worked in gyms, he was a well-known name to us lads over here. He'd been fired for selling roids and counterfeit blues at the gym, so he started up his own training business.'

'Anything else?'

'That's not the best of it, Nicholson had manys a minor charge when he was a teen. I have a colleague who remembers him back then, if you'd like a word some time?'

'Maybe. What was he doing back then?'

'He had some problems with girls. Then it looks like he got into health and fitness and sorted himself out. Happy days, you might say, Nicholson was occupied. But the worst was yet to come.'

'Go on.' I wanted to know what *problems with girls* meant.

'Justin Nicholson was arrested for public indecency.'

'That's strange.'

'Strange indeed, he was only a schoolboy when a woman looked out of her net curtains, middle of the day, tea and *Countdown* and there was Nicholson and the current squeeze having intercourse up against a lamppost in her little suburban cul-de-sac. In school uniform.'

'I don't believe you.'

'A crowd of kids around them all laughing, meanwhile this woman who phoned it in was nearly having a canary.'

'It's not the kind of thing you see every day, to be fair.'

'Yeah, well, he was sixteen then, so was the girl in question, so nothing underage. But that just set the tone. He was cautioned eight times for lewd conduct. Nicholson has a thing for the great outdoors, and doesn't have the wit to wait for the sun to set.'

Detective Amy Campbell came into the room, she gestured that she wanted a word with me.

'Is that everything?' I asked Sarge Moreland.

'It'll get you started at least. If I find anything else, you know the rest ...'

'You'll drop me a line?'

'I will. Hey, what's the weather like over there anyway?'

'I think it's the same here as what you're getting.'

'Don't get sunburnt then,' he said.

'I'll try not to.'

'I do love that Northern Irish accent.'

'You don't sound like you're from Liverpool,' I said.

'I'm from Runcorn. Heard of it?'

'I have. Look, Sergeant, I have to head on.'

'No problem, Detective. Maybe I'll get over there, I fancy coming to Belfast, doing one of those *Game of Thrones* tours. Maybe if I'm over you can show me where's good to get a drink.'

'Maybe,' I said. 'Plenty of places to choose from. I'll have to go, my chief is calling me.'

Campbell shrugged.

'Ah, okay, Harriet, lovely to chat with you.'

'And thank *you* for all your help.'

'You are more than welcome.'

I gritted my teeth and got off the line.

'What the fuck was that?' asked Campbell.

'A sarge in Liverpool, in relation to Justin Nicholson. I think he liked the accent.'

'Fuck me,' said Amy Campbell. 'You'll have to google him, chum, see if he's a looker or not.'

'Sorry, did you want me?'

'Aye, not as much as he did, from the sounds of it. But just to tell you, we have someone in custody for the robbery in the pharmacy. I really don't think it was related to the stabbing of Chloe Taylor.'

'No? I didn't think so either.'

'This fella, he's fucked, really. Has a lot of addiction issues. I'll find out more and let you know, see where he was during the time of Chloe Taylor's murder. My gut is telling me a big no, but it has been wrong before.'

'At least your gut is working, and there's an arrest for the robbery. We'll crack them all.'

'Yes,' said Campbell, 'we'll smash them all. Eventually …'

'Why were Justin and Mary Heaney in the car together?' Sarge Simon asked.

'Mary's widower Craig says he has no idea who Justin is,' I told Fergus Simon what I'd just heard from Dundonald. 'She went by Molly, not Mary.'

'Justin Nicholson is a P.T., he was training her,' said Hewitt, looking at the photo of Molly. 'Harriet, that is definitely the woman we saw him out run with when we were at that townhouse near the Ice Bowl.'

She meant Rebecca Walsh's place.

'Yes,' I said, 'it could be.' I wasn't certain. The context was so different and that day I hadn't been looking at Justin's client much.

'Where did Molly live?' asked Simon.

'In Comber with her husband and three-year-old son.'

'That is a stretch,' he said. 'Would she have been on her way to work, a halfway point?'

'Molly works from home,' I said. 'The widower was adamant she was not having an affair.'

'Isn't the point of an affair,' said Hewitt, 'to keep it secret? Especially from your spouse?'

I told Hewitt what I'd learned from my phone call to Merseyside Police. She listened, then said, 'There's got to be more. I'll phone him and see.'

I handed over Sarge Moreland's number and while she left a message for him, I googled him. He was nice looking, but older, and I thought, if he flirts with her – does the, *I like your Scottish accent* routine on Fleur – I am going to be so pissed off.

But then, before she got a chance, Maisie Hockley called me.

'That photo of the man on news,' she said, 'that man who was shot in Dundonald.'

'Yes, Maisie,' I said, 'Tell me …'

'It could be nothing, but I think …'

'Yes?'

'I think he looks identical to the man who was smiling at me at Optimo. Remember, I said this guy, dark-haired, handsome, he kept smiling at me at the bar. Well, I'm sure that was him.'

Chapter 34

Lizzie was in the hospital keeping vigil by his bedside later that evening. I asked her to come out into the corridor. 'I need to talk to you,' I said. 'I've been looking into places where Justin used to live. I have some concerning news. I'm not sure how much of it you will already know, but some of it concerns you.'

She looked worried.

Nurses and visitors walked by.

'It's alright,' said Hewitt, 'come into this corner, we'll have more privacy.'

'We are worried that you might be in danger,' I said. Lizzie became teary immediately. 'We know what happened when you lived in Coleraine.'

'How do you know we lived there?' she said.

'You mentioned a gardener you had and Justin corrected you and said that was when you lived in Coleraine, remember?'

'Not really.'

'But you *did* live there?' I pushed her.

She pulled her hair back off her face and exhaled. 'Yes.'

'He was hurting you.'

'Yes,' she cried out in relief. 'Yes! He was.'

Officer McMaster from Coleraine PSNI told me she had been called out to what seemed to be *a domestic*, and when they went out to check all was fine. The pair were always calling the police, McMaster said, sometimes it was him, but mostly it was Lizzie.

Coleraine PSNI sent out someone to speak with Lizzie about getting away, about refuges where she could go, support she could get, but she played it down.

Lizzie was fine, she insisted. Then the calls got less frequent, and when they did call, McMaster admitted to me, the police had lost interest.

Then the calls stopped completely. I knew they had moved to Belfast. I could find no record of the police being called out to the bungalow.

'Why are you here for him when he has hurt you like this?' Hewitt asked Lizzie.

'I'm not here because I want to be,' Lizzie said. 'I'm not living with him because I want that either, it's because he told me he'd kill me if I try to leave him.'

I understood. I thought, I have been here. At that moment she was *me*. The me I was three years before.

'I'm here,' said Lizzie, 'because I worry he'll open his eyes and *not* see me. That he'll come home and I'll never hear the end of it. What would he do to me when he's hurt so badly and angry about it, when this is what he does when he loves me, when he's *making love* to me?'

She lifted her top and showed us a three-inch scar.

'Wait,' I said. 'He did that during sex?'

Lizzie began to weep. We helped her to the toilets where she threw water on her face, rubbed her eyes and said, 'Can I show you more?'

'Only if you are happy to, as long as you don't feel compromised.'

'I'm just glad someone is finally listening to me.'

She unbuttoned her boot cut jeans and lowered them until they completely covered her chunky heels. Lizzie's thighs and buttocks were covered in puncture wounds and small scars.

'You are safe now, Lizzie,' said Hewitt.

'Do you need a coffee?' I asked Lizzie.

'I'm jittery already. I've probably had about ten coffees all day.'

'Water then?' said Hewitt.

'Please.'

'Sloane? Water?' Hewitt asked me.

'Yes, I could manage a water,' I said. It was easy to forget to look after yourself on the job, it was warm and I was beyond developing a thirst. Gasping for a glass of Merlot rather than water.

Hewitt left to get us a bottle each.

How, I thought, how is Lizzie okay? Where will she go? What if Justin does survive, will he come after her, stalk her and harass her, like Jason Lucie did to me after my escape?

'Where was Justin the day of Chloe's killing?' I asked Lizzie.

'I don't know. He said he came from the building site, showered and then collected me from Jackie's house.'

We still had questions and not many answers. But we still thought we had enough to bring Drew in and question him about Justin's shooting. And Justin had been identified by Maisie. He could have spiked her drink at any time.

Kayley had left Rocky Place bar with a man and a woman with long dark hair. This could have been Molly Heaney. Justin could have been the man in the car. Her car. A boxy car? A Punto! This could have been the kind of thing they got up to when she told her husband she was training.

Justin had previous and maybe under his influence it was a folie à deux: a lethal combination when the two of them got together.

Maybe Molly and Justin had built up to Chloe. She was vulnerable, often alone.

Or, the shooting could have been Drew's revenge for Chloe, and for Roxanne, and the messages Justin sent her. A paramilitary thing.

Maybe Justin was selling counterfeit Viagra again when that was Drew's turf. Maybe Justin was just an overall nuisance that needed to be silenced. Ince Ross was clearly collateral, but Molly Heaney had to be something more.

Was her husband connected? Was she?

Hewitt returned and handed us our waters.

'This is the time to tell us what you know about Chloe,' I said to Lizzie. 'Did Justin kill her?'

How mad would that be, all the men she blamed, and her man did the deed!

'I don't know,' she said, 'but I do know that he isn't right in the head.'

'We know all about his past. Don't worry.'

She was biting the water bottle in concentration.

'Thank you,' she said, putting her bottle on a chair in the corridor. 'I need to get some air. Do you mind?'

'I'll come with you, if you want,' said Hewitt and the two of them left.

I snuck into Justin's room and stood looking at him, his eyes closed like in sleep, his mouth ajar with tubes coming out of his nose. I quickly got a kit from my bag and swabbed the inside of Justin's mouth and put the swab into a tube, watching over my shoulder the whole time. Then the door opened and she was there.

'Changed my mind,' Lizzie said. 'I can't leave him, this is how scared he has me.'

'He's fit for nothing. Go home and get some rest,' I told her, a sweat breaking on me as I put the travel tube back into my bag with my back to her.

But she said she wasn't ready. She stood and looked out the window at the car park. Hewitt was staring at Justin, her eyes inscrutable.

On the way out I took Lizzie's water bottle and left her mine.

Chapter 35

On Friday Paul was at home and would be off for a few days. 'A large amount of anaesthetic is unaccounted for,' he said, 'They've let me take some time out while they launch in internal investigation in the surgical department.'

'So people won't be having their operations today as a result?' I asked.

'Yes,' he said blankly.

'There'll be a few unhappy campers.'

'I haven't done anything wrong,' he said defensively.

'It's like in my work, it's just procedure.'

'Well, it's never happened to me before.'

'That says it all,' I tried to reassure him. 'It'll be fine.'

Paul asked that the babies stay at home to take his mind off things.

'Nursery's already paid for,' I said. 'You know how much I had to hussle to get those places.'

Paul went to give me a kiss on the lips and got my cheek. He kissed the boys on the tops of their heads, but he looked upset and I had never seen him like that.

'Take yourself out for lunch, or to the cinema,' I said.

'I don't like being alone.'

'Hence why you took me on,' I joked, but I knew it was true.

He said nothing, just helped us out to the car with our luggage, baby bags and two big struggling baby boys, and he watched us drive away before running back into the house in which we had our first date. It was a cute story to tell people, if anybody cared.

If we met anyone who did not know us they assumed we'd been married for years. And that he was the father of the boys. But we were still so new.

I left the babies into the day nursery and drove across the lane to the station. I'd gotten into a habit of watching out for Lizzie as I did it. But she was never there, only that once; the first day I got the kids into the nursery. I knew she was probably at the hospital watching over Justin. I wanted an update on him. If he was dead; if he was hanging on in there.

'We've charged that person, chum,' said Amy Campbell, lingering by the coffee machine.

'Who?' I asked. 'Pour me one too, will you? I need a coffee the size of my ass.'

'Horrible coffee, isn't it?' said Campbell. 'I think there's cocaine in it.' She handed me mine. I took a sip and burned my lip.

'The person who robbed Mayhew's pharmacy,' she said, 'his prints match up with a similar robbery in Sandy Row. He's a drug addict.'

'That's why you're talking about cocaine?'

'Probably.'

'I suspected as much,' I said, 'about the robber being an addict.'

This machete-wielding robber no longer concerned me. Lizzie and Justin were on my mind.

'Good work,' I told Campbell, more to get rid of her, so I could get on with things I did not want her to be around for.

She looked at her notes. 'Brooks Sloane,' she said. 'Any relation?'

'Where is he?' I asked, my heart thumping. I set down my cup.

'Interview room 1.'

Though I had dated Amy's brother in the past she had no idea who mine was; you'd hardly boast about your brother if he was a junkie.

'I need to speak to him,' I said.

'You *are* related?'

'He's the elder of my two brothers. The eldest of us all.'

'Oh shit, Harry. Did you know he does this?'

'No, never. But he's a grown man and this is on him.'

'I feel anxious now,' she said.

'Why, Amy?'

'I hope you don't think I meant to blame you.'

'Don't be stupid,' I said, meaning to sound flippant but sounding rude. 'It's all good, I just need to have a word with him. Find out what is going on.'

Campbell stared at me, and I felt like I needed to explain, or defend him. Brooks had always been so gentle. I hadn't seen him in over a year, but he did these disappearing acts. I'd stopped wondering what was happening to him since I had my sons to worry about. I felt bad; months passed when I didn't think about Brooks at all.

'I hoped he was back in London,' I explained. 'He has children over there.' Not that I'd called them to find out if he had shown up. But I couldn't see him just yet. I would let him stew, I would focus on my job.

He was going nowhere, but at least I knew he was alive. I had work to do, bad coffee to drink and Kate Stile to locate.

Chapter 36

I needed to find Stile, but she was out. The swab in its travel tube and the water bottle were burning holes in my bag.

I received a call from Sergeant Moreland at Merseyside Police.

'Justin Nicholson was working in a gym in Liverpool, he was twenty,' said Moreland, 'living at home when he started a relationship with this girl who was only sixteen. After a workout Nicholson brought her back to his parents' house. They were out at work. And Nicholson then began to sexually victimise her over a long period. She was afraid of him so she went back a few times.'

'What did Nicholson do?'

'Imprisoning her, torturing her, she claimed; making her think he would let her go before resuming the torture.'

He was more like Jason than I'd thought, possibly worse.

'Before the girl withdrew her statement,' said Moreland, 'she said he was nice one minute then horrible. At one point he said, "Will I put you out of your misery?"'

I listened and I wrote it down.

'Then,' the sarge added, 'Nicholson involved knives, and attempted to slice off her nipples.'

'What! That's some serial killer shit.'

'Perhaps he was headed that way.'

'So he's on the DNA database,' I said.

'No and I don't know why not. If it was because the girl withdrew the statement practically as soon as she made it, or if this is a technical fuck up.'

I was in no doubt now that Chloe Taylor's killing was Justin Nicholson's doing. It was not Martin she was seeing, but Justin.

And I could see Justin having an interest in Chloe. She was much younger than him, she wasn't his usual type and he would not have been hers, but that would be the challenge for him. One he would love and would ultimately exploit.

Chapter 37

On the car radio, the news focused on the Repeal vote taking place in Ireland. They were voting on two choices: to give women the right to safe abortions without having to travel over the water, or to make a hard time harder.

I thought about my own abortion, pre-twins, and turned the radio off. I went back into the station and asked to be let into Brooks' cell for a word.

He was sitting there, with his hands all scabby. His face gaunt. Sleepy-eyed.

'When did you get so fucken handy with a machete?' I asked him.

My eldest brother did not register me, he stared off into space. I had not seen him like this in years. He usually kept the deep darkness of his addiction to himself.

'Brooks,' I said. 'I've been going mad worrying about you.' The words felt as hollow as he looked vacuous. I stormed out.

'He shouldn't be here,' I said to Detective Campbell, 'he should be in a facility getting help.'

She looked at me pityingly. 'There is no space, Harry, just huge wait lists. And technically he *has* committed crimes. I know as well as you that it's not fair, but it's all we have to work with.'

I saw Kate Stile from forensics in the distance and chased her into her lab.

'Turns out,' I said to Kate, 'Justin Nicholson has a history of abusing girls, sexually motivated crimes and he also has been involved in selling drugs.'

'Really?' she said. 'Then maybe someone knew that and was putting a stop to it.'

'Could be,' I said, 'but I don't think it's that simple.'

'Is it ever?' Kate sat in front of her microscope and examined a slide. 'I need to do something, Harry, if you don't mind. I prefer quiet to concentrate.'

'Oh yes,' I said, 'no problem. I'll let you get on with your work, but first …'

'Yeah?'

'Erica McClelland.'

'What about her?'

'She was killed on Ballyholme Beach in Bangor,' I said. 'There was a bite on her that nobody knows about. It wasn't in the media, and people in Bangor have had their DNA tested. But they don't know about the bite.'

I took two bags from my handbag. One had a swab tube inside, and the other the plastic water bottle.

'Do you think one of these may be a DNA match?' Kate asked.

'Yes, I really do.' She looked unsure but I was not about to be palmed off again. 'I'm banking on it.'

'Alright,' Stile said, taking them from me. 'It'll be a month until I can get you the results.'

'Do me a favour, Kate,' I said, gritting my teeth. 'Bump me to the front of the queue.'

'I can't do that.'

'I know you did it before.'

'Who for?'

'You do favours for Greg.'

'That's not the same thing, Harry. Can't very well say no to the boss.'

'I won't ask you again,' I pleaded but she still looked unsure. 'Have I ever asked you before, Kate?'

'No you haven't. What's the big rush in this case?'

'Nicholson might die, I'd like to be able to tell him that we know who he is. I don't want him to think he's got off scot-free.'

'This one time!' she said. 'Don't tell anyone or I'll never do anyone a favour again.'

'Kate, you're a star!'

*

At noon we went to the building site on the outskirts of Comber and spoke to Justin's boss, who couldn't vouch for Justin. He said Justin wasn't working there on the day Chloe was killed. 'He doesn't work on Wednesdays, that's when he trains.'

'I thought he trains in the evenings and weekends,' I said.

His boss said, 'No, Justin never works Wednesdays.'

*

Since we were in that neck of the woods, we called in on Craig Heaney. Widower of Mary, or Molly.

'Why did they say "a couple was killed" and a boy?' Craig said, in a gruff Glasgow accent. 'It made them sound like, well, like a couple. My Molly was a married woman.'

'I'm sorry,' said Hewitt. 'That's the media for you. We would have said a man and a woman and they've made that assumption, and that headline.'

'Craig, can you come into the station and talk to us some more?' I asked.

'I can't. I have no one to mind my son.' The little boy was playing in the garden.

'When do you think you will be able to?'

'Tomorrow. My sister is flying over and I'll ask her to mind him.'

'No one available before then?' asked Hewitt. 'A neighbour?'

'No,' Craig said. 'Unless I can bring him with me.'

'We can't have him in the interview room,' said Hewitt. 'There are wires and coffees. It's purely health and safety, man.'

'It will have to be tomorrow, then,' said Craig.

'Maybe we can talk now,' I said, trying to be a bit more accommodating than Fleur. 'We just want to find out a little bit more about Molly.'

'We've had the police out already. They've already done all this.'

'Glasgow man,' said Hewitt.

'Aye,' he said.

'Best place in the world.'

'Really?' he asked. 'Funny how we both ended up here, then.'

'What brought you here?' she asked him.

'I'm a PhD candidate, out of Jordanstown, University of Ulster. It's a funded research place.'

'Oh, that's not bad,' said Hewitt. 'Do you work as well?'

'That is work, and the child. But yes, additionally – some evenings I work as a pizza delivery driver.'

'What about Molly? What did she do for work?'

'She worked from home, she was a market researcher. That way we used no childcare and revolved our work around home, around the wee guy.'

'Can you tell me about the morning leading up to the incident?' I asked Craig.

'Alright,' he said, either on autopilot from telling it so many times or he was emotionally disconnected. 'That morning she was out, so I was the childcare. I was at home, trying to study a little as Gregor played in the garden and I watched.'

'Gregor?' said Hewitt. 'Cute name. Does he ever get Greg for short?'

You'll bookmark that, Fleur, I thought, and bring it up to me later.

'No,' Craig said. 'The full moniker only. We called him after my dad, who died suddenly when Molly was expecting.'

'This is Molly?' I asked Craig. From the photos on the mantel I garnered that Molly had been bigger.

'Yeah. She'd recently got into fitness for her health,' he said, instinctively knowing what I was thinking, where was the double chin and the rounder face? 'To begin it was to get her out of the house. Working from home it's hard to motivate yourself, too. I had this idea she should get herself a personal trainer. I was happy she was exercising and feeling better, I never asked who the trainer was. I thought she'd stopped seeing one, she was gaining again.'

Asshole, I thought. Bereaved asshole, but still …

Chapter 38

I watched the video again of the attempted robbery in Mayhew's Pharmacy. How had I not seen that it was Brooks? He had the height, the gait. But my brother was soft, he would never have harmed Jennifer Crothers, the assistant, and she knew it. Jennifer had been able to take the machete from him so easily. He had let go as soon as she reached for it.

Maybe prison was the best place for him, to get clean. If only prison was clean, but I knew better.

I phoned the hospital for news on Justin when the doctor told me he had 'taken a turn for the worse'.

And when Hewitt and I got to the Ulster Hospital the doctor elaborated that he had been left almost brain dead.

We stood in the room with Justin and looked at his face as he lay in bed. So young it was sad to see; such a waste of a young life. I couldn't see past that. Then I snapped back to reality when Hewitt whispered, 'We should flick a switch and *put him out of his misery.*'

I remembered then everything he had put Lizzie and his victim in Liverpool through, these serial killer tendencies, and I felt a rage surge inside me. And justice. He got what he deserved.

*

Half an hour later we were outside his bungalow. Lizzie was at home. She was watching TV and muted it when we came in. *Love Island,* or one of those dating shows, was on. People in their twenties sat about wearing very little and making everything overdramatic.

'What's up?' she asked, still looking at the TV.

'We've just had a call from the hospital,' said Hewitt.

'And I'm glad to see you aren't there and are here, resting,' I added.

Lizzie snapped a glance at me. 'I'll go and see him later.'

She didn't mention the slip up made by the media, calling Molly and Justin a couple. I didn't want to ask about it either, in case I upset Lizzie.

'That might be an idea, but it's up to you. The doctor told us that the prognosis isn't good.'

'I expected that,' she said.

'He said that Justin has extremely limited brain activity.'

'That's nothing new,' Lizzie said, standing up to get her phone. She rested her other hand on a book that sat on the sideboard.

'We know he was hurting you, Lizzie, and you have a lot to process.'

'I keep getting texts,' Lizzie said, 'colleagues of mine from the residential sending their condolences.'

'That's nice,' I said. 'Get a good network around you now, this is when you need it.'

'Chloe would have been right here with me. My rock. I don't have a big circle of friends like when I was younger.'

'That's the way it goes, hen,' said Hewitt, 'but you have family, don't you? Some close friends? It would be nice to not be alone at this time, for you. I would feel better about it.'

Lizzie didn't reply, she looked at the muted TV screen.

'I saw that you left Chloe's funeral with Drew Taylor,' I said.

She rolled her eyes. 'He just gave me a lift, I already said. He didn't say anything, you know, that strong silent type.'

'I thought he said stuff about Justin?'

'That's *all* he said, something rude about Justin. I hardly want to dwell on that right now when my man might die.'

'I was just surprised,' I said, 'one minute you said you were scared of him, Lizzie, wouldn't like to be alone with him, next you're hopping into his car.'

'Not minutes apart.' She frowned at me. 'And I needed out of there, Jackie was upsetting me.'

'It *was* upsetting, but his daughter was being buried,' I said.

'Cremated!'

'You know what I mean.'

In the past, she had accused Jackie of not caring enough.

'Why are you speaking to me like this, Harriet? *"Hopping into his car!"* Plus, I didn't have my bike and Drew was half-crippled.'

I stared at her. Was I being too pushy?

'But I know what you're getting at,' Lizzie said. 'He can't be trusted and I was desperate.'

'Alright,' said Hewitt.

'You don't think it was Drew Taylor,' said Lizzie, breaking the awkward silence.

'Why do you say that?' Hewitt asked.

'He'd be lifted and charged by now if you did.'

'Lizzie, who do you think has done this to Justin and Molly Heaney, and young Ince Ross?' I asked.

'I thought it was Drew too, but now I think it seems random. Just three people travelling on the same road.'

But they weren't travelling, I thought, Molly Heaney's car was stationary by the side of the road, by a patch of overgrown land. But Lizzie wasn't to know these details.

'I don't know what kind of world we're living in where people think it is okay to just take another person's life,' she said. 'To take that choice, that right away from them.'

'I can see why you and Chloe would have been such good friends,' I told her. 'You have the same values.'

Lizzie smiled sadly.

'How did you meet again?' I meant, tell us again; but it occurred to me that I had not already asked her.

'In a centre,' Lizzie replied.

'What kind of centre?' asked Hewitt pointedly.

'I met her in outpatients at the hospital.'

'Did you work there?' I asked.

'I was an outpatient.'

'When was this?' asked Hewitt.

'June 2016.'

'What was happening with you? I suppose Justin was one thing,' I said. I knew that victims of domestic violence often went on to suffer with mental health issues.

Lizzie nodded. 'I was having problems with anxiety, like women from here have ... from The Troubles. Men and their depression; women and their anxiety. That's why I liked Justin, in the beginning. He seemed lighter than *our men*. I was attracted to that. He wasn't from here. And I'd been through more than most: I'd lost my kids, and then life with Justin got hard, because I read him wrong. I read people wrong all the time.'

I remembered Lizzie saying she taught psychology. But hadn't she also said she hated the job?

'Don't put yourself down, hen,' said Hewitt.

'Men,' said Lizzie. 'They're all as bad, really, they don't need an excuse. They always find one.'

'And Chloe?' I asked her.

'When I met Chloe she was really depressed, and anxious, because someone had been sending her messages online. It got to her. Besides, her mum has mental health problems.'

'That's right,' I said. 'Glynis has bipolar disorder,' I told Hewitt.

'Who said?' asked Lizzie.

'Chloe's mother herself.'

'You spoke to her?' Lizzie looked irritated. I'd seen her possessiveness toward Chloe.

'Yes, of course I did,' I said.

Lizzie shook her head. 'I believe that kind of thing is hereditary and we have no control over it. I come from a similar background that way, so we gelled. Did you ever talk to Dr. Walsh like I recommended?'

'I can't really say.'

'No, it's okay, you can tell me. You know, it was through him Chloe and I met.'

'Oh.'

'Didn't you mention me to him?' she asked.

'Lizzie,' I said, 'I'm sorry, but again I can't talk to you about the specifics of any case.'

'Harriet! I even showed you the photo,' she said it exactly how my twin sister speaks to me.

'Yes, you did,' I said.

'So ...'

'Nothing was going on,' I told Lizzie. 'It was innocent and like I said, I can't talk anymore about it.'

'Didn't you look at the comments on Facebook?'

I looked at her, that self-satisfied face I'd seen a few times, no concern or further mention of Justin, her 'babe'. 'Go on, tell me what I missed,' I said.

'I commented on it, "What a great looking pair you two make". So that's why I wondered if Martin mentioned me.'

'Well, he didn't mention you at all,' said Hewitt, detecting a tone too.

'Okay,' I interjected. 'Do you feel okay about Justin? Maybe you shouldn't be alone right now.'

'Nor you. Nor anyone,' Lizzie replied earnestly. 'There is someone – some paramilitary – running around shooting at men, women and *children*. None of us are safe.'

'We'll keep a patrol car in the area so you feel safer, okay.'

'Thank you. It's not necessary. And I'm sorry. I'm just not myself today. I've been really rude to you.'

'You don't need to apologise,' said Hewitt, 'you've been through a lot in the last week and a half.'

'And the rest,' said Lizzie.

'I have been meaning to ask you,' I said. 'Did you hear from Chloe when she went away for a few months?'

'Her gap half-year?'

'Yes, August '16 – March '17.'

'No.'

'Do you know where she went?'

'I've been sworn to secrecy, sorry.'

'We know she went to Pakistan,' said Hewitt.

'Oh right. There you have it.'

'Did you not think that her family deserved to know the truth and that Chloe may be in danger out there?'

'I wasn't in touch with her then,' said Lizzie, 'she came back and we bumped into each other one day in the street and I thought she'd been in hospital. I'd ask Martin and he would say nothing, say he couldn't. He was annoying like that. He's a bit like you lot, in that respect. I mean, can't always tell you things. I'm not calling you annoying.'

'Oh, we can certainly be annoying, can't we, DI Sloane?' said Hewitt.

'Chloe told me where she'd been,' said Lizzie, ignoring Hewitt. 'We went for a drink and she told me everything. She was a wreck, that's why I took her under my wing.'

'What an interesting experience she must have had.'

'You should go and read about it.' Lizzie laughed.

'Where might I do that?'

'On her blog.'

'It's online?'

'That's generally where blogs are.'

'What is it called?'

'A Modest Traveller.'

'Thanks, Lizzie. You've been very instructive, as usual.'

'You're very welcome.' She smiled. 'Sorry again, for being rude earlier, Harriet.'

'Not to worry,' I said with a smile.

Chapter 39

Late in the afternoon there was a missed call from Father. I ignored it. See how he liked it.

'Shit,' said Hewitt, 'Did I tell you, she would have a diary, or what! And here it is, the most public kind of diary you could have. It's fascinating, Harriet, you should really have a wee read.'

I looked over her shoulder. There was a post all about her experiences that day finding a girl who was in danger of FGM and taking her to a safe location. Below it the comments section was full, people telling her she was amazing, a *shero* doing a great job. A whole online community of admirers.

'The trolls didn't find her there,' I said happily.

*

Later that afternoon, Craig Heaney asked us to call out with him.

'I found this, just now,' said Craig Heaney, he was feeding Gregor spaghetti hoops at the table. 'I was going through Molly's things and at the bottom of her drawer there was this: a basic pay-as-you-go phone.'

'Who does it belong to?'

'Molly. You can look at it. It's proof.'

'Of what?' I asked.

'That I didn't know she was having an affair, until now,' he said.

'How is it proof?'

'Because, earlier, and yesterday, everyone seemed to know, to insinuate that they were sleeping together.'

'I never insinuated that,' said Hewitt.

'No, you did. Maybe you didn't mean to, but you did.'

'I don't think so.'

'So did the officer who called yesterday,' said Craig. 'The media got that Molly and Justin were a couple from you.'

'I assure you they didn't,' I said.

'But now you know differently?' asked Hewitt.

'Molly has had this whole hidden life. Email account, private messages, calls, all so she could talk to him.'

Craig showed a photo, a selfie of them. Molly and Justin, him behind with his arms around her. 'The rest are ... pornographic.'

'I'm sorry,' I said.

'I didn't buy that this was a random act, the local police kept saying *revenge*. But I didn't swallow that, you know ... revenge for what? Who is this cunt my wife let herself get mixed up with?'

'I'd like to take the phone, please.'

'You're welcome to it. I certainly don't want to be able to see it.'

*

That evening we looked through the phone. Chief Dunne said, 'Still on the Chloe Taylor case?'

'Yes, sir,' Hewitt said, 'one of our possible suspects is critically ill. They're going to pull the plug very soon.'

'But what you're investigating is not in our district,' Dunne said. He stood with his hands behind his back, bent his knees as if to ease pain. 'Pass the parcel back to Dundonald and get back to what you are supposed to be doing.'

'Yes, Chief,' I said.

Fleur Hewitt waited until he left and she opened the phone again.

'He's … a lovely fucken guy, isn't he?' she said and apart from her colourful language I would have thought she meant it. Regardless, I felt the need to give a careful reply.

'He's alright,' I said. 'You get on with him well, I see.'

'Do I?' She laughed.

'He likes you.'

'He's in a tough position,' she said, 'with me and him.' She shrugged.

'What?' I asked. This was it, I thought, she'll confide that they're fucking.

'He can't show favouritism, or look like he's singling me out by being harder on me.'

'Why not?'

'Because he's my uncle, isn't he? My mum is Jocelyn's sister. Didn't you know?'

'No, I did not,' I said.

'I'm sure when I first got the post, they were all calling it nepotism.'

'No one told me.'

'Maybe you should get friendlier to your colleagues, hen. You get all the goss that way.'

Now it made sense. They looked alike, her and Jocelyn. I'd picked up on it the moment I saw Hewitt. Then came the relief that they could not be fucking, that here was an attractive woman, mid-thirties. What Greg Dunne had always gone for, according to my ex-partner Diane Linskey. And yet he hadn't. Or couldn't. In this case.

I expected that Greg would move on to the next one, but maybe he hadn't, maybe he was alone. Or as alone as you can be when you are in a long-lived marriage.

Why had the Dunnes sold the villa in Portugal? Did it mean they were splitting up? It bugged me that I still cared. But I had two reminders of Greg in the nursery across the road. It was impossible to forget what I'd had with Greg completely.

Scrolling through the phone we saw that Molly Heaney and Justin were seeing each other since January. We saw their texts, the photos, the erotic ones, the sweet ones. This was one complicated affair.

Lonely, attention-starved woman, suddenly feeling good about herself, takes up with good-looking sexually-incontinent personal trainer, I thought.

Seems it began when they were out running. And there was this empty house, a bungalow, and they would go around the back and have sex. From the photos you could see it was covered with weeds. It became a thing. Cheaper than a hotel. Free.

In more recent messages were real estate ads for the same house. A derelict house. Going by the address, it was right outside that they were shot. The *love shack*, they call it via text. He named it, My Blue Heaven. She talked about cutting back the forest and he talked about painting the whole house blue. She said she was happy to do the door and the window sills, *but the rest of the house, nope!* Then there was talk about what they would do with the rooms. How they would decorate. They had even been talking about leaving their partners; Molly said Craig would forgive her in time; Justin said Lizzie would cut his balls off.

More recently, Justin texted Molly to say:
and after the appointment on Wednesday I've made another one for 11.30 with Moore's in Ballyhack.

That appointment was for the day Chloe died. Around the same time someone inflicted those three stab wounds on her.

'This can't be right,' I said. 'We need to know if he kept that appointment at Moore's.'

'You can. Look, I have some things I need to catch up on,' said Fleur.

'Now?' I said.

'Yes, it doesn't take the both of us. Or do you need me to hold your hand?' She put her hand out and I swatted it away.

Chapter 40

The only Moore's in Ballyhackamore was the estate agents. When I got there it was closed, shutter down, so I phoned Strandtown to get the owner's contact details. Then I called Dom Moore pretending we'd had complaints about his security alarm going off.

It's an old trick. Tends to get a quicker response.

'Your alarm has stopped,' I said when he arrived, 'but do you mind if we go inside and have a word?'

Eyeing the alarm Dom opened up the shutter to expose a blue tiled façade and large windows perfect for property brochures. 'The alarm was definitely going off?' he asked.

'It was. But I'm here to speak with you about something else, so don't worry about the alarm.'

Dom went behind his curved MDF desk and large black monitors. He sat on a leather swivelling chair. 'Well, I'm glad it's stopped,' he said. 'It's my experiment to live life with no technological knowledge whatsoever.' He gestured for me to take a seat at the other side of the desk on one of the non-swivelling thin black seats. 'I'm all ears.'

'The old house you have for sale on the Comber Road,' I said.

'Yes.'

'Your thoughts on it.'

'Honestly?' he asked.

'Please.'

'It's a dive. Little bungalow. Overgrown with trees, can't even see it from the road anymore. I've had a hard time shifting it. £73,000 for three beds, two receptions en suite, etc. Here's the brochure.'

Dom wheeled his way to a wall display and lifted a brochure. He wheeled his way back and pushed it across the desk toward me. The love shack.

Woodchip, net curtains or garishly patterned ones, seventies style. The carpets were just as bad.

'Mature shrubbery, we said.'

'Enclosed rear garden,' I said thinking, sex en plein air.

'And now it's been the scene of a crime; thank god it's already sold.'

'It's sold? When did that happen?'

'Just this week. Is there a problem?'

'Who bought it?' I asked.

'This loved-up young pair, in their early thirties,' said Dom. 'I can get their names, if you need them.'

'Please do.'

He rattled around and found a big red lined book.

'Mary Heaney and Justin Nicholson.'

'Mr. Moore,' I said, 'they are the people who were shot outside the house. Along with that little boy, Ince Ross.'

'Wow, what are the odds. Heard the names, but I didn't register.'

'Mary Heaney was a married woman. Nicholson was in a long-term relationship. Perhaps they were having a look at it when the incident happened.'

'So the sale *has* fallen through, technically,' Dom Moore said.

I was shocked at his callousness.

'Mr. Moore, I'm investigating another homicide, the murder of a young woman by the name of Chloe Taylor.'

'She was stabbed in the PACT office, Upper Newtownards Road, yes?'

'That's right.'

'This place has gone fucken mad, we have a couple of units for sale there too, that's bad for business.'

'And at the time of Ms. Taylor's death you would have had an appointment to see Ms. Heaney and Mr. Nicholson. Mr. Moore, we have their phone records and can see they were planning to come here that morning Chloe was killed.'

'Ah, they must be connected. You must think they are. Some gangland thing?'

'We aren't sure yet,' I said. 'But we're getting closer.'

'Good. Yes, they *were* here but remind me of the date.'

'Wednesday 18th.'

He leafed through a diary. 'Eleven-thirty a.m., they were here, together. I said it needs a lot of work and they brushed me off, all over each other, they were.'

'And so, they put an offer in?'

'Sure did. Then he put down the deposit two days ago.'

'How much was the deposit?'

'Forty grand, in cash.'

I almost stopped breathing. The exact amount of money I had lost from the back of the service car.

'He was so eager,' said Dom Moore, 'standing there waiting for us to open up on Wednesday with all his cash. Now it turns out they were doing one from their partners. Changes things, doesn't it?'

'Changes everything,' I said, absolutely seething.

Chapter 41

By seven I'd clocked off. I took a spin to Lizzie's to update her. Her earlier attitude had been ripping my knitting all day. I wanted to let her know that Justin had been sleeping with Molly Heaney.

Perhaps they had already stolen my money out of the back seat of the service car by the time we saw them out running the evening we called with Rebecca. Maybe they were rubbing my nose in it by passing through again, and chatting like they had nothing to hide.

I looked forward to news of his death.

'I have some bad news,' I said when Lizzie opened the door. 'Some more bad news.'

She turned the TV off and turned on her CD player instead. She looked like she was in for the night. A glass of white wine sat on a little round table beside her seat, and a bottle of chardonnay, more than halfway done.

'Please sit down, Lizzie.'

'Oh God,' she said, 'this doesn't sound good. Is he dead?'

She sat down and I sat in a seat facing hers.

'No. Not that I've heard. Justin, it turns out,' I said, 'was having a relationship with the woman he was in the car with; Mary Heaney.'

'No, he wasn't,' said Lizzie, she lifted a remote control from the coffee table and raised the volume on her CDs.

Michael Bublé played. I found myself gritting my teeth.

'She was not his type. He only likes blondes.'

'They've been having a relationship since the start of the year.'

'Oh yeah,' said Lizzie.

She was looking toward the window and into the distance as if someone was coming but no one was when I followed her gaze.

'I can picture her now; *Molly*,' Lizzie said. 'She has that big forehead, right? Maybe they'll cut a fringe for her to cover up that hole in her head for an open casket. Sorry … did you say you wanted a drink, or not? You hardly want a glass of vino, do you?'

'No.'

'Coffee?' She smacked her lips.

'No, thank you,' I said. I supposed she had a right to be angry. I've never rated fidelity myself.

Lizzie stood. She looked at the book at the sideboard long enough to draw my attention to it, the same as she had done the last time. She might as well have said, 'Here, come and look in here,' and then she was gone into the kitchen for long enough for me to walk over to it, facing the door. I was listening to the kettle starting and cupboards opening, and her cutlery drawer blowing a raspberry as she pushed it shut.

I lifted the book and saw it was not a book at all but a holder of some sort, a box. Inside were photos of Lizzie in her underwear.

I knew she was playing with me. So I played with her in return. Took the photos out and quietly closed the 'book' and returned it to its spot. I put the photos on the sideboard and splayed them out, but not fully. There were eleven in total, but I hadn't had the chance to count them all yet.

I lifted them, one at a time:

In the first one Lizzie was wearing a gold thong and had her hair pulled over her shoulder.

The second one she was wearing huge beige pants.

In the third she had on pink pants.

In the fourth Lizzie wore grey 'boy' shorts and a long dark wig. Long dark hair like the woman who looked after Kayley Molineux at Rocky Place?

These were Kayley's grey underwear. They were token panties. I skipped back to look at the photo before; those pink pants that were probably Maisie's.

The two before, I had no idea.

I looked again at the door. I could hear Lizzie pouring our drinks.

The fifth photo was of her again, this time she had on a blue pair. No takers for those.

The sixth: white pants with a gold heart on the front. Victoria Black's!

Every photo was modelled by Lizzie herself, she had the exact same pose in each, bare up top and holding her breasts with one arm, with the other hand her thumbnail rested between her front two teeth as she smiled coyly. It seemed like the most unnatural pose I had ever seen in my life, she had been programmed to do it from watching rom-coms and skimming old copies of FHM. You know, dressed as a milk maid sucking on a rib of straw, dumbing herself down for her 'babe'. The psycho.

I could hear Lizzie returning but I would not hide the photos when she'd meant for me to find them. She came in with two drinks regardless of me saying I didn't want one.

'Oh,' she said reaching a cup toward me.

'You poor, poor thing,' I said coldly and slowly, trying to muster every drop of sympathy in me and not in me. 'I can't believe he did this to you.' I saw the change, confusion in her eyes. 'Justin,' I said.

She sipped her coffee.

'You won't know about this, Lizzie,' I said, 'but these pants are tokens from crimes. There has been this man drugging women and removing their underwear. It's Justin.

He has brought them home to you, got you to wear them. Sick bastard.' My face registered surprise I did not feel. 'Lizzie, you weren't to know, but Justin was a bad person. In England he *tortured* this young girl.'

'You look like you need a drink,' she said without emotion.

'Yes,' I said, 'in a minute.'

It was still whirling with froth where she'd stirred something into the drink. Then I knew: the coffees! The perpetrator of Chloe Taylor's murder had done this, brought the coffees with them to the PACT office with something in one. They had not bought them in Wee Buns after all. And Chloe Taylor had not touched hers. We found lukewarm cups. So, there had been violence. She had been stabbed in the back and now, I could not turn mine on this other psychopath before me.

'These pants.' I set the cup down and turned a photo to show her. 'They belong to a girl who was found on Dee Street, no one believed she hadn't just drunk too much. I mean, she wasn't physically assaulted.'

'What about Erica?' Lizzie asked.

'Erica who?' I asked. I wanted to let her give it all to me.

'Erica McClelland,' Lizzie said. 'The girl found dead in Ballyholme.'

'What about Erica?'

'Where were her knickers?' Lizzie sipped her coffee.

I shook my head. 'Completely unrelated. That person is still out there. God knows. None of us can be careful enough.'

'What about the next photo?' she asked me.

'I've said enough. I'll have to take these … you don't mind. I know they are revealing, they'll just be used for evidence. No one else will see them.'

'Oh, show them to whoever you have to show them to.'

You'd like that, wouldn't you, Lizzie? I thought.

'But I have to say,' I said, 'sadly, Craig Heaney, Molly's husband, widower – Justin's *mistress's* husband – he showed me a secret phone his wife had hidden in her possession. It was full of photos like these.'

A lie; actually, there were body parts, orifices and appendages. Connections that were biological looking. They were pornographic in nature, just like Craig said, not 'glamour' shots like these ones of Lizzie.

Then I thought, maybe I should be telling Lizzie this instead. Let's see her angry, let's see her real side for once. But I had a better idea.

'I have to say, Lizzie, the texts were very lovey-dovey. Justin was planning to leave you.'

Then I saw her face drop. 'Bullshit.'

'They were planning to move away.'

'Where?' She looked at me with snarky disbelief.

'Five minutes away.' That had to smart.

'Where?'

'Comber Road. You know the house where they were shot outside of?'

Lizzie laughed but I knew then that she had not known.

'The *love shack*,' I said for good measure. 'They called it that in their texts. It didn't look like much of a home, yet.'

'They were shot outside waste land,' said Lizzie.

'No,' I took great pleasure in saying, 'there is a lot of shrubbery but behind it is a house, a little bungalow, it needs a lot of work doing to it, and they were going to fix it up together. Paint it blue.'

'No!' she shouted. I gripped the photos tighter and looked at them, which seemed to remind her that they existed.

'They're not *revealing*' she said. 'I think, they're tasteful.' She took them from me. Looked at them in turn, handed them to me one at a time, same pose, sometimes with a brunette wig, sometimes with a red one, but similar clothing, and more underwear. Ones at the start that I didn't recognise, that were maybe never reported missing.

My stomach dropped to think of all the girls they had drugged, ones who maybe doubted anything had happened. Or blamed themselves.

'And what about those girls, were they abused by Justin?' I asked her. 'Who did the beige pants belong to? Or the thong?'

Lizzie relaxed. She looked at me and then glanced at herself in the mirror on the wall. She wanted to be seen. All this time, these questions, these vague implications, she wanted to be seen. She said that Justin was bad to her, but what I'd seen was all I'd been shown, but what was real was what I had learned.

She was as bad as him. Or worse.

'Justin and Molly put down a deposit for their love shack, but where did they get the money?' I asked.

'What money?'

'Forty grand.'

Lizzie ran up the stairs and I followed her, putting the photos in my pocket. She pulled a box out from behind her bed, there were children's toys in it, rattles, dummies, a camcorder tape, no wads of cash like she was looking for.

'It was mine,' she snapped. 'I had savings and he stole them, didn't he?'

'Where did you get it?' I asked.

She sat on the floor for a moment in shock. Now I believed Lizzie took that cash from the service car. I suddenly remembered how she had gone outside to get the newspaper and had spent some time out there.

'Our delivery boy is a man, and he drives a car. You couldn't make it up!'

But had she? All I heard was another engine and a male voice. It could have been Justin. They could have been working together, opportunistically.

'I was given money from my son's grandparents to stay away,' she said, 'isn't that nice of them!'

'Forty thousand pounds?' I asked her.

Lizzie got up and ran downstairs and I followed her, trying to keep up but not trying to let her know I was. If there was one thing I learned about Lizzie, was that you had to act relaxed and dumb yourself down at every turn while in her presence. I resented it. It reminded me of January 2015.

I was a hostage again.

Lizzie threw herself on the sofa and ran her hands through her hair. She was quiet for a while, then she looked at me and exhaled slowly.

'Even though I've been through so much,' she said, 'there's only one person I feel sorry for. Do you know who that is?'

I shook my head.

'Jackie, lovely Jackie.' She gathered her hair into a ponytail and fastening it with a band she had on her wrist. 'Chloe had a good dad. Must be nice to have a good dad. My dad was a cop too, like yours. I mean, everyone knows your dad.'

My heartbeat thumped again.

'He was always a hit at the nursing home. He liked me.'

'Really?' I said flatly.

'I've worked in them all, Harry. Can I call you Harry, like he does?'

'It's a hard job to work in a nursing home,' I said discretely bringing my thumb to my pager.

'Oh, that's a tangible thought for a selfish person,' she said. 'For someone who was given everything. But I like caring for people. Entertaining them.'

'Some are good at it,' I said.

'I cared for Chloe. She found me entertaining. We laughed and we cried. We both needed that. And I miss it.'

I couldn't act false any longer, my face dropped and Lizzie noticed.

'This is what happens, isn't it?' she asked. 'One person dies and it's oh so important, then it's really not. There's someone else. Then people remember that we're all going to die, sooner or later, so they think about themselves again.'

'We can talk about Chloe,' I said. 'We don't have to talk about Justin if it upsets you. We can talk about you. Just you.'

'I was about to tell you how I had to be good at caring, but there you were interrupting me again,' she said. 'You're always doing that.'

'I'm sorry, Lizzie,' I said surprising myself by how weak I sounded. 'Go on,' I said. Scenes of my kidnapping screeched through my head, I wanted to curl up and cry, but I couldn't. I would have to wait for that, but I sensed I would not leave this house in any normal manner. I knew I wouldn't.

Lizzie laughed. 'I was saying that I was good at caring. Especially when my dad was sick. He wasn't sick like your mum is. It was different, his type of sickness. Not everybody can stomach it. My mum couldn't. She'd have had enough of it, she'd be in the bedrooms packing our stuff then he'd appear in the doorway, gun at his head.' She held her finger to her head and bit her lower lip in anger. 'He'd be saying he'd shoot himself if she tried to leave.'

Her eyes looked dead, then just as suddenly Lizzie lightened and asked, 'This is okay, isn't it? I mean, there's nothing I hate more than self-protecting small talk. *Look at the weather. Blah blah.* I don't want to protect myself anymore, and you even said I should talk about me, Harry.'

'And I want to hear it, Lizzie,' I said.

She played with the fringe on a cushion by her side.

'I was about to tell you about this one night, I was asleep, they were fighting, as usual. Always fighting. He said, "No one's leaving." I could hear him. Then Mum was begging him, don't. "Not her," she said. Me, she meant me. I was little.'

'That's so tough,' I said.

'You know I was in my twenties before I let that memory come all the way back? But that night I opened my eyes and he was aiming a gun at me. 9mm Beretta.' Lizzie stroked the cushion beside her again and looked far away. 'When my second son was taken off me and given to his father, Dad stopped talking to me. What did he want me to do? I went to see him to talk it through. I, at least, didn't want to lose my parents too. But he lifted his hand to me. He smacked me in the face.' Lizzie went silent. 'I loved that poisonous nut-job. When I was little and stupid. You love who you think you should, who they tell you to. One minute my mum was, "Grab your stuff and get away from him," next minute she was like, "You've made your dad feel bad, he can't help it, give him a hug and tell him you love him." But no one has hurt me like he has, Harriet. Not even Justin, or my kids' dads, or the fucken courts. No one will ever hurt me like that again, I'm being for real.'

'And your mum,' I said, 'what did she say about him hitting you, or about the kids?'

'Nothing. I don't care. I hate her more than I hate him. She should have let him blow his rabid brains out. The only time he ever took me under his notice I had a gun in my hand. Dad was impressed with me. Better than the police officers he was training, he said. "You've a good steady hand. Don't know why I didn't get you to do this before," he said, "maybe because you're a girl. But you're good." Suddenly ... he could *see* me.'

She looked at my pocket where the photos were poking out, and she slumped down on the sofa more.

'I'm sorry, Lizzie. We all have our cross to bear,' I said.

Her story brought back the taste of gun metal from Jason's breakdown. I ran my tongue over my chipped tooth, it was not perfectly smooth. I could still feel it after every meal. The reminder of when my life flew apart; my own kidnap and rape at the hands of my nut-job ex-husband. For a second I saw me in Lizzie, me always trying to impress my father. But I had my own family now. Lizzie had nothing and no one, just this capsized life.

'So you haven't seen your father in a long time then?'

'Yeah, years, until Thursday. Drew drove me there.'

'Where?'

'Bangor. A nice little cul-de-sac of bungalows, it's why I like here, it's kind of like their place. He still didn't want to know me, though. Didn't care that I'd just said my final goodbye to my best friend, or that I'd just found out that my man was keeping big important secrets from me.'

When she stopped talking I took the photos and flipped them over. The last photo was a smudge of black. I looked closer, there it was, Lizzie wearing a pair of high heels, bare legs, her bare ass skimmed by a black coat, the sheen of a tiger's sequinned face on it, red belt and cuffs. Chloe's coat.

The one she went out wearing the day she died.

Now I could no longer act trusting. If she had the coat it only meant one thing.

We had never got an alibi for her. Had underestimated her, her power, her pure evilness.

'Lizzie,' I said, 'I'm arresting you for the …'

She grabbed a gun from under a cushion and shot me through the shoulder. It didn't hurt, it was more a shock, a force. Pure heat. I fell on the ground and she got on top of me.

'Finally have the guts to attack someone from the front,' I said, wrestling with her. 'Coward.'

She spat in my face. Went to stand over me when I tripped her up and she crashed onto the floor, the whole time she tried to get that gun to my forehead. After a tussle I got the better of her and cuffed her. Took the gun.

I straddled her back and imagined putting a bullet through her brain. I grabbed a fistful of her stupid hair that I realised was extensions, they came off in my hand. I had no energy to crash her head into the parquet floor.

'Hands above your head, hands above your head,' I growled at her. I pressed the gun into the back of her head and called for backup. 'It was my money. My money, you fucken crazy bitch.'

But it wasn't really. It was money for my children from their own no-good father.

Chapter 42

On Saturday afternoon I was staring out of my hospital window when Hewitt came to visit.

'I can't believe LDM did that,' she said.

'Still think she's good looking?' I asked her wincing.

'Oh hell no. Hotter!'

'I'm leaving here,' I said.

'You are not, you probably need a few days' rest.'

'I can do that at home,' I said.

'Stay here. We have her now. The Sloane girl did good.'

'I've taken a bullet, so now you think I've earned my dues.'

'I'll say *yes*,' said Fleur Hewitt, smiling. 'Do you know that Justin died last night?'

'He did?'

'He was always going to.'

'Aren't we all?' I said. 'It's still a bit of a shock. Have you told Lizzie?'

'Oh no. She'd love that, wouldn't she? I'm letting her sit it out.'

'You haven't interviewed her yet?'

'I want to speak to you first. I found out a few things once you gave me the name of her father last night.'

'I can't even remember last night,' I said. 'But Kinahan, from what I remember from before, was a bit of a psycho, too. I suppose you've got to look at the apple then look at the tree it fell from.'

'Shit doesn't fall far from the asshole, hen,' said Hewitt. 'You were a bit out of it on pain killers after they removed the bullet, Harriet.'

'Tell me,' I said, 'tell me what Pat Kinahan said.'

'Lizzie, or Elizabeth, as he called her, has had both her children taken off her. Two boys. They live with their fathers.'

'Yes.' It came back to me. 'They paid her off to stay away.'

'Oh, they did alright, one of them, a granny of one of the boys. But it's not the half of what I found out about her. Do you know Lizzie attracts very strange relationships? And she has a history of stalking her two most serious exes, and of faking pregnancies. She even stalked her exes' subsequent partners, and their family members. They'd complained to the police but claim they weren't taken seriously.'

'Who are the fathers of her children?' I asked.

'One was an ex, the other a one night stand: that guy maintains that they used a condom but suspects she must have fished it out of the bin after he left. Basting job.'

'Unbelievable!'

'They did a DNA test and the boy was his,' said Hewitt. 'Lizzie acted like they had been having a relationship and wanted to move in with him. In the end, she was at a low ebb and suddenly no mention of her again, then his mum admitted paying her £1,400 to get out of their lives.'

'Is that all a child is worth?' What were mine worth, twenty grand apiece?

'Totally!' said Hewitt. 'Her relationship with her first babydaddy, Stuart, was all about drink and drugs and messing with each other's heads, and with Justin it was exactly the same. Justin would fight men who he thought fancied her.'

'Doesn't surprise me at all, Fleur.'

'When Lizzie and Justin would have sex, knives got involved.'

'We know that.'

'But, listen. That was his kink, if it is a *kink*. Those scars on Lizzie, when I described them to the doctor, said they sounded more consistent with liposuction.'

'Oh my god,' I said.

'Lizzie stabbed Justin, but I reckon it was at his insistence. He had the history of knives. Plus, I saw his dead torso, and it was like a fucken colander.'

'Jesus!'

'They were a headache for police in Coleraine, as you know, then they moved to Belfast, where they had an isolated life. No real friends. Except, for Lizzie, Chloe. But she got covetous, probably, like she had with past relationships. She probably thought that Chloe fancied her boy. I know she smoked a bit of blow but Chloe was straight-laced anyway. I can't see her being part of their games.'

'Definitely not,' I said. 'Chloe was just a trusting soul who trusted the wrong people sometimes.'

'Lizzie had a history of being a bunny boiler long before Justin; he had a history of being abusive and sexually strange, and together …'

'They were a lethal combo. And her past didn't help,' I said. 'Her dad liked to wave his gun around.'

'He who holds a gun talks the loudest.'

'Or, she,' I said. 'Becoming the violent antihero was appealing to Lizzie.'

'And yet, she has a lot going for her,' said Hewitt. 'Sorry, I know she just shot you, Harriet, but still … It seems a bit pointless, the whole thing.'

'So, she shot Justin too?'

'Revenge kill.'

'And his companion, Molly?'

'Jealousy.'

'So she knew about the affair back then?'

'Oh, she'd have tailed him. She clocked his mileage and hacked his Facebook messages.'

'Chloe probably didn't sign Facebook custody over to Lizzie at all.'

'You could be right. We'll check. Maybe. But Justin was always having to report in, take photos of his clients and send them to Lizzie for approval.'

'The before photos!' I said. 'But she definitely did not know about the love shack.'

'No?'

'Definitely not.'

'And the twelve-year-old kid, what?' asked Hewitt. 'Collateral damage.'

'An attempt to make the whole thing look random. Silencing a witness, too.'

'And the gender gap in violence, it closes.'

'She's not the first,' I said. 'But how?'

'On her bike.'

'Really?'

'Nifty, for getting in and out of spots. Plus, it had that little basket, so it looked all sweet and Mary Poppins. And,' said Hewitt, 'a neighbour said they saw a woman on a bike after the shooting, pedalling along, old-fashioned bike at that. Basket in the front ... handy place to hide a gun ...'

'Psycho!'

'Totally! I went to South Eastern Regional College in Bangor, never got the chance to tell you.'

'What did they say? More lies?' I could not picture her having taught there.

'No. She actually wasn't lying,' said Hewitt. 'They had no records of a Lizzie Donegan-Moat working there, but they did have a Beth ... Elizabeth, Lizzie, Beth ... who worked there for a year, she was just out of college herself and about twenty-three or so.'

'Beth Kinahan by any chance?'

'Yep.'

'Where did Donegan-Moat come from?'

'The babydaddies' names, she officially changed her name to theirs: with Stuart Donegan, she had a son called Freddie, he's now eight. With Jamie Moat, she had Benji. Now four.'

'Wow.'

'But get this, Harriet, Lizzie parties with the dudes at the SERC. Every student night she's in the bars. This one dude, she fails him from the course at the end of the year. He goes to the director of the college saying she only did it because he rebuffed her sexual advances. She claimed he never handed in coursework, but the admin was doctored. Lizzie blamed the boy, said that he had the hots for her and she wouldn't go there, but other students said Lizzie was overly-friendly with them, the girls too. She tried to be best friends with them. This one guy, she was always touching him in class. The director didn't know who to believe, but I think we can safely say she was at her work.'

'She was fired?'

'They suspended her. Soon she met a new man, got pregnant, focused all her energy on pinning him down.'

'Nothing surprises me anymore.'

'Nor should it. But that's low down the list of important things now. Just another thing to add, I suppose. Right,' said Hewitt.

'What now?'

'I'll go speak to her. You, in the meantime, rest.'

'Oh no, I'm leaving right now.'

'Leaving to go home, though, hen?'

'Of course, Fleur.'

'Yeah right, I've met your sort before.' Hewitt winked at me.

'Are the results out?' I said.

'What results?'

'The Repeal, from south of the border.'

'They got it,' she said.

'Really?'

'Yeah, the right to safe legal terminations. Who'd have thought Ireland would get it before the North?'

'Not me,' I said.

'It's easier for people here though. I've been with girls who have been given a D&C in the early stages by doctors who know what they're doing and bless them – they're good guys. And there's always travel money.'

'It's still not good enough.'

'I don't disagree. Not that I've had an abortion, I just know it's not fucken black and white.'

'I've had one,' I said, 'I had to do it and don't regret it. I was in a toxic situation, worse than toxic.'

'Even if you weren't, Harriet, it's your body. What a year! And the Belfast Rape trial … Any fucken wonder those other drugged girls didn't report anything.'

*

Paul called in with the twins. I liked seeing him in his professional manner, even though he wasn't working and was just there to say hello, let me see the boys and probably to show the rest of the staff that he had nothing to hide with this audit.

He said he would bring the boys to his mum's for the afternoon. Then I got a call from Kate Stile. 'I have some news,' she said, 'are you sitting down?'

So I got up, and signed myself out of hospital.

Chapter 43

Never leave hospital on a Saturday or you'll end up going back in, Granny Sloane used to say. I ignored that warning and turned on the car radio looking for confirmation of the Irish abortion referendum result. It wasn't time for the news yet. I flicked through stations until I heard Michael Bublé.

Quickly I turned the radio off.

I drove one-handed to Ballyhackamore, walked into the estate agents with my arm in a sling.

'Heard on the radio Justin Nicholson has died,' Dom Moore said.

Repealing the 8th amendment means nothing to you, I thought.

'I wouldn't bother with the Sold sign,' I said. 'And, obviously, the deposit needs returned.'

'Oh, I,' Dom became flustered. 'But who to?'

'Mr. Moore,' I told him sweetly, 'that money was stolen out of a woman's car. So we can play the long game of you going to court and testifying ...'

'I don't have the time for all that.'

'Or, I'll return the money to Justin's victim for you,' I said, 'she won't press charges against you if she gets the money back. You really should have alerted the PSNI with that amount of cash coming in.'

'But I don't have it. It was lodged that same day.'

'You can get it.'

'I can't take that sort of money back out of the bank in one hit.'

'The woman has already told me she would be fine with getting her money back in smaller payments. She's sympathetic to you, too.'

He nodded. 'Alright. We'll do it like that. Weekly instalments?'

'She's elderly,' I said, 'and has mobility issues. I'll call and collect it on her behalf.'

'Scumbag.'

'Sorry?'

'To steal a disabled and elderly person's cash. He deserved that bullet in the head.'

I nodded as neutrally as I could.

*

Carl Higgins was standing in the office when I returned to Strandtown. 'Miss me?' he asked.

'What are you doing here?' I asked.

'I'm off suspension. It was just a misunderstanding. Can't a few officers make the same mistakes without a conspiracy?'

'I'd have thought so. Happens often enough.'

'I hear you were shot,' he said.

I smiled at him.

'And still, you look so pretty.'

'Stop that.'

'No repeat performance of Christmas then?'

'God, no. I didn't appreciate what a good man I have then ... not that I need to explain myself to you.'

'I'm just joking. I'm seeing someone too. I just like to see you squirm.'

'Good, because that could be construed as sexual harassment.'

'What! It was you who kissed me, Harry.'

'Oh, shut up, Carl. We were off the clock,' I said. 'And you copped a feel, don't deny it.'

Higgins laughed.

'Where's Fleur anyway?' I asked.

'Our Flower of Scotland is interviewing Lizzie Moat-Donegan. I suppose you're back with me now.'

'Donegan-Moat! Can this day get any worse?'

'Ah, don't be like that.' Higgins gave me a hug and I almost cried with the pain. 'I'm not copping a feel, okay,' he said, 'I'm just happy to be back. Platonically.'

Chapter 44

I watched Lizzie being interrogated in next room and saw her face on the monitor, the luster of her scowl, the innocent bright-eyed façade she put on, the sense of injury she tried not to let slip.

Chief Dunne came by and asked if I was alright. I said I was.

'The spent bullets and their casings from the Comber Road shooting have been examined by the ballistics expert,' he said.

'And, what were their findings?' I asked.

'They were issued to the PSNI.'

'Pat Kinahan,' I began to tell him.

'Hewitt told me all about that,' Dunne said. 'You look peaky, maybe you should go home.'

'In a minute,' I said.

Sarge Simon was in the interview room, grilling Lizzie with Fleur Hewitt.

'If I wanted Justin dead I'd have killed him,' said Lizzie on the screen. Star of her own show.

'What was your intention?' asked Hewitt.

'So he'd know,' Lizzie said. 'But I didn't want him dead, after all, I'm having his baby.'

'What *was* your intention? Make him suffer? To punish him?'

'Damn straight.'

'The gun you used was a stolen police issue. Explain how it came into your possession,' said Simon.

'I just walked into my childhood home and took it.'

'It belongs to your father, Officer Pat Kinahan, is that right?' Simon asked.

'Right,' said Lizzie.

'He had also reported his car windows smashed during the early hours of Thursday 26 April. Mrs. Kinahan, your mother, reported seeing a light-coloured car driving away from the scene, but it was late and she couldn't tell what colour.'

'That was Justin Nicholson's car. A silver Mercedes,' Hewitt added.

'What were you doing in Bangor then, Lizzie?' Simon asked.

'You tell me,' she replied.

I paged Hewitt at that stage and asked her to come out and talk to me. She looked up at the camera and then paused the interview.

'What in the hell are you doing here?' she asked me in person.

'I have big news,' I told her.

'You should be resting, you nutter.'

'Listen,' I said. 'That bite on Erica McClelland …'

'What about it?'

'It matched Lizzie's DNA, Kate Stile just phoned and told me.'

Fleur looked confused. 'How did you get her DNA?'

'From that water bottle you gave her in the hospital.'

Fleur began to laugh at my gall. 'You must really want this.' She eyed Lizzie on the monitor, then told me to come in with her as she relieved Sarge Simon. He looked at me in surprise too.

A smirk settled on Lizzie's face. She smacked her lips and gave me a smile. 'How are you?' she asked insincerely.

I tried not to recoil. I sat down. 'Great, Elizabeth,' I said. 'All the better for seeing you.'

Hewitt resumed the interview and said, 'We have your DNA on the corpse of Erica McClelland.'

Lizzie was taken aback and it felt good to surprise her, now it was my turn to smirk.

'I have no idea who that even is,' she said.

'Don't you, because your DNA is all over her?'

'I never gave anybody my DNA.' Lizzie narrowed her eyes.

'But you bit Erica on the arm.'

'Did I? Whatever you've done here, it's unethical. I know you can't have my DNA without my consent.'

'No, you definitely gave consent,' I said.

'Ooh! Are you sore?' she asked me.

'Lizzie,' said Hewitt, 'this part is where you tell us what happened, and how Erica McClelland's dead body was found on Ballyholme Beach with your DNA on her.'

'Oh, the one on the beach?' Lizzie cooed. 'The one who thought she was something special? That one?'

'Explain further, if you would?' said Hewitt.

'The one who was flirting with Justin at that gig. That one?'

'So you were at the Vacant Aluminium gig at The Night Kitchen?'

Lizzie had played cat and mouse enough, I could see that even she was tired, she had dark rings around her eyes, and whatever she was going to say about it, to make it seem like Erica's fault, would be a lie and we all knew it. Each girl had been picked up opportunistically.

'We were giving her a lift and she was revealing a lot of skin,' said Lizzie. 'You'll have seen the photos. A right little whore.'

'That's no reason,' I said, but Hewitt put her hand out to stop me saying anything else. Let her hang herself, Hewitt was thinking.

'She was paralytic,' said Lizzie, 'and when she woke in the back seat …'

'What happened then?'

'Justin and I were making love.'

'Where?'

'In the car.'

'Were you having sexual intercourse beside Erica?'

'She was out of it by that stage. Suddenly, she woke all disorientated, and ran. She didn't have to. She could have joined in.' Lizzie laughed. 'Actually, scrub that, joining in was not an option. She wasn't his type. He likes blondes,' Lizzie said this like Fleur and I, two brunettes, should be crying into our pillows. 'Though she could have just asked us to drive her home, but Erica jumped out and ran, down in the direction of the water. I chased her down there and she tripped, we wound up having a tussle and that's when Chloe ...'

'Chloe Taylor?' I said.

'Erica. I mean, Erica! That's when I took a chunk out of her arm. She was trying to headlock me, so it was self-defence.'

'Where was Justin during this?' asked Hewitt.

'He was watching, a little way off. He was encouraging me, supporting me.'

'And then?'

'He went back to the car and got the knife.'

'Who stabbed Erica?'

'Justin gave the knife to me. Erica was in the water. And we were all wet, Justin found it erotic. We went back to the car.'

'After you had stabbed her?' I asked.

'Keep up, Harriet! After that, Justin and I made love on the bonnet of the car.'

'You didn't assault Erica?'

'Sexually? No. But I did assault her, I killed her.' Lizzie laughed.

Hewitt sighed in disgust. 'And tell us what you know about the death of Chloe Taylor.'

'So what happened was …' Lizzie settled down as if she was going to tell us a frilly piece of gossip. Her eyes became sparkly. 'One night Chloe and I got drunk, and were telling each other things, private things, like how she was falling for Martin Walsh, so, sorry, but that was not a lie, you just didn't want to believe it.'

'There was never a relationship between Dr. Walsh and Chloe,' said Hewitt.

Lizzie shrugged. 'Do you want me to tell you what I know or not?'

'What did you tell Chloe?' I asked. 'Did you tell Chloe that you and Justin had been abducting girls and taking their underwear?'

Lizzie laughed. 'Smart,' she said. 'I'm not giving you everything. You'll have to earn that.'

Big deal, I thought, we have you on enough. It's only a matter of time till we get you for everything. Lizzie could have blamed Justin for stabbing Erica, he wouldn't say any different now.

'Two weeks after Erica, we'd sat up talking shit. I woke up with this real dread that I'd told Chloe about that little whore, but I wasn't sure. I'd already been testing her with bits and pieces.'

'Breadcrumbs. Why? To see if you could trust her? To shock Chloe?'

'To see if she would take the bait.'

I could see Lizzie had always been attention seeking, even being around us all the time, she yearned the recognition. How Lucinda Press would have hated her! How I hated her. Lizzie wanted Chloe to know she had killed someone.

She'd been proud and turned on by it, empowered. She was the polar opposite of everything Chloe was and believed in.

'I didn't hear from Chloe for almost a week after,' said Lizzie, 'she was ghosting me. She came round for a drink that Tuesday night but hardly said a word. Spoke more to Drew. She left dead early, saying she had to open up PACT the next morning. So I went to see her at the PACT office. "Let's go for a drink tonight," I said, but she refused. Then I asked, "Why not? What did I tell you?" and she said, "Nothing." So I said, "Why have you been off?" "You know why," she said. That morning, I said I'd nip out and I came back with coffee, put a little something in hers, enough to knock out an epileptic horse. But Chloe refused to drink it, said she was on decaf. For her anxiety.' Lizzie snored. 'Then she had her back to me, and I, whack, whack, whack, located the CCTV tapes, put on her coat, and was gone. Now she's proper *ghosting* me.' Lizzie laughed again.

'And you wrote to the papers, taunting them and us?' said Hewitt. 'And it was you who was trolling Chloe when she was on the TV. You didn't like the attention she was getting with her activist work.'

'I didn't even know her then, you stupid pig.' Lizzie snorted.

I believe that was right. I still wonder if it was Lucinda Press or just another cyber bully. There are a lot of them.

I stared at Lizzie for a moment, almost amused. 'I've looked up your notes,' I said with great pleasure, 'you wanted to get into the police, tried out for years. But you didn't get in because ... why do you think that was?'

'Intelligence.' She pursed her lips.

'Intelligence?'

'I wouldn't have been any good. I'm too intelligent to be a peeler. I mean, what sort of detective leaves alone a bag with tens of thousands of quid in it?'

'We'll cease recording here,' I said.

'What kind of mother is bought out of her kids' lives for less than a grand and a half?' I asked Lizzie as we brought her back to her cell.

'Can I get some tea and toast? Now I'm eating for two,' she asked, ignoring my question.

'You'll be charged with his murder, too,' I said, 'now the father of your *unborn* child is dead.'

I wanted to surprise her.

'Really?' She laughed. 'Is he really dead? But see what I did, Harry, I made him suffer, dragged it out. That was intentional – off the record. Like with you. If I wanted you dead, I've had killed you. But then it would have been game over.'

'It *is* game over,' I said, and louder, 'Any sugar in your tea?' I smiled through gritted teeth.

'No, I'm sweet enough,' she said, 'but plenty of milk, Harry, ta.'

She would have to whistle for it.

*

Drew phoned me. 'I saw on the news that you have Lizzie in custody,' he said.

'We can't give a name right now.'

'But I heard about the shooting at hers. Was it your colleague, the Scottish girl, who was shot?'

'No, Drew, why?'

'Was it you?'

'Yes,' I said. 'I received a gunshot wound.'

'I underestimated you.'

'What is it you want, Drew?' I tried to raise my arm and pain shot right up to my jaw. 'We will update Jackie when we have more to tell him.'

'I have one for you, do you want it?' said Drew.

I shook my head but he couldn't see that. 'If you want to give some information,' I said.

'Okay, but only because I've new respect for you.'

I smiled through the pain. Tough lad Drew Taylor was about to tout on someone.

'Our anniversary breakfast was at The Bell, if you remember ...'

'No, I don't,' I said.

'Me and Roxy's anniversary, the morning Chloe was killed.'

'Yes,' I said, somehow hearing what he'd said as *our anniversary*, mine and his. Maybe I shouldn't have been out of bed. My shoulder was ablaze and I was exhausted.

'Well, they were there at the same time as us.'

'Who was?'

'Justin and his sidepiece.'

'Justin and Mary Heaney?'

'They had a yellow folder on the table and they were looking in it every now and then.'

'Yeah?'

'It's a maternity folder, they'd just been for a scan at the Ulster. The day of Chloe's funeral, I was dropping your woman home, Slabber, when she started to go on about my Roxy.'

'Lizzie? What did she say?'

'She'd seen the Facebook messages her man had sent but Lizzie tried to tell it a different way, as if it was Roxy starting things up. She didn't know I'd already seen them.'

'I see ...'

'I tried to wipe that smile off her face and I told her, "Think you're clever, don't you, girl? But your man is having a child with another girl".'

'What did Lizzie do then?'

'She asked me to drop her to Bangor, but I waited outside for five minutes and she let herself into this wee bungalow. She had a key. And when she came back outside she had boxes of bullets. Oh, and I should have said, I'm not testifying to any of this. I'm just telling you, to help you get the bigger picture.'

Chapter 45

I went to type up notes. Hewitt was about to phone the CPS, but she hung up. 'What was that about money?' she asked me.

'Nothing,' I said.

'It didn't seem like nothing. That's what was in the bag that went missing, all that money, forty g's?'

'No,' I said.

'You don't have to lie to me,' said Hewitt, 'just tell me to butt out.'

'It's not a lie.'

'Then we can get back to business,' she said.

'Good.'

'Only, I saw how you were with Jocelyn, and now this, with Lizzie. Greg gave that money to you. Wanna know how I know that?'

'You're wrong,' I said, 'but go on.'

'Because he gave his kids twenty grand each lately when he sold the Algarve villa, my mum told me.'

'That is far-fetched.' I forced a laugh.

'Do you think I'm buttoned up the back?' Hewitt said. 'But that's your private business. They're your kids and I'm not judging. As long as it's over, one way or another.'

'Oh, it is most definitely over,' I said.

'Except maybe her. Maybe I judge her.' Hewitt nodded at the screen. Lizzie was saying, 'Yes, yes, I did do it,' then singing it, standing up and spinning around her cell.

'Here it comes,' I said.

Hewitt watched for another moment and elbowed me. 'Ah ha, she is clearly mad. That's quite fortunate timing. First a full confession, full cooperation and now the insanity defence starts. Boom!'

'They won't buy it.' I shrugged, the shake of my shoulders reminded me of the bullet she put in me, and that it was out and I would heal but others would not. I popped some painkillers into my mouth.

I saw some sort of crazy kid when I saw Lizzie, which wasn't fair. If it was a man who did all the things she had he'd be called a monster. Lizzie, I could see splashed over the papers, pretty white lady, icy blonde femme fatale, a victim of the men who had damaged her, *them* being made the monsters.

Well, they were both monsters, her and Justin. Her dad was a headbin too. But I doubted that all of her exes were as bad as Nicholson. I was as guilty as anyone I condemned for miscalculating her.

'Drew Taylor just called me,' I told Hewitt. 'He reckons Molly was pregnant, it seems he told Lizzie the news after Chloe's funeral, and that's what made her go postal.'

'Yes,' Hewitt said, 'did I forget to tell you, the autopsy showed a foetus. Sad, isn't it? Lizzie found them with that app.'

'Which app?'

'Find My iPhone. Lead her straight to Justin.'

Hewitt lifted the phone to ring the CPS and give a cold recital of the facts. 'Full confession to the stabbing and killing by drowning of Erica McClelland, full confession to the stabbing and killing of Chloe Taylor, full confession to the shootings and killings of Justin Nicholson, Mary Heaney, and her unborn child … and the shooting and killing of Ince Ross, shooting and maiming of …' She looked at my sling. 'Detective Inspector Harriet Sloane.'

'So Lizzie's pregnant too?' I asked after she'd go the go ahead to keep Lizzie. It was a homerun. No bail.

'I don't think so,' said Hewitt. 'She won't do a test for the doctor. Probably another fake, she's fond of those.'

'Why didn't you add her and Justin's abductions to the tally? Victoria and Kayley … and Maisie?'

'We have enough for now,' Hewitt said. 'The test runs can be added later.'

I had to scoff.

In my bag my mobile was ringing. It was my twin sister, Charly, asking if I was with our father.

'No,' I said. 'He never came to see me in hospital either.'

This fact just came to me. No one had visited me apart from Paul. Not that I had wanted them to, or had stayed in for long enough to warrant visitors. They expected me to be fine. That, or they did not give a hoot.

Where were the calls asking how I was? I'd been bloody well shot.

'None of us can get a hold of him,' Charly told me. 'He visited Mummy this morning then he disappeared.'

'I'll call him,' I said. 'And thanks, I'm fine.'

'Addam's trying him,' said Charly, ignoring me, 'Coral's at the house.'

'What's going on?' I asked her.

'Just come to mine as soon as you can.'

'Is it Mummy?'

'Just come here,' she said with a glimmer of desperation; this was the lobby where she kept me until she threw open the door of the main room, 'Mummy's dead.'

'Is she?' I asked. 'Is she really?'

There was a long pause. 'We can't do this over the phone,' Charly said.

Funny thing was that I was not even surprised. Shocked yes, but I knew all along it would happen.

'Don't worry about Daddy,' I said.

After I rang off, I saw Hewitt looking at me. 'Are you okay?' she asked.

'I have to go; my mother has died,' I said matter-of-factly.

Hewitt went to give me a hug but remembered about my shoulder and patted me gently on the good arm. She gave me a kiss on the cheek. 'What do you need from me, Harry?'

'We need to let Chloe's family know the outcome, and Mary's …'

'And the Rosses and the McClellands,' said Hewitt. 'Yes, yes. I've got Higgins for that donkey work. Don't worry about that now. Just go, hen.'

Epilogue

Today feels like a beach day, same as yesterday.

I don my black vest and a thin cardigan, a silk skirt I have never had the occasion to wear, silver tights, boots and look at myself in my full-length mirrors and I think, who knew this would be that occasion?

Paul comes and puts on his black tie while the babysitter – a nineteen-year-old neighbour of ours who is studying something to do with Early Childhood – insists she doesn't mind that the boys are cranky, and that she's already had chickenpox.

She says she'll bathe the twins later in baking soda if they get too itchy but I know I don't own any. I'm not a baking soda kind of woman.

Then Paul and I leave to go and burn my mother's body. Fuck!

The whole day Sylvia avoids me, and at the ceremony Addam performs his religious speech that only he believes in. I think, Mother would not have wanted this, she was not a believer.

I think of Chloe's funeral and how it was geared solely for her and not a God, and how better it was for it. And the bright colours! Then Addam gives his sales pitch, his come to God moment, and I am mega pissed off when he makes this about recruitment; about, if you don't believe, then good luck to you out there …

Personally, I can't believe there is anything after this. I would like to.

Addam is shaky, and yes, it is his own mother's funeral service he is delivering, but that would not falter my brother. He is very used to death. Each day he spends time with the dead or the dying.

If you didn't know Addam you'd think he is drunk, slurring his words and suddenly I know it. Each of us are fifty-fifty after all. It is the reason we are here, releasing our mother: Addam has Huntington's.

I look at Sylvia, who is watching him with a genuine concern. *This* is why she has had no time for my boys. She has been dealing with this all along. Fuck again!

I try to get Charly's eye but she is wiping her eyes and I can tell she is not taking anything else in. Poor Charlotte, she was the closest of us all to Mother, and it is her birthday today, last day of May. Mine is tomorrow. A new month.

Coral tells me she knows about Addam with one look. She is always trying to get us to take the test; she has and knows she is on the safe side of the fence.

Brooks is here, under escort. He has been allowed compassionate leave from prison to attend.

'How are you, Brooks?' I ask him as we line up.

'I'm sorry,' Brooks says, 'that's what I am. I never got to say goodbye to her.'

'It robbed us all of a goodbye,' I said, because Mother *was* in a limbo for years but we had always been told we would see a decline before she would pass, and she had not gone that way. Just 'fine' one minute and gone the next.

Old neighbours, colleagues and distant cousins of Mother's go along our family line-up to shake our hands and attempt to hug us, whether we are up for it or not.

Even my ex-mother-in-law, Yvonne Lucie, appears. And I have to accept her sympathy until I can slip off to the bar.

Paul comes over and hands me a coffee. I have a habit now of looking for horse medication floating on the top.

'I'm grand with the wine,' I say.

'We're going on a holiday once this is over,' he says.

'We're just back from one.'

'You look like you need another one.'

'The tan *is* fading ...' I look at the back of my hand and spill Merlot on the bar.

'You've been shot, Harry, and your mother has died and you're still running around like a blue-arsed fly. We haven't had any time as a family. You've hardly seen the boys since you went back to work.'

I have the first five grand from Dom Moore at home, I keep it in the safe. I want to buy Paul a Boxster. He shouldn't have to make so many sacrifices. It's not fair on him.

Father sits with some of the old brigade. When he dies he'll have half of the RUC around him, whoever is still knocking about by then. My mother, a woman and a judge, warranted less respect, but more fear. Though only from anyone who knew her outside of the family. She took things more in her stride than I do.

'We've lost an amazing woman,' I say to Paul, a bit drunk, almost tearful. 'Why has no one said that, why has no one said how shite it was that she lived those final years like that, how it was cruel, for her and for us?'

'You just said it,' he replies.

I walk over to my father who turns his face away as the old boys' club tell stories and laugh and guffaw. 'Daddy, why are you avoiding me?' I ask him but he doesn't reply.

'Do you know Lizzie, the woman who shot me? She says she knows you, said she worked in Bethany Nursing Home at one stage.'

'How do I know? They come and go,' he says.

I breathe a sigh of relief. Lizzie made me think there was something between them, but that was Lizzie's talent, making connections where there aren't any.

She had stalked Martin Walsh, *she* had fallen for him. Lizzie had been pushed away by Martin. Then she stood to lose Justin, the only man who didn't push her back.

And that was just because she had shit on him; knew too much about his love of knives.

Some relationships can never end peacefully.

Even her relationship with Chloe had not been as close as she'd made out either. Chloe was afraid of her, and afraid to push her away.

Lizzie had recommended Martin to Chloe solely as a way to hear about him. In the end, he had to take a restraining order out on Lizzie. He never even knew they were friends until Lizzie was charged with her murder, and all the others.

'People falling for their therapist is very common. People are vulnerable, and here's someone who finally cares,' as Rebecca Walsh once told me.

Outside I call after Father one more time but he is away, walking toward his car.

'Look at me,' says Paul.

'What?' I ask him.

Paul moves to the other side of me and stands there and says, 'Just look here, Harry, at me.'

But I turn and look over the road, where a car pulls up, a Skoda, and Greg and the Chief Super from Musgrave Serious Crime Suite both get out and speak to Father. Then Musgrave goes to get cuffs but Greg shakes his head.

'What the hell?' I try to run over and Paul grabs my arm and I wince with the pain in my shoulder.

'Let's relieve the babysitter,' he says.

'What are you talking about?' I ask. I watch as they put Father in the back of the car.

'I'm sorry; they wouldn't wait any longer,' says Paul.

Then they are gone.

'I don't know an easy way to say it,' Paul says. 'Charles stole anaesthetic from the hospital.'

I am confused, waiting for them to return, having realised their mistake. It is his wife's funeral, for God's sake.

'That day your dad called into the hospital to speak with me,' says Paul, 'he was caught on camera. He'd been asking me how much would be too much, would kill a big man with a strong constitution. I thought he was being weird, or a bit senile. I didn't want to worry you.'

The service car does not return. My father has killed my mother, he has put her out of her misery, and I understand now that this was what all his letters and false claims were about. He has wanted a conversation with me about permission; for me to say that it is okay, that I agree it is time to let her go.

He had tried to call me that Friday afternoon before and I had ignored his call. Maybe he was wanting to talk it through with me. Or ask me to do it.

Then he took it into his own hands.

Father has ended a life that ended long ago and given the rest of us our own lives back, even at the cost of his freedom. And in this moment, watching him turn a corner and be gone, I love that man more than I have ever done before.

It is the man standing in front of me I don't love. This 'good' man. My father's traitor. He won't get a penny of my sons' money.

ACKNOWLEDGEMENTS

I owe much gratitude to Ards and North Down Borough Council. It was during a residency funded by ANDBC to the Tyrone Guthrie Centre that this book took hold.

Thank you to the Arts Council of Northern Ireland for recent funding of other projects.

Thank you to my family for their support.

KELLY CREIGHTON
THE BONES OF IT

Thrown out of university, green-tea-drinking, meditation-loving Scott McAuley has no place to go but home: County Down, Northern Ireland. The only problem is, his father is there now too.

Duke wasn't around when Scott was growing up. He was in prison for stabbing two Catholic kids in an alley. But thanks to the Good Friday Agreement, big Duke is out now, reformed, a counsellor.

Squeezed together into a small house, with too little work and too much time to think about what happened to Scott's dead mother, the tension grows between these two men, who seem to have so little in common.

Penning diary entries from prison, Scott recalls what happened that year. He writes about Jasmine, his girlfriend at university. He writes about Klaudia, back home in County Down, who he and Duke both admired. He weaves a tale of lies, rage and paranoia.

Out now in paperback and eBook.

KELLY CREIGHTON
THE SLEEPING SEASON

Book 1 in the Sloane series.

Someone going missing is not an event in their life but an indicator of a problem.

Detective Inspector Harriet Sloane is plagued by nightmares.
Someone from her past watches from a distance.
In East Belfast, four-year-old River vanishes from his room.
Sloane must put her own demons to bed and find the boy.
Before it's too late.

Out now in paperback and eBook.